OUT
ON THE
CUTTING EDGE

G·K
Hall
&Cº

Also published in Large Print
from G.K. Hall by Lawrence Block:

A Walk Among the Tombstones
The Girl with the Long Green Heart
After the First Death
You Could Call It Murder
When the Sacred Ginmill Closes
Coward's Kiss

OUT ON THE ON THE CUTTING EDGE

A Matt Scudder Mystery

———— ◆ ————

Lawrence Block

G.K. Hall & Co.
Thorndike, Maine

Published in 1995 by arrangement with
William Morrow & Co., Inc.

The author gratefully acknowledges permission to include
excerpted lines from the poem "September 1, 1939," by
W.H. Auden from *The English Auden: Poems, Essays and
Dramatic Writings 1927–1939.* Copyright © 1940 by
W.H. Auden. Used with permission of Random House, Inc.,
and Faber and Faber Ltd.

G.K. Hall Large Print Paperback Collection.

The text of this Large Print edition is unabridged.
Other aspects of the book may vary from the original edition.

Set in 16 pt. News Plantin.

Printed in the United States on permanent paper.

Library of Congress Cataloging in Publication Data

Block, Lawrence.
    Out on the cutting edge : a Matt Scudder mystery /
Lawrence Block.
      p.   cm.
    ISBN 0-7838-1177-2 (lg. print : lsc)
    1. Scudder, Matt (Fictitious character) — Fiction. 2. Private
investigators — New York (N.Y.) — Fiction. 3. Large type
books. I. Title.
    [PS3552.L63O9 1995]
    813'.54—dc20   94-42804

For my cousin

Jeffrey Nathan
1943–1988

Acknowledgments

The author is pleased to acknowledge the considerable contribution of William Smart and Karen and Cary Kimble, and indeed of everyone at the Virginia Center for the Creative Arts, where this book was written.

I sit in one of the dives
On Fifty-second Street
Uncertain and afraid
As the clever hopes expire
Of a low dishonest decade:
Waves of anger and fear
Circulate over the bright
And darkened lands of the earth,
Obsessing our private lives;
The unmentionable odor of death
Offends the September night . . .

— W. H. Auden
"September 1, 1939"

When I imagine it, it is always a perfect summer day, with the sun high in a vivid blue sky. It was summer, of course, but I have no way of knowing what the weather was like, or even if it happened during the day. Someone, relating the incident, mentioned moonlight, but he wasn't there either. Perhaps his imagination provided the moon, even as mine chose a bright sun, a blue sky, and a scattering of cottony clouds.

They are on the open porch of a white clapboard farmhouse. Sometimes I see them inside, seated at a pine table in the kitchen, but more often they are on the porch. They have a large glass pitcher filled with a mix of vodka and grapefruit juice, and they are sitting on the porch drinking salty dogs.

Sometimes I imagine them walking around the farm, holding hands, or with their arms around one another's waists. She has had a lot to drink, and it makes her boisterous and flamboyant and a little unsteady on her pins. She moos at the cows, clucks at the chickens, oinks at the pigs, and laughs at the whole world.

Or I'll see them walking through woods, then emerg-

ing at the bank of a stream. There was a Frenchman a couple hundred years ago who always painted idealized rustic scenes, with barefoot shepherds and milkmaids cavorting in nature. He could have painted this particular figment of my imagination.

And now they are naked, there by the stream's side, and they are making love in the cool grass.

My imagination is limited in this area, or perhaps it is simply a respecter of privacy. All it provides is a close-up of her face. Expressions play on her face, and they are like newspaper articles in dreams, shifting and going out of focus just before I can read them.

Then he shows her the knife. Her eyes widen, and something goes out of them. And a cloud moves to cover the sun.

That's how I imagine it, and I don't suppose my imagination comes very close to actual circumstances. How could it? Even eyewitness testimony is notoriously unreliable, and I'm the furthest thing from an eyewitness. I've never seen the farm. I don't even know if there's a stream on the property.

I never saw her, either, except in photographs. I'm looking at one of those photos now, and it seems to me that I can almost see the play of expressions on her face, and her eyes widening. But of course I can see no such thing. As with all photographs, all I can see is a moment frozen in time. It's not a magic picture. You can't read the past in it, or the future. If you turn it over you can read my name and telephone number, but when you turn it over again it's the same pose every time, the lips slightly parted, the eyes looking into the camera, the expression enigmatic. You can stare at it all you want and it's not going to tell you any secrets.

I know. I've looked at it long enough.

1

There are three prominent fraternal organizations for actors in New York, and years ago an actor named Maurice Jenkins-Lloyd had summed them up to anyone who'd listen. "The Players are gentlemen," he'd intoned, "pretending to be actors. The Lambs are actors, pretending to be gentlemen. And the Friars — the Friars are neither, pretending to be both."

I don't know which category Jenkins-Lloyd belonged in. When I knew him he was mostly drunk, pretending to be sober. He used to drink at Armstrong's, which used to be on Ninth Avenue between Fifty-seventh and Fifty-eighth. His drink was Dewar's and soda, and he could drink it all day and all night without showing it much. He never raised his voice, never turned ugly, never fell off his chair. Toward the end of an evening he might slur his words some, but that was about it. Player, Lamb, or Friar, he drank like a gentleman.

And died of it. I was still drinking myself when he died of a ruptured esophagus. It's not the first cause of death you think of for alcoholics, but it doesn't seem to happen to other people. I don't know exactly what causes it, whether it's the cumulative effect of pouring booze down a gullet for all those years or the strain of vomiting a couple of times every morning.

I hadn't thought of Maurice Jenkins-Lloyd in a long time. I thought of him now because I was going to an AA meeting on the second floor of what used to be the Lambs Club. The elegant white building on West Forty-fourth had some years ago become a luxury the Lambs could no longer afford, and they had sold the property and shared space with another club somewhere else in midtown. A church of some sort had bought the property, and it now housed an experimental theater along with facilities for other church activities. On Thursday nights, the Fresh Start group of Alcoholics Anonymous paid a nominal fee for the use of a meeting room.

The meeting ran from eight-thirty to nine-thirty. I got there about ten minutes early and introduced myself to the program chairman. I helped myself to coffee and sat where he indicated. There were eight or ten 6-foot tables arranged in an open rectangle, and my seat was at the far end from the door, next to the chairman's.

By eight-thirty there were about thirty-five people sitting around the tables and drinking coffee out of Styrofoam cups. The chairman opened the meeting and read the preamble, then called on someone to read a portion of the fifth chapter of the Big Book. There were a few announcements — a dance that weekend on the Upper West Side, a group anniversary in Murray Hill, a new meeting added to the schedule at Alanon House. A group that met regularly at a Ninth Avenue synagogue was canceling its next two meetings because of the Jewish holidays.

Then the chairman said, "Our speaker tonight is Matt, from Keep It Simple."

I was nervous, of course. I'd been nervous from the minute I walked into the place. I'm always like that before I lead a meeting, but it passes. When he'd introduced me there was a round of polite applause, and when it died down I said, "Thanks. My name is Matt, and I'm an alcoholic." Then the nervousness was gone, and I sat there and told my story.

I talked for about twenty minutes. I don't re-member what I said. Essentially what you do is tell what it used to be like, what happened, and what it's like now, and that's what I did, but it comes out different every time you tell it.

Some people's stories are inspirational enough for cable television. They'll tell you how they were down and out in East St. Louis and now they're president of IBM with rising expectations. I don't have that kind of story to tell. I still live in the same place and do the same thing for a living. The difference is I used to drink and now I don't, and that's about as inspirational as I get.

When I finished there was another round of polite applause, and then they passed a basket and everyone put in a dollar or a quarter or nothing at all toward the rent and the coffee. There was a five-minute break, and then the meeting resumed. The format varies at different meetings; here they went around the room, and everybody had his turn to say something.

There were maybe ten people in the room I recognized and another half-dozen or so who looked familiar. One woman with a strong jawline and a lot of red hair took off from the fact that I'd been a cop.

"You coulda come to my house," she said. "We had the cops there once a week. My husband and I would drink and fight, and some neighbor'd call the cops, and they'd come. The same cop showed up three times running, and the next thing you knew I was having an affair with him, and before you knew it him and I had a fight, and somebody called the cops. People were always calling the cops on me, even when I was with a cop to start with."

At nine-thirty we said the Lord's Prayer and closed the meeting. A few people came over to shake hands and thank me for leading the meeting. Most of the others hurried out of the building so they could light their cigarettes.

Outside, the night was crisp with early autumn. Summer had been brutal, and the cool nights now were a relief. I walked half a block west, and a man stepped out of a doorway and asked me if I could spare any change. He was wearing mismatched pants and suit jacket and he had wornout tennis sneakers on his feet, and no socks. He looked thirty-five but he was probably younger than that. The street ages you.

He needed a bath and a shave and a haircut. He needed a whole lot more than I could give him. What I did give him was a dollar, fishing a single out of my pants pocket and pressing it into his palm. He thanked me and asked God to bless me. I started walking, and I was almost at the corner of Broadway when I heard someone call my name.

I turned and recognized a fellow named Eddie. He'd been at the meeting, and I'd seen him around now and then at other meetings. Now he was hurrying to catch up with me.

"Hey, Matt," he said. "You want to get some coffee?"

"I had three cups at the meeting. I think I'll just head for home."

"You going uptown? I'll walk you."

We took Broadway to Forty-seventh, walked over to Eighth Avenue, turned right and continued uptown. Of the five people who asked us for money en route, I shook off two of them and gave the others a dollar each and was thanked and blessed in return. After the third one took her dollar and extended her blessing, Eddie said, "Jesus, you gotta be the softest touch on the whole West Side. What are you, Matt, just a boy who can't say no?"

"Sometimes I turn them down."

"But mostly you don't."

"Mostly I don't."

"I saw the mayor on TV the other day. He says we shouldn't give money to people on the street. He says half the time they're addicts, they're just gonna spend the money on crack."

"Right, and the other half'll squander it on food and shelter."

"He says there's beds and hot meals available free of charge to anybody in the city who needs it."

"I know. It makes you wonder why so many people sleep in the streets and eat out of garbage cans."

"He wants to crack down on the window washers, too. You know, guys wipe your windshield whether it needs it or not, then hit you for a handout? He says he doesn't like the way it looks, guys working the street like that."

"He's right," I said. "They're able-bodied guys, too. They ought to be out mugging people or knocking over liquor stores, something that's out of the public eye."

"I guess you're not a big fan of the mayor's."

"I suppose he's all right," I said. "I think he's got a heart the size of a raisin, but maybe that's a requirement, part of the job description. I try not to pay too much attention to who the mayor is or what he says. I give away a few bucks every day, that's all. It doesn't hurt me and it doesn't help anybody very much. It's just what I do these days."

"There's enough of them out there asking for it."

And indeed there were. You saw them all over the city, sleeping in the parks, in the subway tunnels, in the bus- and train-station lobbies. Some of them were mental cases and some were crack addicts, and some of them were just people who had lost a step in the great race and had no place to live. It's hard to get a job when you don't have a residence, hard to keep yourself presentable enough to get hired. But some of them *had* jobs. Apartments are hard to find in New York, and harder to afford; with rent and security and broker's commission to pay, you might need upwards of two thousand dollars to get in the door of an apartment. Even if you could hold a job, how could you save up that kind of money?

"Thank God I got a place," Eddie said. "It's the apartment I grew up in, if you can believe it. A block up and two blocks over, near Tenth. Not the first place I lived in. That's gone now, the building came down, it's where they built the new high school. We moved out of there when I was, I don't know, nine years old? Musta been, because I was in the third grade. You know I done time?"

"Not in the third grade."

He laughed. "No, it was a little later than that. Thing is, the old man died while I was up in Green Haven, and when I got out I didn't have a place to stay, so I moved in with my ma. I wasn't home much, it was just a place to keep my clothes and stuff, but then when she got sick I started staying there with her, and after she died I kept the place.

19

Three little rooms up on the fourth floor, but, you know, it's rent-controlled, Matt. $122.75 a month. A hotel you'd be willing to step into, in this town, shit, you'd pay that for one night."

And, amazingly enough, the neighborhood itself was on its way up. Hell's Kitchen had been a tough, hard-bitten neighborhood for a hundred years, and now the realtors had people calling it Clinton and turning tenement flats into condos and getting six-figure prices for them. I could never figure out where the poor people went, or where the rich people came from.

He said, "Beautiful night, isn't it? Of course before we know it we'll be griping that it's too cold. One day you're dying of the heat and the next minute you're wondering where the summer went. Always the way, huh?"

"That's what they say."

He was in his late thirties, five-eight or -nine and slender, with pale skin and washed-out blue eyes. His hair was light brown and he was losing it, and the receding hairline combined with an overbite to give him a slightly rabbity appearance.

If I hadn't known he'd done time I would probably have guessed as much, although I couldn't tell you why beyond saying that he looked like a crook. A combination, perhaps, of bravado and furtiveness, an attitude that manifested physically in the set of the shoulders and the shiftiness of the eyes. I wouldn't say that it stood out all over him, but the first time I noticed him at a meeting

I had the thought that here was a guy who'd been dirty, a guy who had most likely gone away for it.

He took out a pack of cigarettes and offered me one. I shook my head. He selected one for himself and scratched a match to light it, cupping his hands against the wind. He blew out smoke, then held the cigarette between his thumb and forefinger and looked at it. "I ought to quit these little fuckers," he said. "Sober up and die of cancer, where's the percentage in that?"

"How long are you sober now, Eddie?"

"Coming up on seven months."

"That's great."

"I been coming around the program for close to a year, but it took me a while to put down the drink."

"I didn't catch on right away, either."

"No? Well, I slipped around for a month or two. And then I thought I could still smoke dope, because what the hell, marijuana wasn't my problem, alcohol was my problem. But I guess what I heard at the meetings finally soaked in, and I put down the grass, too, and now I've been completely clean and dry for close to seven months."

"That's terrific."

"I guess."

"As far as the cigarettes are concerned, they say it's not a good idea to try to do too many things at once."

"I know it. I figure when I make my year is time enough to quit these things." He sucked hard on the cigarette and the end glowed red. "This is where I get off. You sure you don't want to get some coffee?"

"No, but I'll walk over to Ninth with you."

We walked the long block crosstown and then stood on the corner talking for a few minutes. I don't remember much of what we talked about. On the corner he said, "When he introduced you he said your home group was Keep It Simple. That's the group meets over at St. Paul the Apostle?"

I nodded. "The official name is Keep It Simple, but everybody just calls it St. Paul's."

"You go there pretty regular?"

"More often than not."

"Maybe I'll see you there. Uh, you got a phone or something, Matt?"

"Sure. I'm at a hotel, the Northwestern. You just call the desk and they'll put you through to me."

I looked at him for a second, then laughed. I had a small stack of wallet-size photos in my breast pocket, each stamped on the back with my name and phone number. I took one out and handed it to him. He said, " 'Matthew Scudder.' That's you, huh?" He turned the card over. "That's not you, though."

"You recognize her?"

He shook his head. "Who is she?"

"A girl I'm trying to find."

"I don't blame you. Find two while you're at it, I'll take one of 'em off your hands. What is it, a job you're working?"

"That's right."

"Pretty girl. Young, or at least she was when this was taken. What is she, about twenty-one?"

"Twenty-four now. The picture's a year or two old."

"Twenty-four's pretty young," he said. He turned the card again. "Matthew Scudder. It's funny how you'll know the most personal things about somebody but you won't know their name. Their last name, I mean. Mine's Dunphy, but maybe you already knew that."

"No."

"I'd give you my phone if I had one. They cut it off for nonpayment a year and a half ago. One of these days I'll have to get it straightened out. It's been good talking to you, Matt. Maybe I'll see you tomorrow night at St. Paul's."

"I'll most likely be there."

"I'll make a point of getting there. You take care now."

"You too, Eddie."

He waited for the light, trotted across the avenue. Halfway across he turned and gave me a smile. "I hope you find that girl," he said.

I didn't find her that night, or any other girl, either. I walked the rest of the way to Fifty-seventh Street and stopped at the desk. There were no messages but Jacob volunteered that I'd had three calls spaced half an hour apart. "Could be it was the same person each time," he said. "He

23

didn't leave no message."

I went up to my room, sat down and opened a book. I read a few pages and the phone rang.

I picked it up and a man said, "This Scudder?" I said it was. He said, "How much is the reward?"

"What reward?"

"Aren't you the man looking to find that girl?"

I could have hung up, but instead I said, "What girl?"

"Her picture's on one side and your name's on the other. Don't you be looking for her?"

"Do you know where she is?"

"Answer my question first," he said. "What's the reward?"

"There might be a small reward."

"How small is small?"

"Not enough to get rich on."

"Say a number."

"Maybe a couple of hundred dollars."

"Five hundred dollars?"

The price didn't really matter. He didn't have anything to sell me. "All right," I agreed. "Five hundred."

"Shit. That's not much."

"I know."

There was a pause. Then he said, briskly, "All right. Here's what you do. You know the corner of Broadway and Fifty-third Street, the uptown corner on the side towards Eighth Avenue. Meet me there in a half hour. And have the money with you. If you don't bring the bread, don't bother coming."

24

"I can't get the money at this hour."

"Ain't you got one of those all-night bank cards? Shit. All right, how much you got on you? You can give me some now and the rest tomorrow, but you don't want to stand around, man, because the chick might not be in the same place tomorrow, you dig what I'm saying?"

"More than you know."

"Say what?"

"What's her name?"

"How's that?"

"What's the chick's name?"

"You the one looking for her. Don't you know her damn name?"

"You don't, do you?"

He thought about it. "I know the name she using *now*," he said. It's the stupidest ones that turn crafty. "That's probably not the name you know."

"What name's she using?"

"Uh-huh. That's part of what you be buying with your five hundred dollars."

What I'd be buying would be a forearm across the windpipe, possibly a knife between the ribs. The ones who have something for you never start out asking about a reward, and they don't want to meet you on streetcorners. I felt tired enough to hang up on him, but he'd just call back again.

I said, "Shut up for a minute. My client's not authorizing any reward until the girl's recovered. You haven't got anything to sell and there's no way you're going to hustle a buck out of me. I don't want to meet you on a streetcorner, but if

I did I wouldn't bring money with me. I'd bring a gun and a set of cuffs and a backup, and then I'd take you somewhere and work on you until I was sure you didn't know anything. Then I'd work on you some more because I'd be pissed at you for wasting my time. Is that what you want? You want to meet me on the corner?"

"Motherfucker — "

"No," I said, "you got that wrong. You're the motherfucker."

I hung up on him. "Asshole," I said aloud, to him or to myself, I'm not sure which. Then I took a shower and went to bed.

2

The girl's name was Paula Hoeldtke and I didn't really expect to find her. I'd tried to tell her father as much but it's hard to tell people what they aren't prepared to hear.

Warren Hoeldtke had a big square jaw and an open face and a lot of wiry carrot-colored hair that was going gray. He had a Subaru dealership in Muncie, Indiana, and I could picture him starring in his own television commercials, pointing at the cars, facing into the camera, telling people they'll get the best possible deal at Hoeldtke Subaru.

Paula was the fourth of the Hoeldtkes' six children. She'd gone to college at Ball State, right in Muncie. "David Letterman went there," Hoeldtke told me. "You probably knew that. Of course that was before Paula's time."

She had majored in theater arts, and immediately after graduation she had come to New York. "You can't make a career in the theater in Muncie," he told me. "Or anywhere in the state, for that matter. You have to go to New York or California.

But I don't know, even if it wasn't that she had the bug to be an actress, I think she would have left. She had that urge to get off on her own. Her two older sisters, they both of them married boys from out of town, and in both cases the husbands decided to move to Muncie. And her older brother, my son Gordon, he's in the car business with me. And there's a boy and a girl still in school, so who knows for sure what they're going to do, but my guess is they'll stay close. But Paula, she had that wanderlust. I was just glad she stuck around long enough to finish college."

In New York she took acting classes, waited tables, lived in the West Fifties, and went on auditions. She had been in a showcase presentation of *Another Part of Town* at a storefront theater on Second Avenue and had taken part in a staged reading of *Very Good Friends* in the West Village. He had copies of the playbills and showed them to me, pointing out her name and the little capsule biographies that ran under the heading of "Who's Who in the Cast."

"She didn't get paid for this," he said. "You don't, you know, when you're starting out. It's so you can perform and people can see you — agents, casting people, directors. You hear all these salaries, this one getting five million dollars for a picture, but for most of them it's little or nothing for years."

"I know."

"We wanted to come for the play, her mother and I. Not the reading, that was just actors stand-

28

ing on the stage and reading lines from a script, it didn't sound very appealing, although we would have come if Paula had wanted it. But she didn't even want us to come to the play. She said it wasn't a very good play and her part was small anyway. She said we should wait until she was in something decent."

They had last heard from her in late June. She had sounded fine. She'd said something about possibly getting out of the city for the summer, but she hadn't gone into detail. When a couple of weeks passed without word from her, they called her and kept getting her answering machine.

"She was hardly ever home. She said her room was tiny and dark and depressing, so she didn't spend much time in it. When I saw it the other day I could understand why. I didn't actually see her room, I just saw the building and the front hall, but I could understand. People pay high prices in New York to live in places that anywhere else would be torn down."

Because she was rarely in, they did not ordinarily call her. Instead, they had a system. She would call every second or third Sunday, placing a person-to-person call for herself. They would tell the operator that Paula Hoeldtke was not at home, and then they would call her back station-to-station.

"It wasn't really cheating them," he said, "because it cost the same as if she called us station-to-station, but this way it was on our phone bill instead of hers. And as a result she wasn't in a hurry to get off the phone, so actually the telephone company came out ahead, too."

But she didn't call, nor did she respond to the messages on her machine. Toward the end of July Hoeldtke and his wife and the youngest daughter gassed up one of the Subarus and took a trip, driving up into the Dakotas to spend a week riding horses at a ranch and seeing the Badlands and Mount Rushmore. It was mid-August when they got back, and when they tried Paula they didn't get her machine. Instead they got a recording informing them that her phone had been temporarily disconnected.

"If she went away for the summer," he said, "she might have had the phone turned off to save money. But would she go away without letting anybody know? It wasn't like her. She might do something on the spur of the moment, but she would get in touch with you and let you know about it. She was responsible."

But not too responsible. You couldn't set your watch by her. Sometimes, during the three years since she'd graduated from Ball State, she'd gone more than two or three weeks between phone calls. So it was possible she'd gone somewhere during the summer and had been too preoccupied to get in touch. It was possible she'd tried to call while her parents were mounted on horses, or hiking along trails in Wind Cave National Park.

"Ten days ago was her mother's birthday," Warren Hoeldtke said. "And she didn't call."

"And that was something she wouldn't have missed?"

"Never. She wouldn't have forgotten and she wouldn't have missed calling. And if she did miss she would have called the next day."

He hadn't known what to do. He called the police in New York and got nowhere, predictably enough. He went to the Muncie office of a national detective agency. An investigator from their New York office visited her last known residence and established that she was no longer living there. If he cared to give them a substantial retainer, they would be glad to pursue the matter.

"I thought, what did they do for my money? Go to the place where she lived and find out she wasn't there? I could do that myself. So I got on a plane and came here."

He'd gone to the rooming house where Paula had lived. She had moved out sometime in early July, leaving no forwarding address. The telephone company had refused to tell him anything beyond what he already knew, that the telephone in question had been disconnected. He'd gone to the restaurant where she'd worked and found out that she'd left that job back in April.

"She may even have told us that," he said. "She must have worked six or seven places since she got to New York, and I don't know if she mentioned every time she changed jobs. She would leave because the tips weren't good, or she didn't get along with somebody, or because they wouldn't let her take off when she had an audition. So she

31

could have left the last job and gone to work some-where else without telling us, or she could have told us and it didn't register."

He couldn't think what else to do on his own, so he'd gone to the police. There he was told that in the first place it wasn't really a police matter, that she had evidently moved without informing her parents and that, as an adult, she had every legal right to do so. They told him, too, that he had waited too long, that she had disappeared al-most three months ago and whatever trail she'd left was a cold one by now.

If he wanted to pursue the matter further, the police officer told him, he'd be well advised to engage a private investigator. Department regu-lations prohibited his recommending a particular investigator. However, the officer said, it was probably all right for him to say what he himself would do if he happened to find himself in Mr. Hoeldtke's circumstances. There was a fellow named Scudder, an ex-cop as a matter of fact, and one who happened to reside in the very neigh-borhood where Mr. Hoeldtke's daughter had been living, and —

"Who was the cop?"

"His name's Durkin."

"Joe Durkin," I said. "That was very decent of him."

"I liked him."

"Yes, he's all right," I said. We were in a coffee shop on Fifty-seventh, a few doors down from my hotel. The lunch hour had ended before we got there, so they were letting us sit over coffee. I'd had a refill. Hoeldtke still had his first cup in front of him.

"Mr. Hoeldtke," I said, "I'm not sure I'm the man you want."

"Durkin said — "

"I know what he said. The thing is, you can probably get better coverage from the people you used earlier, the ones with the Muncie office. They can put several operatives on the case and they can canvass a good deal more comprehensively than I can."

"Are you saying they can do a better job?"

I thought about it. "No," I said, "but they may be able to give the appearance. For one thing, they'll furnish you with detailed reports telling you exactly what they did and who they talked to and what they found out. They'll itemize their expenses and bill you very precisely for the hours they spend on the case." I took a sip of coffee, set the cup down in its saucer. I leaned forward and said, "Mr. Hoeldtke, I'm a pretty decent detective, but I'm completely unofficial. You need a license to operate as a private investigator in this state and I don't have one. I've never felt like going through the hassle of applying for one. I don't itemize expenses or keep track of my hours, and I don't provide detailed reports. I don't have an office, either, which is why we're meeting here over coffee. All I've really got is whatever instincts and abilities I've developed over the years, and I'm not sure that's what you want to employ."

"Durkin didn't tell me you were unlicensed."

"Well, he could have. It's not a secret."

"Why do you suppose he recommended you?"

I must have been having an attack of scruples. Or maybe I didn't much want the job. "Partly because he expects me to give him a referral fee," I said.

Hoeldtke's face clouded. "He didn't mention that either," he said.

"I'm not surprised."

"That's not ethical," he said. "Is it?"

"No, but it wasn't really ethical for him to recommend anyone in the first place. And, to give him his due, he wouldn't have steered you to me unless he thought I was the right person for you to hire. He probably thinks I'll give you good value and a straight deal."

"And will you?"

I nodded. "And part of a straight deal is to tell you in front that you're very likely wasting your money."

"Because — "

"Because she'll probably either turn up on her own or she won't turn up at all."

He was silent for a moment, considering the implications of what I'd just said. Neither of us had yet mentioned the possibility that his daughter was dead, and it looked as though it was going to go unmentioned, but that didn't mean it was all that easy to avoid thinking about it.

He said, "How much money would I be wasting?"

"Suppose you let me have a thousand dollars."

"Would that be an advance or a retainer or what?"

"I don't know what you'd want to call it," I said. "I don't have a day rate and I don't keep track of my hours. I just go out there and do what seems to make sense. There are a batch of basic steps to take for openers, and I'll go through them first, although I don't really expect them to lead anywhere. Then there are a few other things I can do, and we'll see if they get us anyplace or not. When it seems to me that your thousand bucks is used up I'll ask you for more money, and you can decide whether or not you want to pay it."

He had to laugh. "Not a very businesslike approach," he said.

"I know it. I'm afraid I'm not a very businesslike person."

"In a curious way, that inspires confidence. The thousand dollars — I assume your expenses would be additional."

I shook my head. "I don't anticipate a lot in the way of expenses, and I'd rather pay them myself than have to account for them."

"Would you want to run some newspaper ads? I'd thought of doing that myself, either a listing in the personals or an ad with her photo and the offer of a reward. Of course that wouldn't come out of your thousand dollars. It would probably cost that much or more by itself, to do any kind of extensive advertising."

I advised against it. "She's too old to get her

picture on a milk carton," I said, "and I'm not sure ads in the papers are a good idea. You just draw the hustlers and the reward-hunters that way, and they're more trouble than they're worth."

"I keep thinking that she might have amnesia. If she saw her photograph in the newspaper, or if someone else saw it — "

"Well, it's a possibility," I said. "But let's hold it in reserve for the time being."

In the end, he gave me a check for a thousand dollars and a couple of pictures and what information he had — her last address, the names of several restaurants where she'd worked. He let me keep the two playbills, assuring me that they had plenty of copies of both. I copied down his address in Muncie and his phone numbers at home and at the auto showroom. "Call anytime at all," he said.

I told him I probably wouldn't call until I had something concrete to report. When I did, he'd hear from me.

He paid for our coffees and left a dollar for the waitress. At the door he said, "I feel good about this. I think I've taken the right step. You come across as honest and straightforward, and I appreciate that."

Outside, a three-card-monte dealer was working to a small crowd, telling the people to keep their eyes on the red card, keeping his own eye out for cops.

"I've read about that game," Hoeldtke said.

"It's not a game," I told him. "It's a short con, a swindle. The player never wins."

"That's what I've read. Yet people keep playing."

"I know," I said. "It's hard to figure."

After he left I took one of the photos to a copy shop and had them run off a hundred wallet-size prints. I went back to my hotel room, where I had a rubber stamp with my name and number. I stamped each of the photos on the back.

Paula Hoeldtke's last known address was a dingy red brick rooming house on Fifty-fourth Street a few doors east of Ninth Avenue. It was a little after five when I headed over there, and the streets were full of office workers on their way home. There was a bank of doorbells in the entrance hall, over fifty of them, and a single bell marked MANAGER off to the side. Before I rang it I checked the tags on the other bells. Paula Hoeldtke's name wasn't listed.

The manager was a tall woman, rail thin, with a face that tapered from a broad forehead to a narrow chin. She was wearing a floral print housedress and carrying a lit cigarette. She took a moment to look me over. Then she said, "Sorry, I got nothing vacant at the moment. You might want to check back with me in a few weeks if you don't find anything."

"How much are your rooms when you do have something?"

"One-twenty a week, but some of the nicer ones run a little higher. That includes your electric. There's supposed to be no cooking, but you could have a one-ring hotplate and it'd be all right. Each room has a bitty refrigerator. They're small, but they'll keep your milk from spoiling."

"I drink my coffee black."

"Then maybe you don't need the fridge, but it doesn't matter too much, since I got no vacancies and don't expect any soon."

"Did Paula Hoeldtke have a hotplate?"

"She was a waitress, so I guess she took her meals where she worked. You know, my first thought when I saw you was you were a cop, but then for some reason I changed my mind. I had a cop here a couple weeks ago, and then the other day a man came around, said he was her father. Nice-looking man, had that bright red hair just starting to go gray. What happened to Paula?"

"That's what I'm trying to find out."

"You want to come inside? I told the first cop all I knew, and I went over everything for her father, but I suppose you got your own questions to ask. That's always the way, isn't it?"

I followed her inside and down a long hallway. A table at the foot of the stairs was heaped with envelopes. "That's where they pick up their mail," she said. "Instead of sorting it and putting it into fifty-four individual mailboxes, the mailman just drops the whole stack on the table there. Believe it or not, it's safer that way. Other places have mailboxes in the vestibules, and the junkies break into them all the time, looking for welfare checks. Right this way, I'm the last door on the left."

Her room was small but impressively neat. There was a captain's bed made up as a sofa, a straight-backed wooden chair and an armchair, a small maple drop-front desk, a painted chest of drawers with a television set on top of it. The floor was covered with brick-patterned linoleum, most of that covered in turn by an oval braided rug.

I sat on one of the chairs while she opened the desk and paged through the rental ledger. She said, "Here we are. The last day I saw her was when she paid her rent for the last time, and that was the sixth of July. That was a Monday, that's when rents are due, and she paid $135 on the due date. She had a nice room, just one flight up and larger than some of them. Then the following week I didn't see her on the Monday, and on Wednesday I went looking for her. I'll do that, on Wednesdays I go knocking on doors when people haven't come up with the rent. I don't go and evict anybody for being two days late, but I go around and ask for the money, because I've got some that would never pay if I didn't come asking for it.

"I knocked on her door and she didn't answer, and then on my way back downstairs I knocked again, and she still wasn't home. The next morning, that would have been Thursday the sixteenth, I banged on her door again, and when there was no answer I used my passkey." She frowned. "Now why would I do that? She was usually in mornings but not always, and she wasn't but three days late with the rent. Oh, I remember! There was mail for her that hadn't been picked up in a few days, letters I'd seen a couple times over, and between that and the rent being late — anyway, I opened the door."

"What did you find?"

"Not what I was afraid of finding. You hate to open a door that way, you know. You're a cop, I don't have to tell you that, do I? People who live alone in furnished rooms, and you open their doors scared of what you might find. Not this time, thank God. Her place was empty."

"Completely empty?"

"No, come to think of it. She left the bed linen. Tenants have to supply their own linen. I used to furnish it, but I changed the policy, oh, I'd say fifteen years ago. Her sheets and blankets and pillowcase were still on the bed. But there were no clothes in the closet, nothing in the drawers, no food in the refrigerator. No question but that she'd moved out, she was gone."

"I wonder why she left the linen."

"Maybe she was moving someplace where they supplied it. Maybe she was leaving town and only had room to carry so much. Maybe she plain forgot it. When you pack up to leave a motel room you don't take the sheets and blankets, not unless you're a thief, and this is sort of like living in a hotel. I've had them leave linen behind before. Lord, that's not the only thing I've had them leave behind."

She left that hanging there, but I let it lie. I said, "You said she was a waitress."

"Well, that's how she earned her living. She was an actress, or fixing to be one. Most of my people are trying to get into show business. My younger people. I've got a few older folks been with me for years and years, living on pensions and government checks. I've got one woman doesn't pay me but seventeen dollars and thirty cents a week, if you can believe that, and she's got one of the best rooms in the house. *And* I have to climb five flights of stairs to collect her rent, and I'll tell you, there are some Wednesday mornings when it doesn't seem worth the effort."

"Do you know where Paula was working just before she left?"

"I don't even know *that* she was working. If she told me I don't remember, and I doubt she told me. I don't get too close to them, you know. I'll pass the time of day, but that's about all. Because, you know, they come and they go. My old folks are with me until the Lord calls them home, but my young people are in and out of here, in and out. They get discouraged and go home, or they save up some money and get a regular apartment, or they get married or move in with someone, whatever they do."

"How long was Paula here?"

"Three years, or the next thing to it. She moved in just three years ago this week, and I know because I looked it up when her father was here. Of course she moved out two months ago, so she

41

wasn't here the whole three years. Even so, she was with me longer than most. I've got a few have been with me longer than that, besides my rent-controlled old people, I mean. But not many."

"Tell me something about her."

"Tell you what?"

"I don't know. Who were her friends? What did she do with her time? You're an observant woman, you must have noticed things."

"I'm observant, yes, but sometimes I turn a blind eye. Do you know what I mean?"

"I think so."

"I have fifty-four rooms I rent out, and some of the rooms are larger and two girls will share one. I have, I think it's sixty-six tenants at the moment. All I ask is are they quiet, are they decent, do they pay the rent on time. I don't ask how they earn their money."

"Was Paula turning tricks?"

"I have no reason to think that she was. But I couldn't swear on a Bible that she wasn't. I'll say this, I'd bet there's at least four of my tenants earning money that way, and likely more than that, and the thing is I don't know who they are. If a woman gets up and goes out to work, I don't know if she's carrying plates in a restaurant or doing something else in a massage parlor or whatever they call it this year. My tenants can't have guests to their rooms. That's my business. What they do off the premises is their business."

"You never met any of her friends?"

"She never brought anyone home. It wasn't allowed. I'm not stupid, I know people will sneak someone in now and then, but I discourage it enough that no one tries it on a regular basis. If she was friendly with any of the girls in the building, or any of the young men, for that matter, well, I wouldn't know about it."

"She didn't leave you a forwarding address."

"No. I never heard a word from her after the last time she paid her rent."

"What did you do with her mail?"

"Gave it back to the postman. *Gone, no forwarding.* She didn't get much mail. A phone bill, the usual junk mail that everybody gets."

"You got along all right with her?"

"I would say so. She was quiet, she was well-spoken, she was clean. She paid her rent. She was late a few times over the three years." She paged through the ledger. "Here she paid two weeks at once. And here she missed for almost a month, and then she paid an extra fifty dollars a week until she was even with me. I'll let tenants do that if they've been with me for a while and I know they're good for it. And if they don't make a habit of it. You have to carry people some of the time, because everybody has bad times now and then."

"Why do you suppose she left without saying anything to you?"

"I don't know," she said.

"No idea?"

"They'll do that, you know. Just up and disappear, steal out the door with their suitcases in the middle of the night. But they'll generally do that when they're a week or so late with the rent, and she was the next thing to paid up. In fact she may have been completely paid up, because I don't know for sure when she left. At the most she was two days late, but for all I know she paid on the Monday and moved out a day later, because there was ten days that I didn't lay eyes on her between the last time she paid rent and the day I used my passkey."

"It seems odd she would leave without a word."

"Well, maybe it was late when she left and she didn't want to disturb me. Or maybe it was a decent hour but I wasn't home. I'm out at the movies every chance I get, you know. There's nothing I like better than going to the movies in the middle of a weekday afternoon, when the theater's next to empty and there's just you and the picture. I was thinking about getting myself a VCR. I could see any movie I wanted any time of the day, and it doesn't cost but two or three dollars to rent one. But it's not the same, watching on your own set in your own room, and on a bitty TV screen. It's like the difference between praying at home and in church."

3

I spent an hour or so that night going door-to-door in the rooming house, starting at the top floor and working my way down. A majority of the tenants were out. I spoke with half a dozen tenants and didn't learn anything. Only one of the persons I talked to recognized Paula's picture, and she hadn't even realized Paula had moved out.

I called it quits after a while and stopped at the manager's door on my way out. She was watching *Jeopardy*, and she kept me waiting until the commercial. "That's a good program," she said, turning the sound off. "They get smart people to be on that show. You have to have a quick mind."

I asked which room had been Paula's.

"She was in number twelve. I *think*." She looked it up. "Yes, twelve. That's up one flight."

"I don't suppose it's still vacant."

She laughed. "Didn't I tell you I didn't have any vacancies? I don't think it was more than a day before I rented it. Let me see. The Price girl took that room on the eighteenth of July. When did I say Paula moved out?"

"We're not sure, but it was the sixteenth when you found out she was gone."

"Well, there you are. Vacant the sixteenth, rented the eighteenth. Probably rented the seventeenth, and she moved in the following day. My vacancies don't last any time to speak of. I've got a waiting list right now with half a dozen names on it."

"You say the new tenant's name is Price?"

"Georgia Price. She's a dancer. A lot of them are dancers the past year or so."

"I think I'll see if she's in." I gave her one of the photos. "If you think of anything," I said, "my number's on the back."

She said, "That's Paula. It's a good likeness. Your name is Scudder? Here, just a minute, you can have one of my cards."

Florence Edderling, her business card said. *Rooms to Let.*

"People call me Flo," she said. "Or Florence, it doesn't matter."

Georgia Price wasn't in, and I'd knocked on enough doors for the day. I bought a sandwich at a deli and ate it on the way to my meeting.

The next morning I took Warren Hoeldtke's check to the bank and drew out some cash, including a hundred in singles. I kept a supply of them loose in my right front trouser pocket.

You couldn't go anywhere without being asked for money. Sometimes I shook them off. Sometimes I reached into my pocket and handed over a dollar.

Some years back I had quit the police force and left my wife and sons and moved into my hotel. It was around that time that I started tithing, giving a tenth of whatever income I received to whatever house of worship I happened to visit next. I had taken to hanging out in churches a lot. I don't know what I was looking for there and I can't say whether or not I found it, but it seemed somehow appropriate for me to pay out ten percent of my earnings for whatever it gave me.

After I sobered up I went on tithing for a while, but it no longer felt right and I stopped. That didn't feel right either. My first impulse was to give the money to AA, but AA didn't want donations. They pass the hat to cover expenses, but a dollar a meeting is about as much as they want from you.

So I'd started giving the money away to the people who were coming out on the streets and asking for it. I didn't seem to be comfortable keeping it for myself, and I hadn't yet thought of a better thing to do with it.

I'm sure some of the people spent my handouts on drink and drugs, and why not? You spend your money on what you need the most. At first I found myself trying to screen the beggars, but I didn't do that for long. On the one hand it seemed presumptuous of me, and at the same time it felt too much like work, a form of instant detection. When

47

I gave the money to churches I hadn't bothered to find out what they were doing with it, or whether or not I approved. I'd been willing then for my largesse to purchase Cadillacs for monsignors. Why shouldn't I be as willing now to underwrite Porsches for crack dealers?

While I was in a giving mood, I walked over to Midtown North and handed fifty dollars to Detective Joseph Durkin.

I'd called ahead, so he was in the squadroom waiting for me. It had been a year or more since I'd seen him but he looked the same. He'd put on a couple of pounds, no more than he could carry. The booze was starting to show up in his face, but that's no reason to quit. Who ever stopped drinking because of a few broken blood vessels, a little bloom in the cheeks?

He said, "I wondered if that Honda dealer'd get hold of you. He had a German name but I don't remember it."

"Hoeldtke. And it's Subarus, not Hondas."

"That's a real important distinction, Matt. How're you doing, anyway?"

"Not bad."

"You look good. Clean living, right?"

"That's my secret."

"Early hours? Plenty of fiber in your diet?"

"Sometimes I go to the park and gnaw the bark right off a tree."

"Me too. I just can't help myself." He reached up a hand and smoothed his hair back. It was dark brown, close to black, and it hadn't needed smoothing; it lay flat against his scalp the way he'd combed it. "It's good to see you, you know that?"

"Good to see you, Joe."

We shook hands. I had palmed a ten and two twenties, and they moved from my hand to his during the handshake. His hand disappeared from view and came up empty. He said, "I gather you did yourself a little good with him."

"I don't know," I said. "I took some money from him and I'll knock on some doors. I don't know what good it's going to do."

"You put his mind at rest, that's all. At least he's doing all he can, you know? And you won't soak him."

"No."

"I took a picture from him and had them run it at the morgue. They had a couple of unidentified white females since June, but she doesn't match up to any of 'em."

"I figured you'd done that."

"Yeah, well, that's all I did. It's not police business."

"I know."

"Which is why I referred him to you."

"I know, and I appreciate it."

"My pleasure. You got any sense of it yet?"

"It's a little early. One thing, she moved out. Packed everything and took off."

"Well, that's good," he said. "Makes it a little more likely she's alive."

"I know, but there are things that don't make sense. You said you checked the morgue. What about hospitals?"

"You thinking coma?"

"It could be."

"When'd they hear from her last, sometime in June? That's a long time to be in a coma."

"Sometimes they're out for years."

"Yeah, that's true."

"And she paid her rent the last time on the sixth of July. So what's that, two months and a few days."

"Still a long time."

"Not for the person in the coma. It's like the wink of an eye."

He looked at me. He had pale gray eyes that don't show you much, but they showed a little grudging amusement now. " 'The wink of an eye,' " he said. "First she checks out of her rooming house, then she checks into a hospital."

"All it takes is a coincidence," I said. "She moves, and in the course of the move or a day or two later she has an accident. No ID, some public-spirited citizen snags her purse while she's unconscious, and she's Jane Doe in a ward somewhere. She didn't call her parents and tell them she was moving because the accident happened first. I'm not saying it happened, just that it could have."

"I suppose. You checking hospitals?"

"I thought I could walk over to the ones in the neighborhood. Roosevelt, St. Clare's."

"Of course the accident could have happened anywhere."

"I know."

"If she moved, she could have moved anywhere, so she could be in any hospital anywhere in the city."

"I was thinking that myself."

He gave me a look. "I suppose you've got some extra pictures. Oh, that's handy, with your number on the back. I suppose you wouldn't mind if I sent these around for you, asked them all to check their Jane Does."

"That would be very helpful," I said.

"I bet it would. You expect a lot for the price of a coat."

A coat, in police parlance, is a hundred dollars. A hat is twenty-five. A pound is five. The terms took hold years ago, when clothing was cheaper than it is now, and British currency pegged higher. I said, "You'd better look closer. All you got was a couple of hats."

"Jesus," he said. "You're a cheap bastard, anybody ever tell you that?"

She wasn't in a hospital, not in the five boroughs, at any rate. I hadn't expected she would be, but it was the kind of thing that had to be checked. While I was learning this through Durkin's channels, I was walking down other streets on my own. Over the next several days I made a few more visits to Florence Edderling's rooming house, where I knocked on more doors and talked to more

51

tenants when I found them in. There were men as well as women in the building, old people as well as young ones, New Yorkers as well as out-of-towners, but the bulk of Ms. Edderling's roomers were like Paula Hoeldtke — young women, relatively new in the city, long on hope and short on cash.

Few of them knew Paula by name, although most of them recognized her picture, or thought they did. Like her, they spent most of their time away from the rooming house, and when they were in their rooms they were alone, with their doors closed. "I thought this would be like those forties movies," one girl told me, "with a wisecracking landlady and kids gathering in the parlor to talk about boyfriends and auditions and do each other's hair. Well, there used to be a parlor, but they partitioned it years ago and made two rooms out of it and rented them out. There are people I nod to and smile at, but I don't really know a single person in this building. I used to see this girl — Paula? But I never knew her name, and I didn't even know she'd moved out."

One morning I went over to the Actors Equity office, where I managed to establish that Paula Hoeldtke hadn't been a member of that organization. The young man who checked the listings asked me if she'd been a member of AFTRA or SAG; when I said I didn't know, he was nice enough to call the two unions for me. Neither of them had her name on their rolls.

"Unless she used another name," he said. "Her name's not utterly impossible, in fact it looks good in print, but it's the sort of name a great many people would mispronounce, or at least be uncertain about. Do you suppose she went and changed it to Paula Holden or something manageable like that?"

"She didn't say anything about it to her parents."

"It's not always the sort of thing you rush to report to your parents, especially if they have a strong attachment to their name. As parents often do."

"I suppose you're right. But she used her own name in the two shows she was in."

"May I see that?" He took the playbills from me. "Oh, now this might be helpful. Yes, here we are, Paula Hoeldtke. Am I pronouncing it correctly?"

"Yes."

"Good. Actually I can't think how *else* you would pronounce it, but one feels uncertain. She could have just spelled it differently, H-O-L-T-K-Y. But that wouldn't look right, would it? Let's see. 'Paula Hoeldtke majored in theater arts at Ball State University' — oh, the poor darling — 'where she appeared in *The Flowering Peach* and *Gregory's Garden.*' *The Flowering Peach* is Odets, but what the hell do you suppose *Gregory's Garden* might be? Student work, that would be my guess. And that is all they're going to tell us about Paula Hoeldtke. What is this, anyway? *Another Part of*

Town, what a curious choice for a showcase. She played Molly. I barely remember the play, but I don't think that's a principal role."

"She told her parents she had a small part."

"I don't think she exaggerated. Was there anyone in this? Hmmm. 'Axel Godine appears with the permission of Actors Equity.' I don't know who he is, but I can furnish you with his phone number. He played Oliver, so he's probably well up in years, but you never know in a showcase, the casting sometimes tends to be imaginative. Does she like older men?"

"I don't know."

"What's this? *Very Good Friends*. Not a bad title, and where did they do it? At the Cherry Lane? I wonder why I never heard of it. Oh, it was a staged reading, it only had one performance. Not a bad title, *Very Good Friends*, a little suggestive but hardly naughty. Oh, Gerald Cameron wrote it. He's quite good. I wonder how she happened to be in this."

"Is it unusual?"

"Well, sort of. You wouldn't have open auditions for this sort of thing, I wouldn't think. You see, the playwright very likely wanted to get a sense of how his work would play, so he or the designated director got hold of some suitable actors and had them walk through it onstage, possibly in front of prospective backers, possibly not. Some staged readings these days are fairly elaborate, with extensive rehearsals and a fair amount of movement onstage. In others the actors just sit in chairs as if they were doing a radio play. And who directed this? Oh, we're in luck."

"Someone you know?"

"Indeed," he said. He looked up a number, picked up a phone and dialed it. He said, "David Quantrill, please. David? Aaron Stallworth. How *are* you? Oh, really? Yes, well I heard about *that*." He covered the mouthpiece and rolled his eyes at the ceiling. "David, guess what I've got in my hand. No, on second thought don't bother. It's a playbill for a staged reading of *Very Good Friends*. Did that ever get past the staged reading stage, as it were? I see. Yes, I see. I hadn't heard. Oh, that's too bad." His face clouded, and he listened in silence for a moment. Then he said, "David, why I'm calling is there's a fellow with me now who's trying to find one of the actors from the reading. Her name's Paula Hoeldtke and it says here that she read Marcy. Yes. Can you tell me how you happened to use her? I see. Well, look, do you suppose my friend could come and have a word with you? He'll have some questions to ask. It seems our Paula has vanished from the face of the earth and her parents are predictably frantic. Would that be all right? Good, I'll send him right over. No, I don't think so. Shall I ask him? Oh, I see. Thank you, David."

He put the phone down, pressed the tips of two fingers against the center of his forehead, as if trying to suppress a headache. With his eyes lowered he said, "The play hasn't been performed because Gerald Cameron wanted to revise it after the reading, and he hasn't been able to do so because he's been ill." He looked at me. "Very ill."

"I see."

"Everyone's dying. Have you noticed? I'm sorry, I don't mean to do this. David lives in Chelsea, let me write down the address for you. I assumed you'd rather ask him questions yourself than have me try to function as an intermediary. He wanted to know if you were gay. I told him I didn't think so."

"I'm not."

"I suppose he only asked out of habit. After all, what difference could it make? Nobody *does* anything anymore. And it's not as though you have to ask who's gay and who isn't. All you have to do is wait a few years and see who's still alive." He looked at me. "Have you been reading about the seals?"

"I beg your pardon?"

"You know," he said. "The seals." He pressed his elbows against his ribs, clapped his hands together like flippers, and tilted his head to mime a seal balancing a ball on its nose. "In the North Sea, and all along the European coastline. The seals are dying and nobody knows why. Oh, they've isolated a virus, but it's been around for ages, it's the one that causes distemper in dogs, and it's not as though some rottweiler's been racing around biting seals. The best guess seems to be that it's pollution. The North Sea is badly polluted, and they think this has weakened the immune systems of the seals, leaving them with no defense against whatever virus comes along. Do you know what I think?"

"What?"

"The earth has AIDS. We're all whirling merrily through the void on a dying planet, and gay people are just doing their usual number, being shamelessly trendy as always. Right out in front on the cutting edge of death."

David Quantrill had a loft on the ninth floor of a converted industrial building on West Twenty-second Street. It consisted of one enormous high-ceilinged room, the wide board floor painted a glossy white, the walls matte black and sparsely hung with vivid abstract oils. The furniture was white wicker, and there wasn't a great deal of it.

Quantrill was in his forties, pudgy and mostly bald. What hair remained he wore long, curling over his collar. He fussed with a briar pipe and tried to remember something about Paula Hoeldtke.

"You have to remember that it was almost a year ago," he said, "and I never laid eyes or ears on her before or since. Now how did she wind up in *Friends*? Somebody knew her, but who?"

It took him a few minutes to prod the memory loose. He had cast another actress as Marcy, a woman named Virginia Sutcliffe. "Then Ginny called me, very last minute, to say she'd just gotten a call to do two weeks in *Seesaw* in some goddam place. Baltimore? It doesn't matter. Anyway, much as she loved me, et cetera, et cetera. She said there was a girl in a class with her who she swore was just right for Marcy. I said I'd see her, and she came down and read for me, and she was all right." He picked up the photograph. "She's pretty, isn't she, but there's nothing genuinely arresting about her face. Or her stage presence, but she was adequate, and I didn't have the time to chase around the kingdom with a glass slipper, searching for Cinderella. I knew I wouldn't be using her in the actual production. I'd cast Ginny for that, if she turned out to have the right chemistry with the rest of the cast, and assuming I'd forgiven her by then for deserting me and traipsing off to Baltimore."

I asked how I could reach Ginny. He had a number for her, and when it didn't answer he called her service and learned that she was in Los Angeles. He called her agent, got a number for her in California, and called it. He chatted with her for a moment or two, then put me on.

"I barely remember Paula," she said. "I knew her from class, and I just had the thought that she'd be right for Marcy. She has this awkward, tentative quality. Do you know Paula?" I said I didn't. "And you probably don't know the play, so you wouldn't know what the hell I'm talking about. I never saw her after that, so I didn't even know David had used her."

"You were in an acting class with her?"

"That's right. And I didn't really *know* her. It was an improv workshop led by Kelly Greer, two hours every Thursday afternoon in a second-floor studio on upper Broadway. She did a scene, two people waiting for a bus, that I thought was pretty good."

"Was she close to anyone in the class? Did she have a boyfriend?"

"I really don't know any of that. I can't remember ever having an actual conversation with her."

"Did you see her after you got back from Baltimore?"

"Baltimore?"

"I thought you went there for two weeks to be in a play, and that was why you couldn't do the reading."

"Oh, *Seesaw*," she said. "That wasn't two weeks in Baltimore, it was a week in Louisville and a week in Memphis. At least I got to see Graceland. After that I went home to Michigan for Christmas, and when I got back to New York I fell into three weeks of work in a soap, which was a godsend, but it took care of my Thursday afternoons. By the time I was free again there was an opening in one of Ed Kovens's classes, and I'd been wanting to study with him for a long time, and I decided I'd rather do that than more improv work. So I never did see Paula again. Is she in some kind of trouble?"

"It's possible. You said her teacher was Kelly Greer?"

"That's right. Kelly's number's in my Rolodex, which is on my desk in New York, so that's no help to you. But I'm sure it's in the book. Kelly Greer, G-R-E-E-R."

"I'm sure I'll be able to find him."

"Her. I'd be surprised if Paula's still studying with her. You don't usually stay in the same improv workshop forever, it's usually a few months and out, but maybe Kelly will be able to tell you something. I hope Paula's all right."

"So do I."

"I can picture her now, groping her way through that scene. She seemed — what's the word I want? *Vulnerable.*"

Kelly Greer was an energetic little gnome of a woman. She had a mop of gray curls and enormous brown eyes. I found her in the book and reached her at her apartment. Instead of inviting me up she arranged to meet me in a dairy restaurant on Broadway in the low Eighties.

We sat at a table in front. I had a bagel and coffee. She ate an order of kasha varnishkes and drank two tall glasses of buttermilk.

She remembered Paula.

"She wasn't going anyplace," she said. "I think she knew it, which put her ahead of most of them."

"She wasn't any good?"

"She was all right. Most of them are all right. Oh, some of them are hopeless, but most of the ones who get this far have a certain amount of ability. They're not bad. They may even be good, they may even be fine. That's not good enough."

"What else do you need?"

"You need to be terrific. We like to think it's

60

a matter of getting the right breaks, or being generally lucky. Or knowing the right people, or sleeping with the right people. But that's not really what does it. The people who succeed are superb. It's not enough to have some talent. You have to be positively bursting with it. You have to light up the stage or the screen or the tube. You have to glow."

"And Paula didn't."

"No, and I think she knew it, or at least half knew it, and what's more I don't think it broke her heart. That's another thing, besides the talent you have to have the desire. You have to want it desperately, and I don't think she did." She thought for a moment. "She wanted something, though."

"What?"

"I don't know. I'm not sure she knew. Money? Fame? That's what draws a lot of them, especially on the West Coast. They think acting's a way to get rich. It's about the least likely way I can think of."

"Is that what Paula wanted? Money and fame?"

"Or glamour. Or excitement, adventure. Really, how well did I know her? She started coming to my classes last fall and she kept coming around for five months or so. And she wasn't religious about it. Sometimes she didn't show up. That's common enough, they have work or an audition or something that comes up."

"When did she quit?"

"She never quit formally, she just ceased to appear. I looked it up. Her last class was in February."

She had names and phone numbers for a dozen men and women who had studied with her at the same time as Paula. She couldn't remember if Paula had had a boyfriend, or if anyone had ever picked her up after class. She didn't know if Paula had been especially friendly with any of her classmates. I copied down all the names and numbers except for Virginia Sutcliffe, to whom I'd already spoken.

"Ginny Sutcliffe said Paula did an improvisational scene at a bus stop," I said.

"Did she? I use that situation a lot. I can't honestly say I recall how Paula did with it."

"According to Ginny, she had an awkward, tentative quality."

She smiled, but there was no joy in it. " 'An awkward, tentative quality,' " she said. "No kidding. Every year a thousand ingenues descend upon New York, awkward and tentative as all hell, hoping their coltish exuberance will melt the heart of a nation. Sometimes I want to go down to Port Authority and meet the buses and tell them all to go home."

She drank her buttermilk, took up her napkin and dabbed at her lips. I told her Ginny had said that Paula had seemed vulnerable.

"They're all vulnerable," she said.

I called Paula's acting classmates, saw some of them face to face, spoke with others on the phone.

62

I worked my way through Kelly Greer's list, and at the same time I kept knocking on doors at Flo Edderling's rooming house, crossing off names on my list of uninterviewed tenants.

I went, as my client had previously gone, to the restaurant that was Paula's last known place of employment. It was called the Druid's Castle, and it was an English pub-style place on West Forty-sixth. They had dishes like shepherd's pie on the menu, and something called toad-in-the-hole. The manager confirmed that she'd left in the spring. "She was all right," he said. "I forget why she quit, but we parted on good terms. I'd hire her again." There was a waitress who remembered Paula as "a good kid but sort of spacey, like she didn't really have her mind on what she was doing." I walked in and out of a lot of restaurants in the Forties and Fifties, and two of them did turn out to be places where Paula had worked prior to her stint at the Druid's Castle. This was information that might have been useful if I'd planned on writing her biography, but it didn't tell me much about where she'd gone in mid-July.

In a bar at Ninth and Fifty-second, a place called Paris Green, the manager allowed that she looked familiar but said she'd never worked there. The bartender, a lanky fellow with a beard like an oriole's nest, asked if he could see her picture. "She never worked here," he said, "but she used to come in here. Not in the past couple of months, though."

"In the spring?"

"Had to be since April because that's when I started here. What was her name again?"

"Paula."

He tapped the photo. "I don't remember the name, but this is her. I must have seen her in here five, six times. Late. She came in late. We close at two, and it was generally close to that when she came in. Past midnight, anyway."

"Was she alone?"

"Couldn't have been or I would have hit on her." He grinned. "Or at least volleyed, you know? She was with a guy, but was it the same guy every time? I think so but I couldn't swear to it. You have to remember that I never gave her a thought since the last time I saw her, and that's got to be two months ago."

"She was last seen the first week in July."

"That sounds about right, give or take a week or two. Last time I saw her she was drinking salty dogs, they were both drinking salty dogs."

"What did she usually drink?"

"Different things. Margaritas, vodka sours, maybe not that exactly but you get the general idea. Girl drinks. But he was a whiskey drinker and for a change he ordered up a saline canine, and what does that tell me?"

"It was hot out."

"On the nose, my dear Watson." He grinned again. "Either I'd make a good detective or you'd make a good bartender, because we both got the same place with that one. Can I buy you a drink on the strength of that?"

"Make it a Coke."

He drew a beer for himself and a Coke for me. He took a small sip of his and asked what had happened to Paula. I said she'd disappeared.

"People'll do that," he said.

I worked with him for ten minutes or so, and by the time I was through I had a description of Paula's escort. My height, maybe a little taller. Around thirty. Dark hair, no beard or moustache. A casual dresser, a sort of outdoors type.

"Like retrieving lost data from a computer," he said, marveling at the process. "I'm remembering things I never even knew I knew. The only thing that bothers me is the thought that I might be making some of this up without meaning to, just to be obliging."

"Sometimes that happens," I admitted.

"Anyway, the description I gave you would fit half the men in the neighborhood. If he was even from the neighborhood, which I doubt."

"You only saw him the five or six times he was with her."

He nodded. "Add that to the hour they came in, I'd say he picked her up after work or she picked him up after work, or maybe they both worked at the same place."

"And stopped here for a quick one."

"More than one."

"Was she a heavy hitter?"

"He was. She sipped, but she didn't dawdle. Her drinks didn't just evaporate. She didn't show the booze, though. Neither did he. More evidence they worked someplace, and started their drinking here rather than finished it."

He extended the photo. I told him to keep it. "And if you think of anything — "

"I'll call the number."

Dribs and drabs, bits and pieces. By the time I told my story at Fresh Start I'd spent over a week looking for Paula Hoeldtke, and I'd probably given her father a thousand dollars' worth of time and shoe leather, even if I couldn't point to a thousand dollars' worth of results.

I'd talked to dozens of people and I had pages and pages of notes. I'd given out half of the hundred photos I'd had made up.

What had I learned? I couldn't account for her movements after she'd disappeared from her rooming house in the middle of July. I couldn't turn up any evidence of employment subsequent to the waitress job she'd left in April. And the picture I was beginning to develop was a good deal less sharply focused than the one I was handing out all over the neighborhood.

She was an actress, or wanted to be one, but she'd barely worked at all and had evidently stopped going to classes. She'd been in a man's company at a local drinking establishment, late in the evening, perhaps half a dozen times in all. She'd been a loner, but she hadn't spent much time in her room. Where did she go by her lonesome? Did she walk in the park? Did she talk to the pigeons?

4

My first thought the next morning was that I'd been too abrupt with my mystery caller. He wasn't much, but what else did I have?

Over breakfast, I reminded myself that I hadn't really expected to come up with anything. Paula Hoeldtke had dropped out of actressing and waitressing. Then she'd dropped out of Florence Edderling's house and out of her role as her parents' daughter. By now she was probably settled into some new life, and she'd surface when she wanted to. Or she was dead, in which case there wasn't a whole lot I could do for her.

I thought I'd go to a movie, but instead I wound up spending the day talking to theatrical agents, asking the same old questions, passing out pictures. None of them recognized the name or the face. "She probably just went to open auditions," one of them told me. "Some of them look for an agent right away, others buy the trades and go to the cattle calls and try to get a few credits so they have something to impress an agent with."

"What's the best way?"

"The best way? Have an uncle in the business, that's the best way."

I got tired of talking to agents and tried the rooming house again. I rang Florence Edderling's bell and she shook her head as she let me in. "I ought to start collecting rent from you," she said. "You spend more time here than some of my tenants."

"I've just got a few more people to see."

"Take all the time you want. Nobody's complained, and if they don't mind I sure don't."

Of the tenants I hadn't yet interviewed, only one was on the premises. She'd lived in the building since May and didn't know Paula Hoeldtke at all. "I wish I could help," she said, "but she doesn't even look familiar to me. My neighbor across the hall said she'd talked to you, that this girl disappeared or something?"

"It looks that way."

She shrugged. "I wish I could help."

When I was first getting sober I started keeping company with a woman named Jan Keane. I'd known her before, but we'd stopped seeing each other when she joined AA and took up again when I started coming to meetings.

She's a sculptor, living and working in a loft on Lispenard Street, which is in TriBeCa, just south of Canal Street. We began spending a fair amount of time together, seeing each other three or four nights a week, occasionally getting together during the day. Sometimes we went to meetings together, but we did other things as well. We'd go out to dinner, or she would cook for me. She liked to go to galleries, in SoHo or the East Village. This was something I'd never done much of, and I discovered I enjoyed it. I'd always been a little self-conscious in situations like that, never knowing what to say when confronted by a painting or a piece of sculpture, and from her I'd learned that it was perfectly acceptable not to say anything at all.

I don't know what went wrong. The relationship escalated slightly, as relationships do, and we reached a point where I was half living on Lispenard Street, with some of my clothes in her closet and my socks and underwear in one of her dresser drawers. We had conversations in which we speculated gingerly on the wisdom of my maintaining my room at the hotel. Wasn't it a waste to pay rent when I was hardly ever there? On the other hand, was it perhaps valuable as a place to meet clients?

There was a point, I suppose, when it was appropriate for me to give up my room and begin paying my share of the expenses at the loft. And there was a point, too, where we might have gone on to talk about commitment and permanence and, I suppose, marriage.

But we didn't do any of this, and, having left it undone, it became impossible for things to remain as they had been. We disengaged gradually, in little fits and starts. Our times together were increasingly marked by moods and silences, and our times apart became more frequent. We decided — I honestly forget who suggested it — that we ought to see other people. We did, and subsequently found that made us that much more uncomfortable with each other. And at last, gently, and with a surprising lack of drama, I returned a couple of books she had lent me and retrieved the last of my clothing, and I took a cab uptown, and that was that.

It had dragged on long enough for the ending to be something of a relief, but even so I felt lonely a lot of the time, and possessed of a sense of loss. I'd felt less at the breakup of my marriage some years previously, but of course I was drinking then, so I didn't really feel anything.

So I went to a lot of meetings, and sometimes I talked about what I was feeling at meetings, and sometimes I kept it to myself. I had tried dating shortly after the breakup, but I didn't seem to have the heart for it. Now I was beginning to think that it might be time for me to start seeing women again, or a woman. I kept having the thought, but I hadn't yet reached the point of acting on it.

All of which put a curious spin on the business of going door-to-door in a West Side rooming house and making conversation with single women. Most of them were a little young for me, but not all of them were. And there is something about the kind of interview I was conducting that facilitates flirtation. I'd learned this when I was a cop, and a married one at that.

Sometimes, asking my endless questions about the elusive Paula Hoeldtke, I would be aware of a strong attraction to the woman I was questioning. Sometimes I sensed, too, that the current ran in both directions, that the attraction was reciprocal. I wrote little mental scripts, moving us toward emotional intimacy, and from the doorway to the bed.

But I could never bring myself to take the next step. I felt out of sync, and by the time I left the rooming house, having talked to six or ten or a dozen people, my mood had darkened and I felt unutterably alone.

This time all it took was one conversation to bring on the feeling. I went back to my hotel room and sat in front of my TV set until it was time to go to the meeting.

At St. Paul's that night the speaker was a housewife from Ozone Park. She told us how she used to take the first drink of the day as her husband's Pontiac was pulling out of the driveway. She kept her vodka under the sink, in a container that had previously held oven cleaner. "The first time I told this story," she said, "a woman said, 'Oh, dear Jesus, suppose you grabbed the wrong jar and drank the real oven cleaner.' 'Honey,' I told her, 'get real, will you? There was no wrong jar. There was no real oven cleaner. I lived in that house for thirteen years and I never cleaned the oven.' Anyway," she said, "that was my social drinking."

Different meetings have different formats. At St. Paul's the meetings run an hour and a half, and the Friday night meetings are step meetings, centering upon one of the twelve steps of AA's program of recovery. This particular meeting was on the fifth step, but I don't remember what the speaker had to say on the subject or what particular words of wisdom I contributed when it was my turn.

At ten o'clock we all stood to say the Lord's Prayer, except for a woman named Carole who makes a point of not taking part in the prayer. Then I folded my chair and stacked it, dropped my coffee cup in the trash, carried ashtrays up to the front of the room, talked with a couple of fellows, and turned when Eddie Dunphy called my name. "Oh, hello," I said. "I didn't see you."

"I was in the back, I got here a few minutes late. I liked what you had to say."

"Thanks," I said, wondering what I'd said. He asked if I wanted to have coffee, and I said a few of us were going over to the Flame, and why didn't he join us?

We walked a block south on Ninth and wound up at the big corner table with six or seven other people. I had a sandwich and fries and some more coffee. The conversation was mostly about politics. It was less than two months before the election, and people were saying what everybody says every four years, that it was a damned shame there wasn't anybody more interesting to vote for.

I didn't say much. I don't pay any more attention to politics than I have to. There was a woman at our table named Helen who'd been sober about the same length of time I had, and for a while now I'd been toying with the idea of asking her out. Now I placed her under covert surveillance, and I kept coming up with data that got entered in the minus column. Her laugh was grating, she needed some dental work, and every sentence out of her mouth had the phrase *you know* in it. By the time she was done with her hamburger, our romance had died unborn. I'll tell you, it's a great way to operate. You can run through women like wildfire and they never even know it.

A little after eleven I tucked some coins alongside my saucer, said my goodbyes, and carried my check to the counter. Eddie rose when I did, paid his own check and followed me outside. I'd almost forgotten he was there; he'd contributed even less to the conversation than I had.

Now he said, "Beautiful night, isn't it? When the air's like this it makes you want to breathe more. You got a minute? You want to walk a few blocks?"

"Sure."

"I gave you a call earlier. At your hotel."

"What time?"

"I don't know, middle of the afternoon. Maybe three o'clock."

"I never got the message."

"Oh, I didn't leave one. It was nothing important, and anyway you couldn't call me back."

"That's right, you don't have a phone."

"Oh, I got one. It sits right there on the bedside table. It just don't work, that's the only thing wrong with it. Anyway, I just wanted to pass the time of day. What were you doing, looking for the girl some more?"

"Going through the motions, anyway."

"No luck?"

"Not so far."

"Well, maybe you'll get lucky." He took out a cigarette, tapped it against his thumbnail. "What they were going on about back there," he said. "Politics. I have to tell you I don't even know what they were talking about. You gonna vote, Matt?"

"I don't know."

"You gotta wonder why anybody wants to be president. You want to know something? I never voted for nobody in my life. Wait a minute, I just told a lie. You want to know who I voted for? Abe Beame."

"That was a while ago."

"Gimme a minute and I'll tell you the year. That was '73. You remember him? He was a little shrimp of a guy, he ran for mayor and he won. You remember?"

"Sure."

He laughed. "I must of voted twelve times for Abe Beame. More. Maybe fifteen."

"It sounds as though you were highly impressed with him."

"Yeah, his message really moved me. What it

was, some guys from the local clubhouse got hold of a school bus and ran a bunch of us all over the West Side. Every precinct we went to I answered to a different name and they had a voter registration card for me in that name, and I went in the booth and did my civic duty like a little soldier. It was easy, I just voted the straight Democratic ticket like I was told."

He stopped to light his cigarette. "I forget what they paid us," he said. "I was gonna say fifty bucks, but it could have been less than that. This was fifteen years ago and I was just a kid, so it wouldn't take much. Besides, they sprung for a meal, and of course there was free booze for the bunch of us the whole day long."

"Magic words."

"Ain't that the truth? Booze was God's gift even when you had to pay for it, and when it was free, Jesus, there was nothing better."

"There was something about it that defied all logic," I said. "There was a place in Washington Heights where I didn't have to pay for my drinks. I remember taking a cab there from way the hell out in Brooklyn. It cost me twenty dollars, and I drank maybe ten or twelve dollars worth of booze, and then I took a cab home and thought I really put one over on the world. And I didn't just do this once, either."

"It made sense at the time."

"Perfect sense."

He drew on the cigarette. "I forget who it was ran against Beame," he said. "It's funny what you remember and what you forget. This poor bastard, I voted against him fifteen times and I don't remember his name. Here's another thing that's funny. After the first two, three times I voted, I couldn't go in a booth without getting this urge to cross 'em up. You know, vote the other way, take their money and vote Republican."

"Why?"

"Who knows why? I had a couple of belts in me by then and maybe that made it seem like a good idea. And I figured nobody'd know. Secret ballot, right? Only I thought, yeah, there's supposed to be a secret ballot, but there's lots of shit that's supposed to be, and if they can take and vote us fifteen times all over town, maybe they can tell how we're voting. So I did what I was supposed to do."

"The straight ticket."

"You got it. Anyway, that was the first I ever voted. I coulda the year before, I was old enough, but I didn't, and then I voted fifteen times for Abe Beame, and I guess I got it out of my system, because I never done it since."

The light changed and we walked across Fifty-seventh. A blue-and-white patrol car headed north on Ninth with the siren screaming. We turned to follow it with our eyes until it was out of sight. You could still hear it, though, whining faintly over the other traffic noises.

He said, "Somebody must of done something bad."

"Or it's just a couple of cops in a hurry."

"Yeah. Matt, what they were talking about at the meeting. The fifth step?"

"What about it?"

"I don't know. I think maybe I'm afraid of it."

The steps are designed to enable recovering alcoholics to change, to grow spiritually. The founders of AA discovered that people who were willing to grow along spiritual lines tended to stay sober, while those who fought change tended to go back to drinking sooner or later. The fifth step calls for an admission to God, to oneself, and to another human being of the exact nature of one's wrongs.

I quoted the language of the step to Eddie and he frowned. He said, "Yeah, but what does that boil down to? You sit down with somebody and tell him every bad thing you ever done?"

"More or less. Everything that bothers you, everything that weighs on your mind. The idea is that you might drink over it otherwise."

He thought about it. "I don't know if I could do that," he said.

"Well, there's no rush. You're not sober all that long, you don't have to be in a hurry."

"I guess."

"There's a lot of people will tell you that the steps are a load of crap, anyway. 'Don't drink and go to meetings and all the rest is conversation.' You've heard people say that."

"Oh, sure. 'If you don't drink you can't get drunk.' I remember the first time I heard somebody say that. I thought it was the most brilliant remark I ever heard in my life."

"You can't fault it for truth."

He started to say something, but stopped when a woman stepped out of a doorway into our path. She was a haggard, wild-eyed thing, all wrapped in a shawl, her hair stringy and matted. She was holding an infant in one arm, and she had a small child standing next to her, clutching her shawl. She extended one hand, palm up, wordless.

She looked as though she belonged in Calcutta, not New York. I'd seen her before during the past few weeks, and each time I'd given her money. I gave her a dollar now, and she drew back wordlessly into the shadows.

He said, "You hate to see a woman on the street like that. And when she's got her kids with her, Jesus, that's a hell of a thing to see."

"I know."

"Matt, did you ever do it? Take the fifth step?"

"I did, yes."

"You didn't hold nothing back?"

"I tried not to. I said everything I could think of."

He thought about it. "Of course you were a cop," he said. "You couldn't of done anything that bad."

"Oh, come on," I said. "I did a lot of things I'm not proud of, and some of them were acts a person could go to jail for. I was on the force for a lot of years and I took money almost from the beginning. I never lived on what I drew as salary."

"Everybody does that."

78

"No," I said, "everybody doesn't. Some cops are clean and some are dirty, and I was dirty. I always told myself I felt all right about it, and I justified it with the argument that it was clean dirt. I didn't actually shake people down and I didn't overlook homicides, but I took money, and that's not what they hired me to do. It was illegal. It was crooked."

"I suppose."

And I did other things. For Christ's sake, I was a thief. I stole. One time I was investigating a break-in and there was a cigar box next to the cash register that the burglar had somehow missed, and there was close to a thousand dollars in it. I took it and put it in my pocket. I figured the owner'd be covered by insurance, or else it was money he was skimming, in which case I was just stealing from a thief. I had it rationalized, but you can't get around the fact that I was taking money that wasn't mine."

"Cops do that kind of shit all the time."

"They rob the dead, too, and I did that for years. Say you come on a stiff in an SRO hotel or an apartment, and he's got fifty or a hundred dollars on him, and you and your partner divide it up before you zip him into the body bag. What the hell, otherwise it just gets lost in the bureaucratic mill. Even if there's an heir it'll most likely never get to him, and why not just save time and trouble and put it in your pocket? Except that it's stealing."

He started to say something but I wasn't done

yet. "And I did other things. I got guys sent away for things they didn't do. I don't mean I framed any choirboys. Anybody I ever hung anything on was bad to start with. I'd know a guy did a certain job, and I'd know I couldn't touch him for it, but then I might find some eyewitnesses suggestible enough to ID him for something he hadn't done, and that was enough to put him away. Case closed."

"There's a lot of guys in the joint who didn't do what they went away for," he allowed. "Not all of them. I mean, three out of four cons'll swear they were innocent of what they're doing time for, but you can't believe 'em. Cons'll con you. I mean, they lie." He shrugged. "But sometimes it's the truth."

"I know," I said. "I'm not sure I regret putting the right people away for the wrong reason. It got them off the street, and they were people who didn't do the street a whole lot of good. But that didn't necessarily make it the right thing for me to do, so I figured it belonged in my fifth step."

"So you told somebody about it."

"And more. Things that weren't against the law, but that bothered me more than other things that were. Like running around on my wife while I was married. Like not having time for my kids, like walking out on them around the time I left the department. Like not being there for people in general. One time an aunt of mine was dying of thyroid cancer. She was my mother's younger sister, she was all the family I had left, and I kept

80

promising myself I would go and see her in the hospital, and I kept putting it off and putting it off, and the woman died. I felt so bad about not getting to the hospital that I didn't get to the funeral, either. I sent flowers, though, and I went to some fucking church and lit a fucking candle, all of which must have been a hell of a comfort to the dead woman."

We walked in silence for a few minutes, heading west on one of the streets in the low Fifties, then taking a left on Tenth Avenue. We passed a low-down saloon with the door open and that stale beer smell rolled out at us, sickening and inviting all at once. He asked if I'd ever been in the place.

"Not lately," I said.

"It's a real bucket of blood," he said. "Matt? You ever kill anybody?"

"Twice in the line of duty. And once accidentally, and that was line of duty, too. A bullet of mine ricocheted and killed a child."

"You mentioned that last night."

"Did I? Sometimes I do, sometimes I don't. Once after I left the department a guy jumped me on the street in connection with a case I was working on. I threw him and he landed wrong and died of a broken neck. And another time, Christ, I was all of a week sober, and this crazy Colombian charged me with a machete and I emptied a gun into him. So the answer is yes, I've killed four people, five if you count the kid."

"And, except for the kid, I don't think I ever

lost a night's sleep over any of them. And I never agonized over the assholes I sent up for something they didn't do. I think it was wrong to do it, I wouldn't do it that way now, but none of that stuff bothers me anywhere near as much as not visiting Aunt Peg when she was dying. But that's an alcoholic for you. The big stuff is easy. It's the little shit that drives us crazy."

"Sometimes it's the big stuff, too."

"Something eating you, Eddie?"

"Oh, shit, I don't know. I'm a neighborhood guy, Matt. I grew up in these streets. You grew up in Hell's Kitchen, the one thing you learned was not to tell nothing to nobody. 'Don't tell your business to strangers.' My mother was an honest woman, Matt. She found a dime in a pay phone, she'd look around for somebody to give it back to, but I must of heard her say it a thousand times. 'Don't tell nobody your business.' And she walked the walk, God bless her. Two, three times a week till the day he died, the old man'd come home half in the bag and slap her around. And she kept it to herself. Anybody asked her, oh, she was clumsy, she walked into a door, she lost her balance, she fell down a flight of stairs. But most people knew not to ask. If you lived in the Kitchen, you knew what not to ask."

I started to say something but he took my arm and urged me to the curb. "Let's cross the street," he said. "I don't like to walk past that place if I don't have to."

The place in question was Grogan's Open

House. Green neon in the window offered Harp lager and Guinness stout. "I used to hang out there a lot," he explained. "I like to steer clear of it now."

I knew the feeling. There was a time when I drank away the days and nights at Armstrong's, and when I first got sober I'd go out of my way to avoid passing the place. When I had to walk past it I would avert my eyes and speed up my pace, as if I might otherwise be drawn in against my will, like iron filings to a magnet. Then Jimmy lost his lease and relocated a block west at Tenth and Fifty-seventh, and a Chinese restaurant moved into his old spot, and I had one less problem in my life.

"You know who owns that joint, Matt?"

"Somebody named Grogan?"

"Not in years. That's Mickey Ballou's place."

"The Butcher Boy?"

"You know Mickey?"

"Only by sight. By sight and by reputation."

"Well, he's a sight and he's got a reputation. You won't find his name on the license, but it's his store. When I was a kid I was tight with his brother Dennis. Then he got killed in Vietnam. Were you in the service, Matt?"

I shook my head. "They weren't drafting cops."

"I had TB when I was a kid. I never knew it at the time, but there was something showed up on the X ray, kept me out of the service." He threw his cigarette in the gutter. "Another reason

83

to quit these things. But not today, huh?"

"You've got time."

"Yeah. He was okay, Dennis. Then after he died I did some things with Mick. You heard the stories about him?"

"I've heard some stories."

"You heard about him and the bowling bag? And what he had in it?"

"I never knew whether to believe it or not."

"Well, I wasn't there. One time, though, and this was some years ago, I was in a basement two, three blocks from where we're standing now. They had a guy, I forget what he done. Ratted somebody out, it must of been. They're in the furnace room and they got him tied to a post with a clothesline, and a gag in his mouth, and Mickey puts on this long white butcher's apron, covers you from your shoulders down to your feet. The apron's pure white except for the stains on it. And Mickey picks up a ball bat and starts wailing on the guy, and the blood sprays all over the place. Next time I see Mickey he's in the Open House with the apron on. He likes to wear it, like he's a butcher just off work, ducked in for a quick one. 'See that?' he says, pointing to a fresh stain. 'Know what that is? That's rat blood.' "

We had reached the corner a block south of Grogan's Open House, and now we crossed Tenth Avenue again. He said, "I was never no Al Capone, but I done stuff. I mean, shit, voting for Abe Beame's the closest I ever came to an honest day's work. I'm thirty-seven years old and the only time

84

I ever had a Social Security card was in Green Haven. They had me working in the laundry there for whatever it was. Thirty cents an hour? Something ridiculous like that, and they had to take out taxes and Social Security, so you had to get a Social Security card. Up to then I never had one, and after that I never used it."

"You're working now, aren't you?"

He nodded. "Little get-well jobs. Sweeping out a couple of joints after closing, Dan Kelly's and Pete's All-American. You know the All-American?"

"Talk about a bucket of blood. I would duck in there for a quick one, but I never stayed any length of time."

"Like making a pit stop. I used to love that, walk into a bar, have a quick pop, then out again to face the world. Anyway, I go into those two joints late at night or early in the morning, sweep the place out, take out the empties, put the chairs back around the tables. And there's a moving company down in the Village gives me a day's work now and then. Everything's off the books, you don't need no Social Security card for those jobs. I get by."

"Sure."

"My rent's cheap, and I don't eat much, I never ate much, and what am I gonna spend my dough on? Nightclubs? Fancy clothes? Fuel for my yacht?"

"Sounds as though you're doing all right."

He stopped walking, turned to face me. "Yeah,

but I'm just shooting the shit, Matt." He put his hands in his pockets and stood looking down at the pavement. "The point is I done stuff I don't know if I want to tell anybody about. Admitting it to myself, all right, like I already *know* it, right? So it's just a matter of getting honest and facing up to it. And admitting it to God, well, man, if there's no God it don't make no difference, and if there is a God He already knows everything you done, so that part's easy. But coming clean with another person, shit, I don't know, Matt. I done certain things that you could go away for, and in some cases there's other people involved, and I just don't know how I feel about all that."

"A lot of people take the step with a priest."

"You mean like confession?"

"I think it's a little different. You're not seeking formal absolution as much as you're attempting to unburden yourself. You don't have to be a Catholic, and you don't have to go through it in a church. You can even find a priest who's sober in AA and understands what the program's all about. But even if he's not he'd be bound by the seal of the confessional, so you wouldn't have to worry about him saying anything to anybody."

"I couldn't tell you the last time I was in a church. Wait a minute, did you hear what I just said? Christ, I was in a church an hour ago. I been going into church basements once or twice a day for months. But the last time I went to mass, well, I went to a couple weddings over the years, Catholic weddings, but I didn't take communion. I'm sure it's more than twenty years since I made confession."

"It doesn't have to be with a priest. But if you're worried about confidentiality — "

"Is that how you did it? With a priest?"

"I took it with another person from the program. You know him. Jim Faber."

"I don't think I know him."

"Sure you do. He comes to St. Paul's all the time, he was there tonight. He's a few years older than I am. Hair's mostly gray, wears a beat-up army jacket most of the time. You'd know him if you saw him."

"He wasn't at the Flame, was he?"

"Not tonight."

"What is he, a cop or a detective or something?"

"No, he's a printer, he's got his own shop over on Eleventh Avenue."

"Oh, Jim the Printer," he said. "Been sober a long time."

"He's coming up on nine years."

"Yeah, well, that's a long time."

"He would tell you he just did it a day at a time."

"Yeah, that's what they all tell you. It's still nine fucking years, isn't it? No matter how you slice it, divide it into hours and minutes if you want, it still comes to nine years."

"That's the truth."

He took out another cigarette, changed his mind, returned it to the pack. "Is he your sponsor?"

"Not formally. I've never had a sponsor in any formal way. I've never been very good at doing things the way you're supposed to. Jim's the person I call when I want to talk about something. If I call anybody."

"I got a sponsor when I was about two days out of detox. I got his number next to my phone. The phone doesn't work and I've never called him anyway. We go to different meetings, so I never see him, either."

"What's his name?"

"Dave. I don't know his last name, and I have to say I'm beginning to forget what he looks like, it's so long since I saw him. But I've never yet thrown his number away, so I guess he's still my sponsor. I mean, I could call him if I had to, right?"

"Sure."

"I could even take the step with him."

"If you felt comfortable with him."

"I don't even know him. Do you have anybody that you sponsor, Matt?"

"No."

"You ever hear anybody's fifth step?"

"No."

There was a bottle cap on the sidewalk and he kicked at it. "Because I guess that's what I'm leading up to. I can't believe it, a crook looking to confess to a cop. Of course you're not with the department no more, but would you still, you know, be bound to report anything I said?"

"No. I wouldn't have the legal right to withhold

information, the way a priest or a lawyer might, but that's how I'd treat it. As privileged information."

"Would you be willing? It'd be a whole load of shit once I got started, you might not want to sit through it."

"I'll force myself."

"I feel funny asking."

"I know. I felt the same way."

"If it was just me involved," he began, then broke off the sentence. He said, "What I want to do, I want to take a couple of days, sort things out in my mind, think some things through. Then if you're still willing we can get together and I can talk some. If that's all right with you."

"There's no hurry," I told him. "Wait until you're ready."

He shook his head. "If I wait till I'm ready I'll never do it. Gimme the weekend to sort it out and then we'll sit down and do it."

"Sorting it out is part of it. Take all the time you need."

"I been doing that," he said. He grinned, put a hand on my shoulder. "Thanks, Matt. That's my block coming up and I think I'll say good night."

" 'Night, Eddie."

"Have a good weekend."

"You too. Maybe I'll run into you at a meeting."

"St. Paul's is just Monday through Friday, right? I'll probably get there Monday night, anyway.

Matt? Thanks again."

He headed for his building. I walked up a block on Tenth, walked east on one of the cross streets. A few doors from the corner of Ninth Avenue, three young men in a doorway went silent at my approach. Their eyes followed me all the way to the corner, and I could feel their stares like darts between my shoulder blades.

Halfway home a hooker asked me if I felt like partying. She looked young and fresh, but they mostly do these days; drugs and viruses keep them from lasting long enough to fade.

I told her we'd have to make it some other time. Her smile, at least as enigmatic as the Mona Lisa's, stayed with me all the way home. At Fifty-sixth Street a black man, bare to the waist, asked me for spare change. Half a block farther, a woman stepped out of the shadows and made the same request. She had lank blond hair and the face of an Okie out of one of those Depression photographs. They each got a dollar from me.

There were no messages at the hotel desk. I went up to my room and took a shower and got into bed.

Some years back three brothers named Morrissey owned a small four-story brick building on West Fifty-first half a block from the river. They lived in the top two stories, rented out the ground floor to an Irish amateur theater, and sold beer and whiskey after hours on the second floor. There was a time when I went there a lot, and there may have been half a dozen occasions when Mickey Ballou and I were there at the same time. I don't know that we ever exchanged a word, but I remember seeing him there, and knowing who he was.

My friend Skip Devoe had said of Ballou that, if he had ten brothers and they all stood around in a circle, you'd think you were at Stonehenge. Ballou had that megalithic quality, and he had too an air of wild menace just held in check. There was a man named Aronow, a manufacturer of women's dresses, who one night spilled a drink on Ballou. Aronow's apology was immediate and profuse, and Ballou mopped himself up and told Aronow to forget it, and Aronow left town and didn't come back for a month. He didn't even go home and pack, he took a cab straight to the airport and was on a flight within the hour. He was, we all agreed, a cautious man, but not overly cautious.

Lying there, waiting for sleep to come, I wondered what was on Eddie's mind and what it might have to do with the Butcher Boy. I didn't stay up late worrying about it, though. I figured I'd find out soon enough.

5

The good weather held all weekend. Saturday I went to a ball game. The Mets and the Yankees had both had a shot at it. The Mets were still leading their division, in spite of the fact that nobody was hitting. The Yankees had slipped to six or seven out and it didn't look as though they were going to turn it around. That weekend the Mets were in Houston for three games with the Astros. The Yankees were coming to the end of a home stand, hosting the Mariners, and I got to see Mattingly win it with a double down the line in the eleventh.

Coming home, I stayed on past my stop and rode down to the Village. I had dinner at an Italian place on Thompson Street, caught a meeting, made an early night of it.

Sunday I went over to Jim Faber's apartment and watched the Mets on the cable sports channel. Gooden held the Astros to three scratch hits through eight innings, but the Mets couldn't get any runs across for him, and Johnson pulled him in the top of the ninth for a pinch hitter, Mazzilli, who promptly flied out to deep short. "I think that was a mistake," Jim said softly, and in the bottom of the ninth the Houston second baseman walked, stole second, and scored on a sharp single through the middle.

We ate at a Chinese restaurant Jim had been wanting to try, then went to a meeting at Roosevelt Hospital. The speaker was a shy woman with an expressionless face and a voice that didn't carry past the first two rows. We were in the back and it was impossible to hear a word. I gave up trying and let my mind wander. I started thinking about the game and wound up thinking about Jan Keane and how she'd enjoyed going to ball games even though she had only a vague notion of what they were doing out there on the field. She told me once that she liked the perfect geometry of the game.

I took her to the fights once but she hadn't cared for that. She said she found it all exhausting to watch. But she loved hockey. She had never seen a match until we went together, and she wound up liking it far more than I do.

I was glad when the meeting ended, and I went straight home afterward. I didn't feel like being around people.

Monday morning I earned a couple of dollars. A woman who'd sobered up at St. Paul's had moved in a few months ago with a fellow in Rego Park. He'd been sober at the time, but he'd slipped around for years, drifting in and out of the program, and he picked up a drink again shortly after they set up housekeeping. It took six or eight weeks and one good beating for her to realize that she'd made a mistake and that she didn't have to go on taking it, and she'd moved back to the city.

But she'd left some things at the apartment and she was afraid to go back there by herself. She asked what I would charge to ride shotgun.

I told her she didn't have to pay me. "No, I think I should," she said. "This isn't just an AA favor. He's a violent son of a bitch when he drinks, and I don't want to go out there without someone who's professionally qualified to deal with that sort of thing. I can afford to pay you and I'll be more comfortable doing it that way."

She arranged for a cabbie named Jack Odegaard to run us out and back. I knew him from meetings, but I hadn't known his last name until I read it on the hack license posted over the glove box.

Her name was Rosalind Klein. The boyfriend's name was Vince Broglio, and he wasn't a terribly violent son of a bitch that afternoon. He mostly just sat around chuckling ironically to himself and sucking on a longneck Stroh's while Roz packed up a couple of suitcases and a brace of shopping bags. He was watching game shows on TV, using the remote control to hop back and forth between the channels. The whole apartment was littered with boxes of half-eaten pizza from Domino's and those little white cartons of takeout food from Chinese restaurants. And empty beer and whiskey bottles. And overflowing ashtrays, and empty cigarette packs wadded up and tossed into corners.

At one point he said, "You my replacement? The new boyfriend?"

"Just along for the ride."

He laughed at that. "Aren't we all? Along for the ride, I mean."

A few minutes later, without taking his eyes off the Sony, he said, "Women."

"Well," I said.

"If they didn't have pussies there'd be a bounty on 'em." I didn't say anything, and he glanced my way, looking to read my expression. "Now that," he said, "might be construed to be a sexist remark." He had a little trouble getting his tongue around *construed;* and he got interested in the word and let go of his original train of thought. "Construed," he said. "I gotta get construed, blewed and tattooed. My whole problem, see, is I got misconstrued once. How's that for a problem?"

"It's a pretty good one."

"Let me tell you something," he said. "*She's* the one with a problem."

Jack Odegaard drove us back to the city, and he and I helped Roz get her stuff into her apartment. Before the move she'd lived on Fifty-seventh a few doors from Eighth Avenue. Now she was in a high-rise at Seventieth and West End. "I had a big one-bedroom," she said, "and now I'm in a studio, and my rent's more than double what it used to be. I ought to have my head examined for letting go of my old place. But I was moving into a beautiful two-bedroom in Rego Park. You saw the apartment, if you can imagine what it looked like before the shit hit the fan. And if you're going to commit to a relationship you have to show some faith in it, don't you?"

She gave Jack fifty bucks for the trip and paid me a hundred for my hazardous duty. She could afford it, just as she could handle the higher rent; she made good money working in the news department of one of the TV networks. I don't know what exactly she did there, but I gather she did it well.

I thought I might see Eddie at St. Paul's that night but he wasn't there. Afterward I walked down to Paris Green to talk to the bartender who'd recognized Paula Hoeldtke's picture. I thought he might have remembered something, but he hadn't.

The next morning I called the telephone company and was told that Paula Hoeldtke's phone had been disconnected. I was trying to find out when this had happened and for what reason, but I had to go through channels before I could find somebody who was authorized to tell me. The service had been terminated at the customer's request, a woman told me, and then asked me to hold the line for a moment. She returned to inform me further that there was an outstanding final balance in the customer's favor. I asked how that could be; had she overpaid the final bill?

"She never received her final statement," the woman told me. "She evidently didn't leave a forwarding address. She had put down a deposit prior to installation, and the final bill came to less than the funds on deposit. In fact — "

"Yes?"

"According to the computer, she hadn't paid anything since May. But her charges were low, so she still hadn't exceeded the amount of deposit."

"I see."

"If she'll supply us with her current address, we can forward the balance due to her. She may not want to be bothered, it only comes to four dollars and thirty-seven cents."

I told her that was probably low on Paula's list of priorities. "There's one other thing you could help me with," I said. "Could you tell me the exact date when she requested termination of service?"

"Just a moment," she said, and I waited. "That was July twentieth," she said.

That sounded wrong, and I checked my notebook to make sure. I was right — Paula had paid rent for the last time on the sixth, Florence Edderling had entered the room and found it empty on the fifteenth, and Georgia Price moved in on the eighteenth. That meant Paula would have waited a minimum of five days after quitting the premises before calling to have her telephone cut off. If she waited that long, why call at all? And, if she was

97

going to call, why not provide a forwarding address?

"That doesn't square with my figures," I said. "Is it possible that she requested termination earlier and it took a few days before the order was carried out?"

"That's not how it works. When we receive a disconnect order, we put it through right away. We don't have to send somebody out to disconnect, you know. We do it electronically from a distance."

"That's strange. She'd already vacated the premises."

"Just a minute. Let me punch it up on the screen again and see what it says." I didn't have a long wait. "According to this," she said, "the phone was still in service until we received instructions to disconnect on 7/20. Of course there's always the possibility of computer error."

I had a cup of coffee and read through my notebook. Then I put through a collect call to Warren Hoeldtke at his auto showroom. I said, "I've run into a minor inconsistency here. I don't think it amounts to anything, but I want to check it out. What I'd like to get from you is the date of your last telephone call to Paula."

"Let me see. It was sometime in late June, and — "

"No, that was the last time you talked with her. But you called her several times after that, didn't you?"

"Yes, and we were ultimately advised that the service had been disconnected."

"But first there were some calls where you reached her answering machine. I want to know when the last one of those went through."

"I see," he said. "Gee, I'm afraid I haven't got that kind of memory. It was toward the end of July when we took our trip, and right after we got back we called and learned the phone was disconnected, so that would have been the middle of last month. I think I told you all that."

"Yes."

"But as for our last call when we got the machine, that would have been before we left for the Black Hills, but I wouldn't be able to tell you the date."

"You've probably got a record."

"Oh?"

"Do you keep your phone bills?"

"Of course. My accountant would have a fit if I didn't. Oh, I see. I was thinking there would be no record of a call if we didn't get through to her, but of course if the machine answered it would be a complete call. So it would be on our statement."

"That's right."

"I don't have the paid bills here, I'm afraid. My wife will know right where they are, though. Do you have my home phone number?" I said I did. "Let me call her first," he said, "so she'll have everything at hand when you call."

"While you're at it, tell her I'll be calling collect.

I'm at a pay phone."

"That's no problem. In fact, I have a better idea. Give me the number of the pay phone and she can call you."

I was calling from a phone on the street and I didn't want to relinquish possession of it. After he rang off I stood there still holding the receiver to my ear so that I would look as though I were using the phone. I allowed a little time for Hoeldtke to reach his wife and another few minutes for her to thumb through her file of paid phone bills. Then, still holding the receiver to my ear, I hung one hand on the hook so she'd be able to get through to me when she called. A couple of times someone would linger a few yards away, waiting to use the phone when I got off it. Each time I turned and said apologetically that I expected to be a while.

The phone rang, though not before I'd begun to tire of my little exercise in street theater. I said hello, and a confident female voice said, "Hello, this is Betty Hoeldtke, and I'm calling for Matthew Scudder." I identified myself and she said that her husband had told me what I was trying to determine. "I have the July statement in front of me," she said. "It shows three calls to Paula. Two of them were two-minute calls and one was three minutes. I was just now trying to imagine how it could have taken three minutes to leave a message asking her to call us, but of course first we would have had to listen to her message, wouldn't we? Although I sometimes think the phone company's computers bill you for more minutes than you actually stay on the phone."

"What were the dates of the calls, Mrs. Hoeldtke?"

"July fifth, July twelfth, and July seventeenth. And I looked up the June calls, and the last time we spoke with Paula was June the nineteenth. That's on our statement because she would call us and we would call her back."

"Your husband told me about the code you used."

"I feel a little funny about it, although we weren't really cheating the phone company out of anything. But it always seems — "

"Mrs. Hoeldtke, what was the date of the last call to Paula?"

"July seventeenth. She usually called on a Sunday, and July fifth when we first called and got the machine was a Sunday, and then the twelfth was a week later, and the seventeenth, let me see — twelve thirteen fourteen fifteen sixteen seventeen, Sunday Monday, Tuesday Wednesday Thursday Friday — the seventeenth would have been a Friday, and — "

"You reached her answering machine on the seventeenth of July."

"We must have, because that was the three-minute conversation. I probably left a longer message than usual to tell her that we were leaving for the Dakotas the middle of next week, and to please call us before we left."

"Let me make some notes," I said, and jotted

down what she'd told me in my notebook. Something didn't add up. All it very likely meant was that somebody's records were wrong, but I would spend as much time as I had to ironing out the inconsistency, like a bank teller working three hours overtime to search out a ten-cent discrepancy.

"Mr. Scudder? What's happened to Paula?"

"I don't know, Mrs. Hoeldtke."

"I've had the most awful feeling. I keep having the thought that she's — " The pause stretched. "Dead," she said.

"There's no evidence of that."

"Is there any evidence that she's alive?"

"She seems to have packed up and left her room under her own power. That's a favorable sign. If she'd left her clothes in the closet I'd be less optimistic."

"Yes, of course. I see what you mean."

"But I can't get much sense of where she may have gone, or what her life might have been like during the last few months she lived on West Fifty-fourth Street. Did she give any indication of what she was doing? Did she mention a boyfriend?"

I asked other questions in that vein. I couldn't draw anything much out of Betty Hoeldtke. After a while I said, "Mrs. Hoeldtke, one of my problems is I know what your daughter looks like but I don't know who she is. What did she dream about? Who were her friends? What did she do with her time?"

"With any of my other children that would be

a much easier question to answer. Paula was a dreamer, but I don't know what it was that she dreamed. In high school she was the most normal and average child you could imagine, but I think that was just because she wasn't ready yet to let her own light shine. She was hiding who she was, and maybe from herself as well." She sighed. "She had the usual high school romances, nothing very serious. Then at Ball State I don't think she had a real boyfriend after Scott was killed. She kept — "

I interrupted to ask who Scott was and what had happened to him. He was her boyfriend and unofficial fiancé during her sophomore year, and he'd lost control of his motorcycle on a curve.

"He was killed instantly," she remembered. "I think something changed in Paula when that happened. She had boys she was friendly with after that, but that was when she got really interested in theater and the boys were friends of hers from the theater department. I don't think there was much question of romance. The ones she spent the most time with, my sense was that they weren't interested in romance with girls."

"I see."

"I worried about her from the day she left for New York. She was the only one who left, you know. All my others stayed nearby. I kept it hidden, I didn't let on to her, and I don't think Warren had any idea how I worried. And now that she's dropped off the face of the earth — "

"She may turn up just as abruptly," I offered.

103

"I always thought she went to New York to find herself. Not to be an actress, it never seemed that important to her. But to find herself. And now my fear is that she's lost."

I had lunch at a pizza stand on Eighth Avenue. I got a thick square of the Sicilian and shook a lot of crushed red pepper onto it and ate it standing up at the counter, washing it down with a small Coke. It seemed quicker and more predictable than, say, walking down to the Druid's Castle and finding out for myself what toad-in-the-hole was.

There was a noon meeting Tuesdays at St. Clare's Hospital, and I remembered that Eddie had mentioned it as one he went to fairly regularly. I got there late but stayed right through to the prayer. He didn't show up.

I called my hotel to see if there were any messages. Nothing.

I don't know what made me go looking for him. Cop instinct, maybe. I'd been expecting to see him at St. Paul's the night before and hadn't. He could have changed his mind about doing his fifth step with me, or might simply have wanted more time to weigh the idea, and might have stayed away from the meeting to avoid encountering me before he was ready. Or he might have decided he wanted to watch something on television that night, or gone to another meeting, or for a long walk.

Still, he was an alcoholic and he'd been troubled, and those conditions could have inclined him to forget all the fine reasons he knew for staying away from a drink. Even if he'd started drinking, that was no call for me to go after him. The only time to help somebody is when he asks for it. Until then, the best thing I could do for him was leave him alone.

Maybe I was just tired of trying to cut the cold trail of Paula Hoeldtke. Maybe I went looking for Eddie because I figured he'd be easy to find.

Even so, it took some doing. I knew what street he was on but I didn't know the building, and I didn't much feel like going door-to-door trying to read the nameplates on doorbells and mailboxes. I checked a phone book to see if he was still listed in spite of his phone having been disconnected. I couldn't find him.

I called an Information operator and identified myself as a police officer and made up a shield number. That's a misdemeanor, but I don't suppose it's the sort of thing you can go to hell for. I wasn't asking her to do anything illegal, just trying to get her to do me a favor she'd probably have denied a civilian. I told her I was trying to find a listing a year or two old. It wasn't in her computer, but she found an old White Pages and looked it up for me.

I'd told her I was looking for an E. Dunphy in the 400 block of West Fifty-first Street. She didn't have that, but she showed a P. J. Dunphy at 507 West Fifty-first, which could put him three or four doors west of Tenth Avenue. That sounded likely. It had been his mother's apartment, and he wouldn't have bothered to change the way the phone was listed.

Number 507 was like its neighbors, an old-law tenement six stories tall. Not all of the bells and mailboxes had nameplates, but there was a slip of white cardboard in the slot next to the bell for 4-C with DUNPHY hand-lettered on it.

I rang his bell and waited. After a few minutes I rang it again and waited some more.

I rang the bell marked SUPER. When the buzzer sounded in response I pushed the door and let myself into a dim hallway that smelled of mice and cooked cabbage and stagnant air. Down at the end of the hall a door opened and a woman emerged. She was tall, with straight shoulder-length blond hair secured with a rubber band. She wore blue jeans that were starting to go at the knee and a plaid flannel shirt with the sleeves rolled to the elbow and the top two buttons unbuttoned.

"My name's Scudder," I told her. "I'm trying to locate one of your tenants. Edward Dunphy."

"Oh, yes," she said. "Mr. Dunphy's on the fourth floor. One of the rear apartments. I think it's 4-C."

"I tried his bell. There was no answer."

"Then he's probably out. Was he expecting you?"

"I was expecting him."

She looked at me. She'd appeared younger from a distance but at close range you could see that she had to be crowding forty. She carried the years

106

well enough. She had a high broad forehead with a sharply defined widow's peak, a jawline that was strong but not severe. Good cheekbones, interesting facial planes. I had kept company with a sculptor long enough to think in those terms, and the breakup had been too recent for me to have lost the habit.

She said, "Do you think he's upstairs? And not answering his bell? Of course it's possible that it's out of order. I fix them when the tenants report them, but if you don't get many visitors you wouldn't necessarily know that your bell wasn't functioning. Do you want to go up there and knock on his door?"

"Maybe I'll do that."

"You're worried about him," she said. "Aren't you?"

"I am, and I couldn't tell you why."

She made up her mind quickly. "I have a key," she said. "Unless he's changed the lock, or put on an extra one. God knows I would, in a city like this one."

She returned to her own apartment, came back with a ring of keys, then double-locked her own door and led the way up the stairs. Other smells joined the mouse and cabbage scents in the stairwell. Stale beer, stale urine. Marijuana. Latin cooking.

"If they change the locks, or add new ones," she said, "I'm supposed to get the key. There's actually a clause to that effect in the lease, the landlord has the right of access to all apartments.

But nobody pays any attention to it, and the owner doesn't care, and *I* certainly don't care. I've got a key that's marked 4-C, but that doesn't mean it's likely to open anything."

"We'll try it."

"That's all we can do."

"Well, it's not quite all," I said. "Sometimes I'm not too bad at opening a lock without the key."

"Oh, really?" She turned to give me a look. "That must be very useful in your profession. What are you, a locksmith or a burglar?"

"I used to be a cop."

"And now?"

"Now I'm an ex-cop."

"No kidding. You told me your name but I lost it."

I told her again. As we climbed, I learned that her name was Willa Rossiter and that she'd been the building's superintendent for some twenty months. She received the apartment rent-free in exchange for her services.

"But it doesn't really cost the landlord anything," she said, "because he wouldn't be renting it anyway. There are three empty apartments in the building beside mine. They're not for rent."

"You'd think they'd go fast."

"They'd go in a minute, and they'd bring a thousand a month, crazy as it sounds. But he'd rather warehouse the empty apartments. He wants to turn the building into a co-op, and every untenanted apartment is ultimately a vote on his side, and an apartment he can sell for whatever the traffic will bear."

"But in the meantime he loses a thousand a month on each vacancy."

"I guess it's worth it to him in the long run. If we go co-op, he'll get a hundred thousand dollars for each of these rabbit warrens. But that's New York. I don't think there's anyplace else in the country where you could get that for the whole building."

"Anywhere else in the country, the building would be condemned."

"Not necessarily. It's a solid building. It's over a hundred years old, and these old tenements were cheap working-class housing when they went up. They're not like the brownstones in Park Slope and Clinton Hill that were very grand in their day. Even so, this is a sound structure. And that's Mr. Dunphy's door. In the rear on the right."

She got to his door and knocked on it, a good strong knock. When no answer came she knocked again, louder. We looked at each other, and she shrugged and fitted her key into the lock. She turned it twice around, first to disengage the dead bolt, then to snick back the spring lock.

As soon as she cracked the door I knew what we were going to find. I gripped her shoulder.

"Let me," I said. "You don't want to see this."

"What's that smell?"

I pushed past her and went to look for the body.

The apartment was a typical tenement railroad

flat, with three little rooms lined up in a row. The hall door led into a living room furnished with a matching couch and armchair and a table-model TV. The armchair's seat was sprung, and the fabric was worn through on its arms, and on the arms of the couch. There was an ashtray on the table that held the television set. It had a couple of butts in it.

The next room was the kitchen. The stove and sink and refrigerator were in a row against the wall, and over the sink was a window looking out on an airshaft. Away from the appliances stood a large old-fashioned claw-foot bathtub. Some of its porcelain exterior had chipped away to reveal black cast iron. A plywood top, painted a glossy off-white, converted the tub into a dining table. There was an empty coffee cup on top of the tub-table, and another dirty ashtray. There were dishes stacked in the sink, and clean ones in a wire strainer on the drainboard.

The last room was the bedroom, and that was where I found Eddie. He was sitting on the edge of his unmade bed, slumped forward. He was wearing a plain white T-shirt and nothing else. There was a stack of glossy magazines beside him on the bed, and one in front of him on the linoleum-covered floor, this last open to a double-page spread shot of a young woman with her wrists and ankles bound and ropes wrapped elaborately around her body. Her large breasts were tightly wrapped with lamp cord, or something that looked like it, and her face was contorted in an unconvincing grimace of pain and terror.

There was a rope around Eddie's neck, a noose fashioned from a length of plastic-coated clothesline. Its other end was fastened to a pipe running the length of the ceiling.

"My God!"

It was Willa, come to see for herself. "What happened?" she demanded. "Jesus God, what happened to him?"

I knew what had happened.

6

The cop's name was Andreotti. His partner, a light-skinned black patrolman, was downstairs getting a statement from Willa. Andreotti, a bear of a man with shaggy black hair and bushy eyebrows, had followed me up three flights to Eddie's apartment.

He said, "You were on the job once yourself, so I assume you followed the procedures. You didn't touch anything or change the position of any article on the scene, right?"

"That's right."

"He was a friend of yours and he didn't show up. What was it, he had an appointment with you?"

"I was supposed to see him yesterday."

"Yeah, well, he woulda been in no condition to show up. The AME'll fix a time of death, but I can tell you right now it's more than twenty-four hours. I don't care what the book says, I'm opening a window. Why don't you get the one in the kitchen?"

I did, and the living room window as well. When

I came back he said, "So he didn't show and then what? You called him?"

"He didn't have a phone."

"What's that there?" There was an upended orange crate serving as a bedside bookshelf, and on top of it stood a black telephone with a rotary dial. I said that it was out of order.

"Oh yeah?" He held the receiver to his ear, cradled it. "So it is. It unplugged or what? No, it oughta work."

"It had been disconnected some time ago."

"What was he doing, keeping it as an art object? Shit, I wasn't supposed to touch it. Not that anybody's gonna dust the place. We'll close this one right away, it looks pretty open and shut, don't you think?"

"From the looks of it."

"I seen a couple of these. Kids, high school, college age. First one I seen, I thought, shit, this ain't no way to kill yourself. 'Cause this is a teenage kid that we found in his own clothes closet, if you can picture it, and he's sitting on an upside-down milk crate, one of those plastic milk crates? And there's this knotted bedsheet around his neck, and it's looped around the whatchacallit, the horizontal bar the clothes hangers hang on. Now say you're gonna hang yourself, that's not how to do it. 'Cause all you gotta do is stand up the minute you lose your nerve and you take the weight off the rope, or in his case the bedsheet. And if there's real weight put on, enough to strangle you fast or snap your neck, it's gonna pull the whole bar down.

"So I was ready to go off half-cocked, figuring somebody strangled the kid and tried to fake a suicide, and did a real ass-backward job of it, too, when fortunately the guy I'm partnered with puts me wise. First thing he points out is the kid's naked. 'Autoerotic asphyxiation,' he tells me.

"I never heard of it before. What it is, it's a new way to masturbate. You cut off your air by half strangling yourself and it boosts the thrill. Except when you do it wrong like this poor bastard did, and then you're dead meat. And this is how your family finds you, with your eyes bulging and your cock in your hand."

He shook his head. "He was a friend of yours," he said, "but I bet you never knew he was into shit like this."

"No."

"Nobody ever knows. High school kids, sometimes they tell each other. With adults, shit, can you picture a grown man telling another guy, 'Hey, I found this great new way to beat my meat?' So you weren't expecting to find what you found. You just figured maybe he had a heart attack, something like that?"

"I was just generally worried that something was wrong."

"So, she opened the door with her passkey. It was locked?"

"Double-locked. The spring lock and the deadbolt."

"And all the windows shut. Well, that's pretty

clear cut, you ask me. He got any family ought to be notified?"

"His parents were dead. If he had anybody else, he never mentioned it."

"Lonely people dyin' alone, it'd break your heart if you let it. Look how thin he is. The poor son of a bitch."

In the living room he said, "You willing to make a formal identification? In the absence of next of kin, we ought to have somebody ID him."

"He's Eddie Dunphy."

"Okay," he said. "That's good enough."

Willa Rossiter was in 1-B. It was a rear apartment and had the same floor plan as Eddie's, but it was on the east side of the building so everything was reversed. And someone had modernized the plumbing in her unit, and there was no tub in her kitchen. Instead she had a two-foot-square stall shower in the small water closet off the bedroom.

We sat in her kitchen at an old tin-topped table. She asked me if I'd like something to drink and I said I'd welcome a cup of coffee.

"All I've got is instant," she said. "And it's decaf at that. Are you sure you wouldn't rather have a beer?"

"Instant decaf is fine."

"I think I want something stronger myself. Look at me, how I'm shaking." She held out a hand, palm toward the floor. If it was in fact trembling it didn't show. She went to the cupboard over the sink and got out a fifth of Teacher's and poured about two ounces into a Flintstones jelly glass. She sat down at the table with the bottle and the glass in front of her. She picked up the glass, looked at it, then drank off half the whiskey in a single swallow. She coughed, shuddered, heaved a sigh.

"That's better," she said.

I could believe it.

The kettle whistled and she fixed my coffee, if you could call it that. I stirred it and left the spoon sitting in the cup. It's supposed to cool faster that way. I wonder if it really does.

She said, "I can't even offer you milk."

"I drink it black."

"There's sugar, though. I'm positive of that."

"I don't use any."

"Because you don't want to mask the true flavor of the instant decaf."

"Something like that."

She drank the rest of her scotch. She said, "You recognized the smell right away. That's how you knew what you would find."

"It's not a smell you forget."

"I don't expect to forget it. I suppose you walked into a lot of apartments like that when you were a cop."

"If you mean apartments with dead bodies in them, yes, I'm afraid I did."

"I guess you get used to it."

"I don't know if you ever get used to it. You generally learn to mask your feelings, from others and from yourself."

"That's interesting. How do you do that?"

"Well, drinking helps."

"Are you sure you won't — "

"No, I'm positive. How else do you stop yourself from feeling anything? Some cops get angry at the deceased, or express contempt for him. When they bring the body downstairs, more often than not they drag the bag so the body bounces down the steps. You don't want to see that when the guy in the body bag was a friend of yours, but for the cops or the morgue crew, it's a way to dehumanize the corpse. If you treat him like garbage, you won't agonize as much over what happened to him, or have to look at the fact that it could happen to you someday."

"God," she said. She added whiskey to her glass. It showed Fred Flintstone with a goofy grin on his face. She capped the bottle, took a drink.

"How long since you were a cop, Matt?"

"A few years."

"What do you do now? You're too young to be retired."

"I'm a sort of private detective."

"Sort of?"

"I don't have a license. Or an office, or a listing in the Yellow Pages. Or much of a business, as far as that goes, but people turn up from time to time wanting me to handle something for them."

"And you handle it."

"If I can. Right now I'm working for a man from Indiana whose daughter came to New York to be an actress. She lived in a rooming house a few blocks from here, and a couple of months ago she disappeared."

"What happened to her?"

"That's what I'm supposed to be trying to find out. I don't know a hell of a lot more than I did when I started."

"Is that why you wanted to see Eddie Dunphy? Was he involved with her?"

"No, there was no connection."

"Well, there goes my theory. I had a flash just now that he'd gotten her to pose for one of those magazines, and the next thing you knew she was in a snuff film, and you can take it from there. Do they really exist?"

"Snuff films? Probably, from what I hear. The only ones I ever came into contact with were pretty obvious fakes."

"Would you watch a real one? If someone had a print and invited you to watch it."

"Not unless I had a reason."

"Curiosity wouldn't be enough of a reason?"

"I don't think so. I don't think I'd have that much curiosity on the subject."

"I wonder what I would do. Probably watch it and then wish I hadn't. Or not and wish I had. What's her name?"

"The girl who disappeared? Paula Hoeldtke."

"And there was no connection between her and Eddie Dunphy?" I said there wasn't. "Then why did you want to see him?"

"We were friends."

"Longtime friends?"

"Fairly recent."

"What did the two of you do, go shopping for magazines together? I'm sorry, that's a callous thing to say. The poor man's dead. He was your friend and he's dead. But the two of you seem like unlikely friends."

"Cops and criminals sometimes have a lot in common."

"Was he a criminal?"

"He used to be, in a small-time way. It was an easy thing to grow up into, raised in these streets. Of course this neighborhood used to be a lot rougher than it is now."

"Now it's getting gentrified. Yuppified."

"It's still got a ways to go. There are some hard people living on these blocks. The last time I saw Eddie he told me about a homicide he'd witnessed."

She frowned, her face troubled. "Oh?"

"One man beat another to death with a baseball bat in a basement furnace room. It happened some years ago, but the man who swung the bat is still around. He owns a saloon a few blocks from here."

She sipped her whiskey. She drank like a drinker, all right. And I don't think it was her first of the day. I'd noticed something on her breath earlier, probably beer. Not that that meant she was a lush. When you stop drinking, you become unnaturally sensitive to the smell of the stuff on other people. She'd probably just had a beer with her lunch, the way most of the world does.

Still, she drank neat whiskey like an old hand. No wonder I liked her.

"More coffee, Matt?"

"No thanks."

"You sure? It's no trouble, the water's still hot."

"Not just yet."

"It's pretty lousy coffee, isn't it?"

"It's not that bad."

"You don't have to worry about hurting my feelings. I haven't got a whole lot of ego tied up in my coffee, not when it comes out of a jar. There was a time I used to buy beans and grind my own. You should have known me then."

"I'll settle for knowing you now."

She yawned, extending her arms overhead, stretching like a cat. The movement drew her breasts into relief against the front of her flannel shirt. A moment later she had lowered her arms and the shirt was once again loose on her, but I remained aware of her body, and when she excused herself to go to the bathroom I watched her as she walked from the table. Her jeans were tight on her butt, worn almost white on the cheeks, and I stared after her until she was out of the room.

Then I looked at her empty glass, and the bottle standing next to it.

When she came back she said, "I can still smell it."

"It's not in the room, it's in your lungs. It'll take a while to get rid of it. But the windows are open up there and the apartment'll air out fast enough."

"It doesn't matter. He won't let me rent it."

"Another one for him to warehouse?"

"I expect so. I'll have to call him later, tell him he lost a tenant." She gripped the base of the bottle with one hand, spun the oversize cap with the other. There were no rings on her fingers, no polish on her nails. She wore a digital watch with a black plastic strap. Her fingernails were clipped short, and one thumbnail showed a white spot near the base.

She said, "How long has it been since they took the body out? Half an hour? Any minute now there'll be somebody ringing my bell, asking if his apartment's available. People are like vultures in this town." She poured a little whiskey into her glass and Fred Flintstone grinned his silly grin. "I'll just say it's rented."

"And meanwhile people sleep in the subway stations."

"And on park benches, but it's getting too cold for that now. I know, I see them all over, Manhattan's starting to look like a Third World country. But the people on the streets couldn't rent one of these apartments. They haven't got a thousand a month."

"And yet the ones who do get city housing wind up costing more than that. The city pays something like fifty dollars a night to house people in single rooms in welfare hotels."

"I know, and they're filthy and dangerous. The

121

welfare hotels, I mean. Not the people." She sipped her drink. "Maybe the people, too. As far as that goes."

"Maybe."

"Filthy and dangerous people," she sang tunelessly, *"in filthy and dangerous rooms.* Now there's an urban folk song for the Eighties." She put both hands behind her head and fiddled with the rubber band that was holding her hair in place. Once again her breasts pushed against the front of her shirt, and again I was drawn to them. She unfastened the rubber band, combed her hair with her fingers, gave her head a shake. Loose, her hair fell past her shoulders and framed her face, softening its lines. Her hair was several different shades of blond, ranging from very light tones to a medium brown.

She said, "The whole thing is crazy. The whole system is rotten. That's what we used to say, and it looks as though we were right all along. About the problem, if not about the solution."

"We?"

"Hell, yes, all two dozen of us. Christ."

She was, it turned out, a woman with a past. Twenty years ago she'd been a college kid in Chicago for the Democratic Convention. She'd lost two teeth to a police baton when Daley's cops lost it and rioted. Already radicalized, the incident propelled her into an SDS offshoot, the Progressive Communist Party.

"In all innocence," she said, "we wound up with

the same initials as angel dust. Of course this was twenty years ago and dust didn't amount to much, but then neither did we. Our total membership never exceeded thirty. And we were going to start a revolution, we were going to turn the country around. Government ownership of the means of production, complete elimination of class lines, an end to discrimination on the basis of age or sex or color — the thirty of us were going to lead the rest of the country to heaven. I think we really believed it, too."

She gave the movement years of her life. She would move to some city or town, get a job waitressing or working in a factory, and do whatever she was ordered to do. "The orders didn't necessarily make sense, but unquestioning obedience to party discipline was part of the deal. You weren't supposed to notice if the instructions made sense or not. Sometimes two of us would be ordered to move to Dipshit, Alabama, and rent a house and live as man and wife. So two days later I'd be shacked up in a trailer with somebody I barely knew, sleeping with him and fighting about who'd do the dishes. I'd say he was trapped in his old sexist roles if he expected me to do all the housework, and he'd remind me that we were supposed to blend in with our surroundings, and how many househusbands with elevated consciousness were you going to find in your average redneck trailer park? And then two months later, when we'd just about got it worked out, they'd send him to Gary, Indiana, and me to Oklahoma City."

123

Sometimes she was ordered to talk to fellow workers with the goal of recruiting new members. A few times she'd performed unfathomable acts of industrial sabotage. Often she went someplace to await further instructions, and no instructions came; finally she'd be moved somewhere else, and told to wait some more.

"I can't really convey what it was like," she said. "Maybe I should say that I can't really *remember* what it was like. The party became your whole life. You were isolated from everything else because you were living a lie, so you never got past the surface stage in relationships outside the party. Friends and neighbors and fellow workers were just part of the scenery, props and stage dressing in the false front you were presenting to the world. Besides, they were just pawns in the great chess game of history. They didn't know what was really going on. That was the heady part, the drug — you got to believe that your life was more significant than other people's."

Five years ago she'd begun to get profoundly disillusioned, but it took a while before she was ready to write off such a big portion of her life. It was like a poker game — you were reluctant to fold a hand when you already had so much invested in it. She fell in love finally with someone who was not in or of the movement, and defied party discipline by marrying him.

They moved to New Mexico, where the marriage fell apart. "I realized the marriage was just a way out of the PCP," she said. "If that's what it took, so be it. You know what they say about ill winds. I got a divorce. I moved here. I became a super because I couldn't figure out how else to get my hands on an apartment. How about you?"

"What about me?"

"How'd you get here? And where is it you've got to?"

I'd been asking myself the same goddamned questions for years.

"I was a cop for a long time," I said.

"How long?"

"Close to fifteen years. I had a wife and kids, I lived in Syosset. That's on Long Island."

"I know where it is."

"I don't know that you could say I got disillusioned. One way or another the life stopped suiting me. I quit the police force and I moved out, got a room on Fifty-seventh Street. I'm still there."

"A rooming house?"

"A little better than that. The Northwestern Hotel."

"You're either rich or rent-controlled."

"I'm not rich."

"You live alone?" I nodded. "Still married?"

"The divorce went through a long time ago."

She leaned forward and put a hand on top of mine. Her breath was richly seasoned with scotch. I wasn't sure I liked smelling it that way, but it was a lot easier to take than the smell in Eddie's apartment.

She said, "Well, what do you think?"

"About what?"

"We looked on death side by side. We told each other the story of our lives. We can't get drunk together because only one of us is drinking. You live alone. Are you involved with anybody?"

I had a sudden sense-memory of sitting on the sofa in Jan's loft on Lispenard Street, with Vivaldi chamber music playing and the smell of coffee brewing.

"No," I said. "I'm not."

Her hand pressed down on mine. "Well, what do you think, Matt? Do you want to fuck?"

7

I was never a smoker. During the drinking years, every once in a while I would get the urge and buy a pack of cigarettes and smoke three or four of them, one right after the other. Then I would throw the pack away and it would be months before I touched another cigarette.

Jan didn't smoke. Toward the end, when we decided to see other people, I had a couple of dates with a woman who smoked Winston Lights. We never went to bed together, but one night we exchanged a couple of kisses, and it was quite startling to taste tobacco on her mouth. I felt a flicker of revulsion. I felt, too, a brief yearning for a cigarette.

The taste of whiskey on Willa's mouth was far more profound in its effects. This was to be expected; after all, I didn't have to go to meetings every day to keep from picking up a cigarette, and if I did pick one up it wasn't odds-on to put me in a hospital.

We embraced in the kitchen, both of us standing. She was only a couple of inches shorter than

I, and we fit well together. I had already been wondering what it would be like to kiss her, before she said what she'd said, before she put her hand on mine.

The whiskey taste was strong. I mostly drank bourbon, scotch only rarely, but it didn't make any difference. It was the alcohol that sang to me, mixing memory with desire.

I felt a dozen feelings, all of them too well interwoven to be sorted out. There was fear, and a deep sadness, and of course there was the longing for a drink. There was excitement, a great rush of excitement, some of it owing to her whiskey mouth, but another greater strain of it issuing directly from the woman herself, the soft firmness of her breasts against my chest, the insistent heat of her loins against my thigh.

I put a hand on her ass and gripped her where her jeans were thin. Her hands dug into my shoulders. I kissed her again.

After a moment she drew away and looked at me. Our eyes locked. Hers were wide open, I could see all the way in.

I said, "Let's go to bed."

"God, yes."

The bedroom was small and dark. With the curtains drawn, hardly any light came through the little window. She switched the bedside lamp on, then switched it off again and took up a book of matches instead. She scratched one into flame and tried to light a candle, but the wick sputtered and the match went out before she could get it going. She tore out another match and I took the match and the candle away from her and set them aside. The dark was light enough.

Her bed was a double. There was no bedstead, just a box spring on the floor with a mattress on it. We stood next to it looking at each other and getting out of our clothes. There was an appendectomy scar on the right side of her abdomen, a dusting of freckles on her full breasts.

We found our way to the bed, and to each other.

Afterward she went into the kitchen and came back with a can of light beer. She popped the top and took a long drink. "I don't know why the hell I bought this," she said.

"I can think of two reasons."

"Oh?"

"Tastes great and less filling."

"Funny man. Tastes great? It tastes like nothing at all. I always liked strong tastes, I've never wanted light anything. I like Teacher's or White Horse, the dark heavy scotches. I like those rich Canadian ales. When I smoked I could never stand anything with a filter on it."

"You used to smoke?"

"Heavily. The party encouraged it. It was a way to bond with the working people — offer a cigarette, accept a cigarette, light up, and smoke your brains out in solidarity and comradeship. Of course once the revolution was accomplished, smoking would wither away like the dictatorship of the proletariat. The corrupt tobacco trust would be smashed and the farmers in the Piedmont would be reeducated to grow something dialectically correct. Mung beans, I suppose. And the working class, free from the stresses of capitalistic oppression, would no longer have the need for periodic whiffs of nicotine."

"You're making this up."

"The hell I am. We had a position on everything. Why not? We had plenty of time for it, we never fucking *did* anything."

"So you smoked for the good of the revolution."

"Bet your ass. Camels, a couple of packs a day. Or Picayunes, but they were hard to find."

"I never heard of them."

"Oh, they were wonderful," she said. "They made Gauloises taste like nothing at all. They would rip your throat out and turn your toenails brown. You didn't even have to light them. You could get cancer just carrying a pack in your purse."

"When did you quit?"

"In New Mexico, after my marriage broke up. I was so miserable anyway I figured I wouldn't even notice cigarette withdrawal. I was dead wrong about that, as it turned out, but I stuck with it anyway. You don't drink at all?"

"No."

"Did you ever?"

"Oh, yes."

"He said emphatically. You drank, therefore you don't."

130

"Something like that."

"I sort of figured as much. Somehow you don't remind me of any of the lifelong abstainers I've known. I don't usually get along too well with that type."

She was sitting crosslegged on top of the bed. I was lying on my side, propped up on one arm. I reached out a hand and touched her bare thigh. She rested her hand on top of mine.

"Does it bother you that I don't drink?"

"No. Does it bother you that I do?"

"I don't know yet."

"When you find out, be sure and let me know."

"All right."

She tilted the can, drank a little beer. She said, "Is there anything I can offer you? I can make coffee, such as it is. Do you want some?"

"No."

"I don't have any fruit juice or soft drinks, but it wouldn't take me a minute to run to the corner. What would you like?"

I took the beer can out of her hand and put it on the table next to the bed. "Come here," I said, easing her down onto the mattress. "I'll show you."

Around eight I groped around until I found my shorts. She had dozed off, but she woke up while I was dressing. "I have to go out for a while," I told her.

"What time is it?" She looked at her watch and made a clucking sound with her tongue. "Already," she said. "What a lovely way to while away the hours. You must be starving."

"And you must have a short memory."

Her laugh was richly lewd. "For nourishment. Why don't I make us something to eat."

"I have to be someplace."

"Oh."

"But I'll be done around ten. Can you hold out until then? We'll go out for hamburgers or something. Unless you're too ravenous to wait."

"That sounds good."

"I'll be back around ten-thirty, no later than that."

"Just ring my bell, honey. And, incidentally, you do. Loud and clear."

I went to St. Paul's. I walked down the steps to the basement entrance, and the minute I got inside I felt a sense of relief, as if I'd been holding something in check and could let go of it now.

I remember, years ago, waking up and needing a drink bad. And going downstairs to McGovern's, just next door to the hotel, where they opened early and where the man behind the stick knew what it was like to need a morning drink. I can remember how it felt in my body, the pure physical need for a drink, and how that need was actually slaked before I got the drink down. As soon as it was poured, as soon as I had my hand on the glass, some inner tension relaxed. The simple knowledge that relief was just a swallow away banished half the symptoms.

Funny how it works. I needed a meeting, I needed the company of my fellows, I needed to hear the wise and foolish things that got said at meetings. I needed, too, to talk about my day as a way of releasing it, and thus integrate the experience.

I hadn't done any of this yet, but I was safe now, I was in the room, and it would get done in due course. So I felt better already.

I went over to the coffee urn and drew myself a cup. It wasn't a great deal better than the instant decaf I'd had at Willa's. But I drank it down and went back for more.

The speaker was a member of our group, celebrating a two-year anniversary. Most of the people in the room had heard her drinking story at one time or another, so she talked instead about what her life had been like during the past two years. It was an emotional qualification, and the applause when she finished was more than perfunctory.

I raised my hand after the break and talked about finding Eddie's body, and about spending the rest of the day with someone who was drinking. I didn't go into detail, just spoke about what I'd felt then, and what I was feeling now.

After the meeting several members came up to me with questions. Some of them weren't too clear on who Eddie was and wanted to determine if he was someone they knew. He wasn't a regular at St. Paul's, and he didn't speak up a lot, so not many people knew who I was talking about.

Several who did wanted to know the cause of death. I didn't know how to answer that. If I said he'd hanged himself they'd assume he'd committed suicide. If I explained further I'd have to get into a deeper discussion of the matter than I felt comfortable with. I was deliberately vague, saying that the cause of death hadn't been officially determined, that it looked like accidental death. That was the truth, if not the whole truth.

A fellow named Frank, long sober himself, had only one question. Had Eddie died sober?

"I think so," I told him. "There weren't any bottles around the room, nothing to suggest he was on a slip."

"Thank God for that," Frank said.

Thank God for what? Drunk or sober, wasn't he just as dead?

Jim Faber was waiting for me at the door. We walked out together and he asked me if I was going for coffee. I said I had to meet someone.

"The woman you spent the afternoon with? The one who was drinking?"

"I don't think I mentioned it was a woman."

"No, you didn't. 'This person was drinking, which was fairly natural under the circumstance. There's no reason to think they have a problem with it.' This person, they — you don't make that kind of grammatical error, not unless you're trying to avoid saying *she*."

I laughed. "You should have been a detective."

"No, it's the printer in me. It gives you a wonderful awareness of syntax. You know, it doesn't really matter how much she drinks, or whether she's got a problem with it. It's what the effect is on you."

"I know."

"You ever been with a woman who was drinking?"

"Not since I've been sober myself."

"I didn't think so."

"I haven't really been with anybody aside from Jan. And the few dates I've had have been with women in the program."

"How'd you feel this afternoon?"

"I enjoyed being with her."

"How'd you feel being around the booze?"

I thought over my answer. "I don't know where the woman stopped and the booze started. I was nervous and excited and edgy, but I might have felt a lot of that if there hadn't been a drink anywhere in the building."

"Did you have the urge to drink?"

"Sure. But I never considered acting on it."

"You like her?"

"So far."

"You on your way to see her now?"

"We're going out for a bite."

"Not the Flame."

"Maybe someplace a little nicer than that."

"Well, you've got my number."

"Yes, Mother. I've got your number."

He laughed. "You know what old Frank would

say, Matt. 'Lad, there's a slip under every skirt.' "

"I'll bet he would. And I'll bet he hasn't looked under too many skirts lately. You know what he did say? He asked me if Eddie died sober, and when I said he did, he said, 'Well, thank God for that.' "

"So?"

"He's just as dead either way."

"That's true," he said, "but I've got to go along with Frank on this one. If he had to go, I'm glad he went out sober."

I hurried back to my hotel, grabbed a fast shower and shave, and put on a sport jacket and tie. It was twenty to eleven by the time I rang Willa's bell.

She had changed, too. She was wearing a light blue silk blouse over a pair of white Levi's. She had braided her hair, and the braid was coiled across the front of her head like a tiara. She looked cool and elegant, and I told her so.

"You look nice yourself," she said. "I'm glad you're here. I was getting paranoid."

"Was I very late? I'm sorry."

"You weren't more than ten minutes late, and I started getting paranoid forty-five minutes ago, so it had nothing to do with the time. I just decided you were too good to be true and I was never going to see you again. I'm glad I was wrong."

Outside, I asked if there was any place special she wanted to go. "Because there's a restaurant not far from here I've been wanting to try. It has a sort of French bistro atmosphere, but they have more ordinary pub fare on the menu, too, along with the French food."

"It sounds good. What's it called?"

"Paris Green."

"On Ninth Avenue. I've passed it but I've never been inside. I love the name."

"It gets the feel of the place across. The French atmosphere, and all the plants hanging from the ceiling."

"Don't you know what Paris green is?"

"Evidently not."

"It's a poison," she said. "It's an arsenic compound. Arsenic and copper, if I remember right, and that would account for the color."

"I never heard of it."

"You might have if you were a gardener. It used to get a lot of use as an insecticide. You would spray it on plants to kill chewing insects. They absorbed it through their stomachs and died. They don't use arsenicals in the garden these days, so I don't suppose it's been around for years."

"You learn something every day."

"Class isn't over yet. Paris green was also used as a coloring agent. To color things green, predictably enough. They used it primarily in wallpaper, and consequently a lot of people have died over the years, most of them children with a bent for oral experimentation. I want you to promise me that you won't put chips of green wallpaper in your mouth."

"You have my word."

"Good."

"I'll try to find other channels for my bent for oral experimentation."

"I'm sure you will."

"How do you know all this, anyway? About Paris green?"

"The party," she said. "The Progressive Commies. We learned everything we could about toxic substances. I mean, you never know when somebody's going to decide that it's tactically correct to poison the municipal water system of Duluth."

"Jesus."

"Oh, we never did anything like that," she said. "At least I didn't, and I never heard of anyone who did. But you had to be prepared."

The tall bearded bartender was behind the stick when we walked in. He gave me a wave and a smile. The hostess led us to a table. When we were seated Willa said, "You don't drink and you've never eaten here, and you walk in and the bartender greets you like a cousin."

"It's not really all that mysterious. I was in here asking some questions. I told you about that young woman I've been trying to find."

"The actress, and you told me her name. Paula?"

"He recognized her, and described the man she was with. So I came in a second time hoping he'd remember more. He's a nice fellow, he's got an interesting mind."

"Is that what you were doing earlier tonight?

138

Working on your case? Do you call it a case?"

"I suppose you could."

"But you don't."

"I don't know what I call it. A job, I guess, and one I'm not doing particularly well with."

"Did you make any progress this evening?"

"No. I wasn't working."

"Oh."

"I was at a meeting."

"A meeting?"

"An AA meeting."

"Oh," she said, and she was going to say something else, but the waitress, with a great sense of timing, showed up to take our drink orders. I said I'd have a Perrier. Willa thought for a moment and ordered a Coke with a piece of lemon.

"You could have something stronger," I said.

"I know. I already had more to drink than I usually do, and I was a little headachey when I woke up. I don't think you mentioned earlier that you were in AA."

"I don't generally tell people."

"Why? You can't think it's something to be ashamed of."

"Hardly that. But the idea of anonymity is sort of bound up in the whole program. It's considered bad form to break somebody else's anonymity, to tell people that the person in question is in AA. As far as breaking your own anonymity is concerned, that's more of an individual matter. I suppose you could say that I keep it on a need-to-know basis."

"And I need to know?"

"Well, I wouldn't keep it a secret from some-one I was involved with emotionally. That would be pretty silly."

"I guess it would. Are we?"

"Are we what?"

"Emotionally involved."

"I'd say we're on the verge."

"On the verge," she said. "I like that."

The food was pretty good considering that the place was named after a lethal substance. We had Jarlsberg cheeseburgers, cottage fries, and salad. The burgers were supposedly grilled over mesquite, but if there was a difference between that and ordinary charcoal, it was too subtle for me. The potatoes were hand-cut and fried crisp and brown. The salad contained sunflower seeds and radish sprouts and broccoli florets, along with two kinds of lettuce, neither of them ice-berg.

We talked a lot during the meal. She liked foot-ball, and preferred the college game to the pros. Liked baseball but wasn't following it this year. Liked country music, especially the old-time twangy stuff. Used to be addicted to science fiction and read shelves of it, but now when she read at all it was mostly English murder mysteries, the country house with the body in the library and butlers who had or hadn't done it. "I don't really give a damn who did it," she said. "I just like to slip into a world where everybody's polite and well-spoken and even the violence is neat and almost gentle. And everything works out in the end."

"Like life itself."

"Especially on West Fifty-first Street."

I talked a little about the search for Paula Hoeldtke and about my work in general. I said it wasn't much like her genteel English mysteries. The people weren't that polite, and everything wasn't always resolved at the end. Sometimes it wasn't even clear where the end was.

"I like it because I get to use some of my skills, though I might be hard put to tell you exactly what they are. I like to dig and pick at things until you begin to see some sort of pattern in the clutter."

"You get to be a righter of wrongs. A slayer of dragons."

"Most of the wrongs never get righted. And it's hard to get close enough to the dragons to slay them."

"Because they breathe fire?"

"Because they're the ones in the castles," I said. "With moats around them, and the drawbridge raised."

Over coffee she asked me if I'd become friendly with Eddie Dunphy in AA. Then she put her hand to her mouth. "Never mind," she said. "You already told me it was against the rules to break another member's whatchamacallit."

"Anonymity, but it doesn't matter now. Being dead means never having to remain anonymous.

Eddie started coming to meetings about a year ago. He'd stayed completely sober for the past seven months."

"How about you?"

"Three years, two months, and eleven days."

"You keep track to the day?"

"No, of course not. But I know my anniversary date, and it's not hard to figure the rest out."

"And people celebrate anniversaries?"

"Most people make it a point to speak at a meeting on their anniversary, or within a few days of it. At some groups they give you a cake."

"A cake?"

"Like a birthday cake. They present it to you, and everybody has some after the meeting. Except for the ones on diets."

"It sounds — "

"Mickey Mouse."

"I wasn't going to say that."

"Well, you could. It does. In some groups they give you a little bronze medallion with the number of years in roman numerals on one side and the serenity prayer on the other."

"The serenity prayer?"

" 'God grant me the serenity to accept the things I cannot change, courage to change the things I can, and the wisdom to know the difference.' "

"Oh, I've heard that. I didn't know it was an AA prayer."

"Well, I don't think we have exclusive title to it."

"What did you get? A cake or a medallion?"

"Neither. Just a round of applause and a lot of people telling me to remember it's still a day at a time. I guess that's why I belong to that group. No-frills sobriety."

" 'Cause you're just a no-frills kind of guy."

"You bet."

When the check came she offered to split it. I said I'd get it, and she didn't put up a fight. Outside, it had turned a little colder. She took my hand when we crossed the street, and went on holding it after we reached the curb.

When we got to her building she asked me if I wanted to come in for a few minutes. I said I thought I'd go straight home, that I wanted to get an early start the next morning.

In the vestibule she fitted her key in the lock, then turned to me. We kissed. There was no alcohol on her breath this time.

Walking home, I kept catching myself whistling. It's not something I'm much given to.

I gave out dollar bills to everyone who asked.

8

I woke up the next morning with a sour taste in my mouth. I brushed my teeth and went out for breakfast. I had to force myself to eat, and the coffee had a metallic taste to it.

Maybe it was arsenic poisoning, I thought. Maybe there had been shreds of green wallpaper in last night's salad.

My second cup of coffee didn't taste any better than the first, but I drank it anyhow and read the *News* along with it. The Mets had won, with a new kid just up from Tidewater going four-for-four. The Yankees won, too, on a home run by Claudell Washington in the ninth inning. In football, the Giants had just lost the best linebacker in the game for the next thirty days; something illicit had turned up in his urine, and he was suspended.

There had been a drive-by shooting at a street-corner in Harlem which the paper had characterized as much frequented by drug dealers, and two homeless persons had fought on a platform of the East Side IRT, one hurling the other into the path of an oncoming train, with predictable results. In Brooklyn, a man in Brighton Beach had been arrested for the murder of his former wife and her three children by a previous marriage.

There was nothing about Eddie Dunphy. There wouldn't be, unless it was a very slow day for news.

After breakfast I set out to walk off some of the loginess and lethargy. It was overcast, and the weather forecast called for a forty percent chance of rain. I'm not sure just what that's supposed to mean. *Don't blame us if it rains,* they seem to be saying, and *don't blame us if it doesn't.*

I didn't pay much attention to where I was going. I wound up in Central Park, and when I found an empty bench I sat on it. Across from me and a little to the right, a woman in a thrift-shop overcoat was feeding pigeons from a sack of bread crumbs. The birds were all over her and the bench and the surrounding pavement. There must have been two hundred of them.

They say you just exacerbate a problem by feeding pigeons, but I was in no position to tell her to stop. Not as long as I went on handing out dollar bills to panhandlers.

She ran out of bread crumbs, finally, and the birds left, and so did she. I stayed where I was and thought about Eddie Dunphy and Paula Hoeldtke. Then I thought about Willa Rossiter, and I realized why I'd awakened feeling lousy.

I hadn't had time to react to Eddie's death. I'd

145

been with Willa instead, and when I might have been sad for him I was instead exhilarated and excited by whatever was growing between us. And the same thing was true, in a less dramatic way, with Paula. I'd gone as far as some conflicting data relating to her telephone, and then I'd put everything on hold so that I could have a romantic encounter.

There wasn't necessarily anything wrong with that. But Eddie and Paula had been stowed somewhere under the heading of Unfinished Business, and if I didn't deal with them I was going to keep having a sour taste in my mouth, and my coffee was going to have a metallic aftertaste.

I got up and got out of there. Near the entrance at Columbus Circle a wild-eyed man in denim cut-offs asked me for money. I shook him off and kept walking.

She'd paid her rent on July 6. On the thirteenth it was due again, but she didn't show up. On the fifteenth Flo Edderling went to collect and she didn't answer the door. On the sixteenth Flo opened the door and the room was empty, nothing left behind but the bed linen. On the seventeenth her parents called and left a message on her machine, and that same day Georgia arranged to rent the just-vacated room, and a day later she took possession. And two days after that, Paula called the phone company and told them to disconnect her phone.

The woman I'd spoken to originally at the phone

company was a Ms. Cadillo. We had established a pleasant working relationship the previous day, and now she remembered me right away. "I hate to keep bothering you," I said, "but I'm having a problem reconciling data from a few different sources. I know she called for a disconnect on July twentieth, but what I'd like to do is find out where she called from."

"I'm afraid we wouldn't have that on record," she said, puzzled. "In fact we'd never know that in the first place. As a matter of fact — "

"Yes?"

"I was going to say that my records wouldn't show whether she phoned us to order cessation of service or whether she might have written to us. Almost everyone phones, but she could have written. Some people do, especially if they've enclosed a final payment. But we didn't receive any payment from her at that time."

I'd never even thought that the disconnect order could have been mailed in, and for a moment that seemed to clear everything up. She could have put a note in the mail long before the twentieth; given the state of the postal service, it might still be en route.

But that wouldn't explain her parents' call to her on the seventeenth.

I said, "Isn't there a record kept of all calls made from a given number?"

"There is, but — "

"Could you tell me the date and time of the last call she made? That would be very helpful."

"I'm sorry," she said. "I really can't do that. I'm not able to retrieve that information myself, and it's a violation of policy to do it."

"I suppose I could get a court order," I said, "but I hate to put my client to the trouble and expense, and it would mean wasting everybody's time. If you could see your way clear to helping me out, I'd make sure no one ever knew where it came from."

"I really am sorry. I might bend the rules if I could, but I don't have the codes. If you really do need a record of her local calls, I'm afraid you'd have to have that court order."

I almost missed it. I was in the middle of another sentence when it registered. I said, "Local calls. If she made any toll calls — "

"They'd be on her statement."

"And you can access that?"

"I'm not supposed to." I didn't say anything, giving her a little slack, and she said, "Well, it *is* a matter of record. Let me see what I can punch up. There are no toll calls at all during the month of July — "

"Well, it was worth a try."

"You didn't let me finish."

"I'm sorry."

"There are no calls at all during July, no toll calls, until the eighteenth. There are two calls on the eighteenth and one on the nineteenth."

"And none on the twentieth?"

"No. Just those three. Would you like the numbers that she called?"

"Yes," I said. "Very much."

There were two numbers. She'd called one both days, one just on the nineteenth. They both had the same area code, 904, and I checked the book and found that was nowhere near Indiana. It was north Florida, including the panhandle.

I found a bank and bought a ten-dollar roll of quarters. I went back to my pay phone and dialed the number she'd called twice. A recording told me how much money to put in, and I did, and a woman answered on the fourth ring. I told her my name was Scudder and that I was trying to get in touch with Paula Hoeldtke.

"I'm afraid you have the wrong number," she said.

"Don't hang up, I'm calling from New York. I believe a woman named Paula Hoeldtke called this number the month before last and I'm trying to trace her movements since then."

There was a pause. Then she said, "Well, I don't rightly see how that can be. This is a private residence and the name you mentioned isn't familiar to me."

"Is this 904-555-1904?"

"It most certainly is not. The number here is — wait a moment, what was that number you just read?"

I repeated it.

"That's my husband's place of business," she said. "That's the number at Prysocki Hardware."

"I'm sorry," I said. I had read the wrong listing

from my notebook, the number she'd called only once. "Your number must be 828-9177."

"How did you get that other number?"

"She called both numbers," I said.

"Did she. And what did you say her name was?"

"Paula Hoeldtke."

"And she called this number *and* the store?"

"My records may be wrong," I said. She was still asking questions when I broke the connection.

I walked to the rooming house on Fifty-fourth Street. Halfway there a kid in jeans with a scraggly goatee asked me for spare change. He had the wasted look of a speed freak. Some of the crack addicts get that look. I gave him all my quarters. "Hey, thanks!" he called after me. "You're beautiful, man."

When Flo came to the door I apologized for bothering her. She said it was no bother. I asked if Georgia Price was in.

"I'm sure I don't know," she said. "Didn't you get to talk to her yet? Though I don't know what help she could be. I couldn't hardly rent her the room before Paula was out of it, so how would she know her?"

"I spoke to her. I'd like to talk to her again."

She gestured toward the staircase. I walked up a flight, stood in front of the door that had been Paula's.

There was music playing within, with an insistent if not infectious beat. I knocked, but I wasn't sure she could hear me over the noise. I went to knock again when the door opened.

Georgia Price was wearing a leotard, and her forehead glowed with perspiration. I guess she had been dancing, practicing steps or something. She looked at me, and her eyes widened when she placed me. She took an involuntary step backward and I followed her into the room. She started to say something, then stopped and went to turn off the music. She turned back to me, and she looked scared and guilty. I didn't think she had much cause for either emotion, but I decided to press.

I said, "You're from Tallahassee, aren't you?"

"Just outside."

"Price is a stage name. Your real name is Prysocki."

"How did you — "

"There was a phone here when you moved in. It hadn't been disconnected."

"I didn't know I wasn't supposed to use it. I thought the phone came with the room, like a hotel or something. I didn't know."

"So you called home, and you called your father at his store."

She nodded. She looked terribly young, and scared to death. "I'll pay for the calls," she said. "I didn't realize, I thought I would get a bill or something. And then I couldn't get a phone installed right away, they couldn't send someone to connect it until Monday, so I waited until then to have it disconnected. When the installer came he just hooked the same phone up, but with a

151

different number so I wouldn't get any of her calls. I swear I didn't mean to do anything wrong."

"You didn't do anything wrong," I said.

"I'll be happy to pay for the calls."

"Don't worry about the calls. You were the one who ordered the phone disconnected?"

"Yes, was that wrong? I mean, she wasn't living here, so — "

"That was the right thing for you to do," I told her. "I'm not concerned about a couple of free phone calls. I'm just trying to find a girl who dropped out of sight."

"I know, but — "

"So you don't have to be afraid of anything. You're not going to get in trouble."

"Well, I didn't exactly think I was going to get in trouble, but — "

"Was there an answering machine hooked up to the phone, Georgia? A telephone answering machine?"

Her eyes darted involuntarily to the bedside table, where an answering machine stood alongside a telephone.

"I would have given it back when you were here before," she said. "If I even thought of it. But you just asked me a couple of quick questions, what was in the room and did I know Paula and did anybody come looking for her after I moved in, and by the time I remembered the machine you were gone. I didn't mean to keep it, only I didn't know what else to do with it. It was here."

"That's all right."

"So I used it. I was going to have to buy one, and this one was already here. I was just going to use it until I could afford to buy one of my own. I want to get one with a remote, so you can call from another phone and get your messages off it. This one doesn't have that feature. But for the time being it's okay. Do you want to take it with you? It won't take me a minute to disconnect it."

"I don't want the machine," I said. "I didn't come here to pick up answering machines, or to collect money for calls to Tallahassee."

"I'm sorry."

"I want to ask you a few questions about the phone, that's all. And about the machine."

"Okay."

"You moved in on the eighteenth and the phone was on until the twentieth. Did Paula get any calls during that time?"

"No."

"The phone didn't ring?"

"It rang once or twice but it was for me. I called my friend and gave her the number here, and she called me once or twice over the weekend. That was a local call so it didn't cost anything, or if it did all it cost was a quarter."

"I don't care if you called Alaska," I told her. "If it'll put your mind at rest, the calls you did make didn't cost anybody anything. Paula's deposit came to more than her final bill; so the calls were paid for out of money that would have been refunded to her, and she's not around to claim the refund anyway."

"I know I'm being silly about this," she said.

"That's all right. The only calls that came in were for you. How about when you were out? Were there any messages on her machine?"

"Not after I moved in. I know because the last message was from her mother, all about how they were going to be out of town, and that message must have been left a day or two before I moved in. See, as soon as I figured out it was her phone and not one that came with the room, I unplugged the answering machine. Then about a week later I decided she wasn't coming back for it and I might as well use it, because I needed one. When I hooked it up again I played her messages before I set the tape to record."

"Were there messages besides the ones from her parents?"

"A few."

"Do you still have them?"

"I erased the tape."

"Do you remember anything about the other messages?"

"Gee, I don't. There were some that were just hang-ups. I just played the tape once through trying to figure out how to erase it."

"What about the other tape, the one that says nobody's home but you can leave a message? Paula must have had one of those on the machine."

"Sure."

"Did you erase it?"

"It erases automatically when you record a new

message over it. And I did that so I could leave a message in my own voice when I started using the machine." She chewed at her lip. "Was that wrong?"

"No."

"Would it have been important? It was just the usual thing. 'Hello, this is Paula. I can't talk to you right now but you can leave a message at the sound of the tone.' Or something like that, that's not word-for-word."

"It's not important," I said. And it wasn't. I just would have liked a chance to hear her voice.

9

"I'm surprised you're still on it," Durkin said. "What did you do, call Indiana and shake some more dough out of the money tree?"

"No. I probably should, I'm putting in a lot of hours, but I'm not getting much in the way of results. I think her disappearance is a criminal matter."

"What makes you think so?"

"She never officially moved out. She paid her rent one day, and ten days later her landlady cracked the door and the room was empty."

"Happens all the time."

"I know that. The room was empty except for three things. Whoever cleaned it out left the phone, the answering machine, and the bed linens."

"And what does that tell you?"

"That somebody else packed the stuff and carried it off. A lot of rooming houses furnish bed linen. This one didn't. Paula Hoeldtke had to supply her own linen, so she would have known to take it with her when she left. Someone else who

156

didn't know might have assumed it was supposed to stay with the room."

"That's all you've got?"

"No. The answering machine was left behind, and it was hooked up to continue answering the phone and telling people to leave their messages. If she'd left on her own she'd have called and had the phone disconnected."

"Not if she left in a hurry."

"She probably would have called in somewhere along the line. But let's say she didn't, let's say she was enough of an airhead to forget it altogether. Why would she leave the machine?"

"Same thing. She forgot it."

"The room was left empty. No clothes in the drawers, nothing in the closet. There wasn't a whole lot of clutter around for things to get lost in. All that was left was the bed linen, the phone, and the answering machine. She couldn't have not noticed it."

"Sure she could. Lots of people leave the phone when they move. I think you're supposed to leave the phone, unless it's one that you bought outright. Anyway, people leave them. So she's gonna leave her phone. So the answering machine — where is it, it's next to the phone, right?"

"Right."

"So she looks over there and she doesn't see something separate, an answering machine, a household appliance, keeps you in touch with your friends and associates, ends your worry of missing calls, di dah di dah di dah. What she sees is part of the phone."

I thought about it. "Maybe," I said.

"It's part of the phone, it goes with the phone. And, since the phone stays, it stays with the phone."

"And why doesn't she come back for it when she realizes it's missing?"

"Because she's in Greenland," he said, "and it's cheaper to buy a new machine than to get on a plane."

"I don't know, Joe."

"I don't know either, but I'll tell you this, it makes as much sense as looking at a phone and an answering machine and two sheets and a blanket and trying to make a kidnapping case out of it."

"Don't forget the bedspread."

"Yeah, right. Maybe she moved somewhere that she couldn't use the linen. What was it, a single bed?"

"Larger than that, somewhere between a single and a double. I think they call it a three-quarter."

"So she moved in with some slick dude with a king-size water bed and a twelve-inch cock, and what does she need with some old sheets and pillowcases? What does she even need with a phone, as far as that goes, if she's gonna be spending all her time on her back with her knees up?"

"I think somebody moved her out," I said. "I think somebody took her keys and let himself into her room and packed up all her things and slipped out of there with them. I think — "

"Anybody see a stranger leave the building with

a couple of suitcases?"

"They don't even know each other, so how would they spot a stranger?"

"Did anybody see *anybody* toting some bags around that time?"

"It's too long ago, you know that. I asked the question of people on the same floor with her, but how can you remember a commonplace event that might have taken place two months ago?"

"That's the whole point, Matt. If anybody left a trail, it's ice-cold by now." He picked up a Lucite photo cube, turned it in his hands and looked at a picture of two children and a dog, all three beaming at the camera. "Go on with your script," he said. "Somebody moves her stuff out. He leaves the linen because he doesn't know it's hers. Why does he leave the answering machine?"

"So anybody who calls her won't know she's gone."

"Then why doesn't he leave everything, and even the landlady won't know she's gone?"

"Because eventually the landlady will figure out that she's not coming back, and the matter might get reported to the police. Cleaning out the room tidies a potential loose end. Leaving the answering machine buys a little time, gives the illusion she's still there to anybody at a distance, and makes it impossible to know exactly when she moved. She paid her rent on the sixth and her room was found to be vacant ten days later, so that's the best I can narrow down the time of her disappearance, and that's because he left the machine on."

"How do you figure that?"

"Her parents called a couple of times and left messages. If the machine hadn't picked up they would have kept calling until they reached her, and when they didn't reach her no matter what time they called, they would have been alarmed, they would have thought something happened to her. In all likelihood her father would have come to see you two months earlier than he did."

"Yeah, I see what you mean."

"And it wouldn't have been a cold trail then."

"I'm still not sure it would have been a police matter."

"Maybe, maybe not. But if he'd hired somebody private back in the middle of July — "

"You'd have had an easier time of it. No argument." He thought for a moment. "Say she left the machine behind herself, not by accident but because she had a reason."

"What reason?"

"She moved out but she doesn't want somebody to know she's gone. Her parents, say, or somebody else she's trying to duck."

"She'd just keep the room. Pay the rent and live elsewhere."

"All right, say she wants to move out and skip town but she wants to be able to get her calls. She could — "

"She couldn't get her calls from a distance."

"Sure she could. They've got this gizmo, you just call your machine from any touch-tone phone and punch in a code and the machine plays back your messages."

"Not all machines have the remote-pickup feature. Hers didn't."

"How do you know that? Oh, right, you saw the machine, it's still in the room." He splayed his fingers. "Look, what's the point going over this again and again? You were a cop long enough, Matt. Put yourself in my position."

"I'm just saying that — "

"Put yourself in my fucking position, will you? You're sitting at this desk and a guy comes in with a story about bed linen and a telephone answering machine. There's no evidence that a crime has been committed, the missing person is a mentally competent adult, and nobody's seen her for over two months. Now what am I supposed to do?"

I didn't say anything.

"What would *you* do? In my position."

"What you're doing."

"Of course you would."

"Suppose it was the mayor's daughter."

"The mayor doesn't have a daughter. The mayor never had a hard-on in his life, so how could he have a daughter?" He pushed his chair back. "Of course it's a different matter if it's the mayor's daughter. Then we put a hundred men on it and work around the clock until something breaks. Which doesn't mean something necessarily does, not after all this time and with so little to go on. Look, what's the big fear here? Not that she went to Disney World and the Ferris wheel got stuck

161

with her at the top of it. What are you and her parents really afraid of?"

"That she's dead."

"And maybe she is. People die all the time in this city. If she's alive she'll call home sooner or later, when the money runs out or her head clears up, whatever it takes. If she's dead there's nothing anybody can do for her, you or me or anybody else."

"I suppose you're right."

"Of course I'm right. Your problem is you get like a dog with a bone. Call the father, tell him there's nothing to run with, he should have called you two months ago."

"Right, make him feel guilty."

"Well, you could find a better way to put it. Jesus, you already gave it more than most people would and took it as far as it would go. You even dug up some decent clues, the phone calls and everything, the answering machine. The trouble is they're not attached to anything. You pull them and they come off in your hand."

"I know."

"So let go of it. You don't want to put in any more hours or you wind up working for chump change."

I started to say something but his phone rang. He talked for a few minutes. When he hung up he said, "What did we do for crime before we had cocaine?"

"We made do."

"Did we? I guess we must have."

I walked around for a few hours. Around one-thirty it started raining lightly. Almost immediately the umbrella sellers turned up on the streetcorners. You'd have thought they had existed previously in spore form, springing miraculously to life when a drop of water touched them.

I didn't buy an umbrella. It wasn't raining hard enough to make it worthwhile. I went into a bookstore and killed some time without buying anything, and when I left the rain still didn't amount to much more than a fine mist.

I stopped at my hotel, checked at the desk. No messages, and the only mail was an offer of a credit card. "You have already been approved!" the copy blared. Somehow I doubted this.

I went upstairs and called Warren Hoeldtke. I had my notebook at hand, and I gave him a quick rundown on what lines of investigation I'd pursued and what little I'd managed to determine. "I've put in a lot of hours," I said, "but I don't think I'm much closer to her than I was when I started. I don't feel as though I've accomplished anything."

"Do you want more money?"

"No. I wouldn't know how to go about earning it."

"What do you think has happened to her? I realize you don't have any hard knowledge, but don't you have some sense of what went on?"

"Only a vague one, and I don't know how much weight to attach to it. I think she got mixed up with somebody who appeared exciting and turned out to be dangerous."

"Do you think — "

He didn't want to say it, and I couldn't blame him. "She may be alive," I said. "Maybe she's out of the country. Maybe she's mixed up in something illegal. That might explain why she hasn't been able to get in touch with you."

"It's hard to imagine Paula involved with criminals."

"Maybe it just looked like an adventure to her."

"I suppose that's possible." He sighed. "You don't leave much room for hope."

"No, but I wouldn't say you have grounds for despair yet, either. I'm afraid all you can do is wait."

"That's all I've done from the beginning. It's . . . hard."

"I'm sure it must be."

"Well," he said. "I want to thank you for your efforts, and for being straight with me. I'll be happy to send you more money if you think there's any point at all in putting in more time."

"No," I said. "I'll probably put in a few more days on this anyway, just on the chance that something'll loosen up. In which case you'll hear from me."

"I didn't want to take any more money from him," I told Willa. "The original thousand had put me under more obligation than I wanted to be. If I accepted any more of his money I'd have his daughter around my neck for the rest of my life."

"But you're doing more work. Why shouldn't you get paid for it?"

"I got paid already, and what did I give him in return?"

"You did the work."

"Did I? In high school physics they taught us how to measure work. The formula was force times distance. Take an object that weighs twenty pounds, move it six feet, and you've done a hundred and twenty foot-pounds worth of work."

"Foot-pounds?"

"That was the unit of measurement. But if you stood and pushed against a wall all day and didn't budge it, you hadn't performed any work. Because you'd moved the wall a distance of zero, so it didn't matter how much the wall weighed, the product was zero. Warren Hoeldtke paid me a thousand dollars and all I did was push a wall."

"You moved it a little."

"Not enough to matter."

"Oh, I don't know," she said. "When Edison was working on the light bulb, somebody said he must be discouraged because he wasn't making any progress. Edison said he'd made great progress, because now he knew twenty thousand materials that you couldn't use for a filament."

"Edison had a better attitude than I have."

"And a good thing, too, or we'd all be in the dark."

We *were* in the dark, and seemed none the worse

165

for it. We were in her bedroom, stretched out on her bed, a Reba McIntyre tape playing in the kitchen. Through the bedroom window you could hear the sounds of a quarrel in the building behind hers, loud voices arguing a point in Spanish.

I hadn't intended to drop in on her. I'd gone out walking after my call to Hoeldtke. I was passing a florist and had the impulse to send her flowers, and after he'd written up the order I found out he couldn't deliver until the following day. So I'd delivered them myself.

She put the flowers in water and we sat in the kitchen with them on the table between us. She made coffee. It was instant, but it was a fresh jar of a premium brand and no killjoy had taken the caffeine out of it.

And then, without needing to discuss the matter, we'd moved to the bedroom. Reba McIntyre had been singing when we entered the bedroom and she was still hard at it, but we had heard some of the songs more than once. The tape reversed automatically, and would play over and over if you let it.

After a while she said, "Are you hungry? I could cook something."

"If you feel like it."

"Shall I tell you a secret? I never feel like it. I'm not a great cook, and you've seen the kitchen."

"We could go out."

"It's pouring. Don't you hear it in the airshaft?"

"It was raining very lightly earlier. What my Irish aunt used to call a soft day."

166

"Well, it turned hard, from the sound of it. Suppose I order Chinese? They don't care what the weather's like, they hop on their kamikaze bicycles and ride through hailstorms if they have to. 'Neither rain nor snow nor heat nor gloom of night shall keep you from your moo goo gai pan.' Except I don't want moo goo gai pan. I want — would you like to know what I want?"

"Sure."

"I want sesame noodles and pork fried rice and chicken with cashews and shrimp with four flavors. How does that sound?"

"Like enough food for an army."

"I bet we eat all of it. Oh."

"What's the matter?"

"Are you going to have time? It's twenty to eight, and by the time they deliver and we eat it'll be time for your meeting."

"I don't have to go tonight."

"Are you sure?"

"Positive. I have a question, though. What's shrimp with four flavors?"

"You've never had shrimp with four flavors?"

"No."

"Oh, my dear," she said. "Are you ever in for a treat."

We ate at the tin-topped table in the kitchen. I tried to move the flowers to give us more room but she wouldn't let me. "I want them where I can see them," she said. "There's plenty of room."

167

She had gone shopping that morning, and besides coffee she'd stocked up on fruit juice and soft drinks. I had a Coke. She got out a bottle of Beck's for herself, but before she opened it she made sure it wouldn't bother me.

"Of course not," I said.

"Because nothing goes with Chinese food like beer. Matt, is it all right to say that?"

"What, that beer goes well with Chinese food? Well, it may be a controversial statement, and I suppose there are some wine growers somewhere who'd give you an argument, but so what?"

"I wasn't sure."

"Open your beer," I said. "And sit down and eat."

Everything was delicious, and the shrimp dish was the treat she'd promised. They'd included disposable chopsticks with our order and she used a pair. I had never learned to handle them and stuck with a fork. I told her she was good with the chopsticks.

"It's easy," she said. "It just takes practice. Here. Try."

I made an effort, but my fingers were clumsy. The sticks kept crossing and I couldn't get any food to my mouth. "This would be good for someone on a diet," I said. "You'd think somewhere along the way they could have invented the fork. They invented everything else. Pasta, ice cream, gunpowder."

"And baseball."

"I thought that was the Russians."

168

We finished everything, just as she'd predicted. She cleared the table, opened a second bottle of Beck's. "I'll have to learn the ground rules," she said. "I feel a little funny about drinking in front of you."

"Do I make you uncomfortable?"

"No, but I'm afraid I'll make *you* uncomfortable. I didn't know if it was all right to talk about how great beer is with Chinese food because, oh, *I* don't know. Is it all right to talk about booze that way?"

"What do you think we do at meetings? We talk about booze all the time. Some of us spend more time talking about it than we used to spend drinking it."

"But don't you tell yourselves how terrible it was?"

"Sometimes. And sometimes we tell each other how wonderful it was."

"I never would have guessed that."

"That didn't surprise me as much as the laughter. People tell about the damnedest things that happened to them, and everybody breaks up."

"I wouldn't think they'd talk about it, let alone laugh. I guess I thought it would be like mentioning rope in the house of the hanged."

"In the house of the hanged," I said, "that's probably the chief topic of conversation."

Later she said, "I keep wanting to bring the flowers in here. That's crazy, there's no room for them. They're better in the kitchen."

"They'll still be there in the morning."

"I'm like a kid, aren't I? Can I tell you something?"

"Sure."

"God. I don't know if I should tell you this. Well, with that preamble, I guess I have to, don't I? Nobody ever gave me flowers before."

"That's pretty hard to believe."

"Why is it so hard to believe? I spent twenty years devoting myself heart and soul to revolutionary politics. Radical activists don't give each other flowers. I mean, talk about your bourgeois sentimentality, your late capitalist decadence. Mao said let a thousand flowers bloom, but that didn't mean you were supposed to pluck a handful and take them home to your sweetie. You weren't even supposed to have a sweetie. If a relationship didn't serve the party, you had no business in it."

"But you got out of there a few years ago. You were married."

"To an old hippie. Long hair and fringed buckskin and love beads. He should have had a 1967 calendar on his wall. He was locked in the sixties, he never knew they'd ended." She shook her head. "He never brought home flowers. Flowering tops, yes, but not flowers."

"Flowering tops?"

"The most potent part of the marijuana plant. *Cannabis sativa,* if you want to be formal. Do you smoke?"

"No."

"I haven't in years, because I'm afraid it would lead me right back to cigarettes. That's funny, isn't it? They try to scare you that it'll lead to heroin, and I'm afraid it might lead to tobacco. But I never liked it that much. I never liked feeling out of control."

The flowers were still there in the morning.

I hadn't intended to stay the night, but then I hadn't planned on dropping in on her in the first place. The hours just slipped away from us. We talked, we shared silences, we listened to music, and to the rain.

I awoke before she did. I had a drunk dream. They're not uncommon, but I hadn't had one in a while. The details were gone by the time I got my eyes open, but in the dream someone had offered me a beer and I had taken it without thinking. By the time I realized I couldn't do that, I'd already drunk half of it.

I woke up not sure if it was a dream and not entirely certain where I was. It was six in the morning and I wouldn't have wanted to go back to sleep even if I could, for fear of slipping back into the dream. I got up and dressed, not showering to keep from waking her. I was tying my shoes when I felt that I was being watched, and I turned to see her looking at me.

"It's early," I said. "Go back to sleep. I'll call you later."

I went back to my hotel. There was a message for me. Jim Faber had called, but it was far too early to call him back. I went upstairs and showered and shaved, then stretched out on the bed for a minute and surprised myself by dozing off. I hadn't even felt tired, but I wound up sleeping for three hours and woke up groggy.

I took another shower and shook off the grogginess. I called Jim at his shop.

"I missed you last night," he said. "I was just wondering how you were doing."

"I'm fine."

"I'm glad to hear it. You missed a great qualification."

"Oh?"

"Guy from Midtown Group. Very funny stuff. He went through a period where he kept trying to kill himself and couldn't get it right. He couldn't swim a stroke, so he rented a flat-bottom rowboat and rowed for miles. Finally, he stood up, said, 'Goodbye, cruel world,' and threw himself over the side."

"And?"

"And he was on a sandbar. He was in two feet of water."

"Sometimes you can't do a single thing right."

"Yeah, everybody has days like that."

"I had a drunk dream last night," I said.

"Oh?"

"I drank half a beer before I realized what I was doing. Then I realized, and I felt horrible, and I drank the rest of it."

"Where was this?"

"I don't remember the details."

"No, where was it you spent the night?"

"Nosy bastard, aren't you? I stayed over with Willa."

"That's her name? The super?"

"That's right."

"Was she drinking?"

"Not enough to matter."

"Not enough to matter to whom?"

"Jesus Christ," I said. "I was with her for about eight hours, not counting the time we slept, and in all that time she had two beers, one with dinner and one after. Does that make her an alcoholic?"

"That's not the question. The question is does it make you uncomfortable."

"I can't remember when I last spent a more comfortable night."

"What brand of beer was she drinking?"

"Beck's. What's the difference?"

"What did you drink in your dream?"

"I don't remember."

"What did it taste like?"

"I don't remember the taste. I wasn't aware of it."

"That's a hell of a note. If you're going to drink in your dreams, at least you ought to be able to taste it and enjoy it. You want to get together for lunch?"

"I can't. I've got some things I have to do."

"Maybe I'll see you tonight, then."

"Maybe."

I hung up, irritated. I felt as though I was being treated like a child, and my response was to turn childishly irritable. What difference did it make what kind of beer I drank in my dream?

10

Andreotti wasn't on duty when I got over to the precinct house. He was downtown, testifying before a grand jury. The guy he'd been partnered with, Bill Bellamy, couldn't understand what I wanted with the medical examiner's report.

"You were there," he said. "It's open and shut. Time of death was sometime late Saturday night or early Sunday morning, that's according to the preliminary report from the man on the scene. All evidence on the scene supports a finding of accidental death by autoerotic asphyxiation. Everything — the pornography, the position of the body, the nudity, everything. We see these all the time, Scudder."

"I know."

"Then you probably know it's the best-kept secret in America, because what paper's going to print that the deceased died jerking off with a rope around his neck? And it's not just kids. We had one last year, this was a married guy and his wife found him. Decent people, beautiful apartment on West End Avenue. Married fifteen years! Poor woman didn't understand, couldn't understand. She couldn't even believe that he masturbated, let alone that he liked to strangle hisself while he did it."

"I understand how it works."

"Then what's your interest? You got some kind of an insurance angle, your client can't collect if you get a suicide verdict?"

"I haven't got a client. And I doubt he had any insurance."

"Because I remember we had an insurance investigator come up in connection with the gentleman from West End Avenue. He had a whole lot of coverage, too. Might have been as much as a million dollars."

"And they didn't want to pay it?"

"They were going to have to pay something. Suicide'll only nullify a policy for a certain amount of time after it's taken out, to prevent you from signing up when you've already decided to kill yourself. This case, he'd had the policy long enough so suicide didn't cancel it. So what was the hook?" He frowned, then brightened. "Oh, right. He had that double indemnity clause where they pay you twice as much for accidental death. I have to say I never saw the logic to that. I mean, dead is dead. What's the difference if you have a heart attack or wreck your car? Your wife's got the same living expenses, your kid's college is gonna cost the same. I never understood it."

"The insurer didn't want to accept a claim of accidental death?"

"You got it. Said a man puts a rope around his neck and hangs hisself, that's suicide. The wife got herself a good lawyer and they had to pay the whole amount. Man had the intention of hanging hisself, but he did not have the intention of killing hisself, and that made it an accident and not a suicide." He smiled, liking the justice of it, then remembered the matter at hand. "But you're not here about insurance."

"No, and I'm pretty sure he didn't have any. He was a friend of mine."

"Interesting friend for you to have. Turns out he had a sheet on him longer than his dick."

"Mostly small-time, wasn't it?"

"According to what he got collared for. Far as what he got away with, how could you say? Maybe he kidnapped the Lindbergh baby and went scot-free."

"I think it was a little before his time. I have a fair idea of the kind of life he used to lead, although I don't know the details. But for the past year he's been staying sober."

"You're saying he was an alcoholic."

"A sober one."

"And?"

"I want to know if he died sober."

"What difference does it make?"

"It's hard to explain."

"I got an uncle used to be a terrible alcoholic. He quit drinking and now he's a different person."

"It works that way sometimes."

"Used to be you didn't want to know the man,

and now he's a fine human being. Goes to church, holds a job, acts right with people. Your friend, it didn't look like he'd been drinking. There was no bottles laying around."

"No, but he might have done some drinking elsewhere. Or he could have taken other drugs."

"You mean like heroin?"

"I would doubt it."

"Because I didn't see no tracks. Still, there's more than you think that'll snort it."

"Any drugs," I said. "They're doing a complete autopsy, aren't they?"

"They got to. The law requires it."

"Well, could I see the results when you get them?"

"Just so you'll know if he died sober?" He sighed. "I guess. But what does it matter? They got some rule, he's got to be sober when he dies or they won't bury him in the good section of the cemetery?"

"I don't know if I can explain it."

"Try."

"He didn't have much of a life," I said, "and he didn't have much of a death, either. For the past year he's been trying to stay sober a day at a time. He had a lot of trouble at the beginning and it never got to be what you could call easy for him, but he stayed with it. Nothing else ever worked for him. I just wanted to know if he made it."

"Give me your number," Bellamy said. "That report comes in, I'll call you."

I heard an Australian qualify once at a meeting down in the Village. "My head didn't get me sober," he said. "All my head ever did was get me into trouble. It was my feet got me sober. They kept taking me to meetings and my poor head had no choice but to follow. What I've got, I've got smart feet."

My feet took me to Grogan's. I was walking around, up one street and down another, thinking about Eddie Dunphy and Paula Hoeldtke and not paying much attention to where I was going. Then I looked up, and I was at the corner of Tenth Avenue and Fiftieth Street, right across from Grogan's Open House.

Eddie had crossed the street to avoid the place. I crossed the street and went in.

It wasn't fancy. A bar, on the left as you entered, ran the length of the room. There were dark wooden booths on the right, and a row of three or four tables between them. There was an old-fashioned tile floor, a stamped tin ceiling that needed minor repairs.

The clientele was all male. Two old men sat in silence in the front booth, letting their beers go flat. Two booths back there was a young man wearing a ski sweater and reading a newspaper. There was a dart board on the back wall, and a fellow wearing a T-shirt and a baseball cap was playing by himself.

At the front end of the bar, two men sat near a television set, neither paying attention to the picture. There was an empty stool between them. Toward the back, the bartender was leafing through a tabloid, one of the ones that tell you Elvis and Hitler are still alive, and a potato chip diet cures cancer.

I walked over to the bar and put my foot on the brass rail. The bartender looked me over for a long moment before he approached. I ordered a Coke. He gave me another careful look, his blue eyes unreadable, his face expressionless. He had a narrow triangular face, so pale he might have lived all his life indoors.

He filled a glass with ice cubes, then with Coke. I put a ten on the bar. He took it to the register, punched *No Sale,* and returned with eight singles and a pair of quarters. I left my change on the bar in front of me and sipped at my Coke.

The television set was showing *Santa Fe Trail,* with Errol Flynn and Olivia de Havilland. Flynn was playing Jeb Stuart, and an impossibly young Ronald Reagan was playing George Armstrong Custer. The movie was in black and white, with the commercials in color.

I sipped my Coke and watched the movie, and when the commercials came on I turned on my stool and watched the fellow in back shoot darts. He would toe the line and lean so far forward I kept thinking he would be unable to keep his balance, but he evidently knew what he was doing; he stayed on his feet, and the darts all wound up in the board.

After I'd been there twenty minutes or so, a black man in work clothes came in wanting to know how to get to DeWitt Clinton High School. The bartender claimed not to know, which seemed unlikely. I could have told him, but I didn't volunteer, and no one else spoke up, either.

"Supposed to be around here somewhere," the man said. "I got a delivery, and the address they gave me ain't right. I'll take a beer while I'm here."

"There's something wrong with the pressure. All I'm getting is foam."

"Bottled beer be fine."

"We only have draught."

"Guy in the booth has a bottle of beer."

"He must have brought it with him."

The message got through. "Well, shit," the driver said. "I guess this here's the Stork Club. Fancy place like this, you got to be real careful who you serve." He stared hard at the bartender, who gazed back at him without showing a thing. Then he turned and walked out fast with his head lowered, and the door swung shut behind him.

A little while later the dart player sauntered over and the bartender drew him a pint of the draught Guinness, thick and black, with a rich creamy head on it. He said, "Thanks, Tom," and drank, then wiped the foam from his mouth onto his sleeve. "Fucking niggers," he said. "Pushing in where they're not wanted."

The bartender didn't respond, just took money

and brought back change. The dart player took another long drink of stout and wiped his mouth again on his sleeve. His T-shirt advertised a tavern called the Croppy Boy, on Fordham Road in the Bronx. His billed cap advertised Old Milwaukee beer.

To me he said, "Game of darts? Not for money, I'm too strong a player, but just to pass the time."

"I don't even know how to play."

"You try to get the pointed end into the board."

"I'd probably hit the fish." There was a fish mounted on the wall above the dart board, and a deer's head off to one side. Another larger fish was mounted above the back bar; it was a sailfish or marlin, one of the ones with a long bill.

"Just to pass the time," he said.

I couldn't remember the last time I'd thrown a dart, and I hadn't been good at it then. Time had by no means improved my skills. We played a game, and as hard as he worked to look bad, I still didn't come out looking good. When he won the game in spite of himself, he said, "You're pretty good, you know."

"Oh, come on."

"You've got the touch. You haven't played and your aim's not sharp, but you've got a nice light wrist. Let me buy you a beer."

"I'm drinking Coca-Cola."

"That there is why your aim's off. The beer relaxes you, lets you just think the dart into the board. The black stuff's the best, the Guinness.

It works on your mind like polish on silver. Takes the tarnish right off. That do you, or would you rather have a bottle of Harp?"

"Thanks, but I'll stay with Coke."

He bought me a refill, and another black pint for himself. He told me his name was Andy Buckley. I gave him my name, and we played another game of darts. He foot-faulted a couple of times, showing a clumsiness he hadn't revealed when he was practicing. When he did it a second time I gave him a look and he had to laugh. "I know I can't hustle you, Matt," he said. "You know what it is? It's force of habit."

He won the game quickly and didn't coax when I said no to another. It was my turn to buy a round. I didn't want another Coke. I bought him a Guinness, and had a club soda for myself. The bartender rang the "No Sale" key and took money from my stack of change.

Buckley took the stool next to mine. On the television screen, Errol Flynn was winning De Havilland's heart and Reagan was being gracious in defeat. "He was a handsome bastard," Buckley said.

"Reagan?"

"Flynn. In like Flynn, all he had to do was look at them and they wet their pants. I don't think I've seen you here before, Matt."

"I don't come around very often."

"You live around here?"

"Not too far. You?"

"Not far. It's quiet, you know? And the beer's

good, and I like the darts."

After a few minutes he went back to the dart board. I stayed where I was. A little later the bartender, Tom, glided over and topped up my glass of soda water without asking. He didn't take any money from me.

A couple of men left. One came in, conferred with Tom in an undertone, and went out again. A man in a suit and tie came in, had a double vodka, drank it right down, ordered another, drank that right down, put a ten-dollar bill on the bar, and walked out. This entire exchange was carried out without a word from him or the bartender.

On the television set, Flynn and Reagan went up against Raymond Massey's version of John Brown at Harper's Ferry. Van Heflin, rotten little opportunist that he was, got what was coming to him.

I got out of there while the credits were rolling. I scooped up my change, put a couple of bucks back on the bar for Tom, and left.

Outside, I asked myself what the hell I'd thought I was doing there. Earlier I'd been thinking of Eddie, and then I'd looked up and found myself in front of the place he'd been afraid to get near. Maybe I went in myself in order to get a sense of who he'd been before I knew him. Maybe I was hoping for a peek at the Butcher Boy himself, the notorious Mickey Ballou.

What I'd found was a ginmill, and what I'd done

was hang out in it.

Strange.

I called Willa from my room. "I was just looking at your flowers," she said.

"They're your flowers," I said. "I gave them to you."

"No strings attached, huh?"

"No strings. I was wondering if you felt like a movie."

"What movie?"

"I don't know. Why don't I come by for you around six or a little after? We'll see what's playing on Broadway and get a bite later."

"On one condition."

"What's that?"

"It's my treat."

"It was your treat last night."

"What was last night? Oh, we had Chinese. Did I pay for that?"

"You insisted."

"Well, shit. Then you can pay for dinner."

"That was my plan."

"But the movie's on me."

"We'll split the movie."

"We'll work it out when you get here. What time? Six?"

"Around then."

She wore the blue silk blouse again, this time over loose khaki fatigues with drawstring cuffs. Her hair was braided in twin pigtails, in the style of an Indian maiden. I took hold of her pigtails and held them out at the sides. "Always different," I said.

"I'm probably too old for long hair."

"That's ridiculous."

"Is it? I don't even care, anyway. I wore it short for years. It's fun to be able to do things with it."

We kissed, and I tasted scotch on her breath. It wasn't shocking anymore. Once you got used to it, it was a pleasant taste.

We kissed a second time. I moved my mouth to her ear, then down along her neck. She clung to me and heat flowed from her loins and breasts.

She said, "What time's the movie?"

"Whenever we get there."

"Then there's no hurry, is there?"

We went to a first-run house on Times Square. Harrison Ford triumphed over Palestinian terrorists. He was no match for Errol Flynn, but he was a cut above Reagan.

Afterward we went to Paris Green again. She tried the filet of sole and approved of it. I stayed with what I'd had the other night, cheeseburger and fries and salad.

She had white wine with her meal, just a glass of it, and brandy with her coffee.

We talked a little about her marriage, and then a little about mine. Over coffee I found myself talking about Jan, and about how things had gone wrong.

"It's a good thing you kept your hotel room," she said. "What would it cost if you gave it up and then wanted to move back in?"

"I couldn't do it. It's inexpensive for a hotel, but they get sixty-five dollars a night for their cheapest single. What does that come to? Two thousand dollars a month?"

"Around there."

"Of course they'd give you some kind of a monthly rate, but it would still have to be well over a thousand dollars. If I had moved out I couldn't possibly afford to move back in. I'd have had to get an apartment somewhere, and I might have had trouble finding one I could afford in Manhattan." I considered. "Unless I got serious and found some kind of real job for myself."

"Could you do that?"

"I don't know. A year or so ago there was a guy who wanted me to go in with him and open a bona fide detective agency. He thought we could get a lot of industrial work, trademark infringement, employee pilferage control, that sort of thing."

"You weren't interested?"

"I was tempted. It's a challenge, making a go of something like that. But I like the space in the life I lead now. I like to be able to go to a meeting whenever I want, or just take a walk in the park or sit for two hours reading everything in the paper. And I like where I live. It's a dump, but it suits me."

"You could open a legitimate agency and still

stay where you are."

I nodded. "But I don't know if it would still suit me. People who succeed usually want the trappings of success to justify the energy they have to put into it. They spend more money, and they get used to it, and then they *need* the money. I like the fact that I don't need very much. My rent's cheap, and I really like it that way."

"It's so funny."

"What is?"

"This city. Start talking about anything and you wind up talking about real estate."

"I know."

"It's impossible to avoid. I put a sign by the doorbells, *No Apartments Available.*"

"I saw it earlier."

"And I still had three people ring the bell to make sure I didn't have something for rent."

"Just in case."

"They thought maybe I just kept the sign there all the time to cut down the volume of inquiries. And at least one of them knew I'd just lost a tenant, so maybe he figured I hadn't gotten around to taking down the sign. There was a piece in the *Times* today, one of the major builders is announcing plans to build two middle-income projects west of Eleventh Avenue to house people with family incomes under fifty thousand dollars. God knows it's needed, but I don't think it'll be enough to make any difference."

"You're right. We started talking about relationships and we're talking about apartments."

She put her hand on mine. "What's today? Thursday?"

"For another hour or so?"

"And I met you when? Tuesday afternoon? That seems impossible."

"I know."

"I don't want this to go too fast. But I don't want to put the brakes on, either. Whatever happens with us — "

"Yes?"

"Keep your hotel room."

When I first got sober there was a midnight meeting every night at the Moravian Church at Thirtieth and Lexington. The group lost the space, and the meeting moved to Alanon House, a sort of AA clubhouse occupying an office suite just off Times Square.

I walked Willa home and then headed over to Times Square and the midnight meeting. I don't go there often. They get a young crowd, and most of the people who show up have more drugs than alcohol in their histories.

But I couldn't afford to be choosy. I hadn't been to a meeting since Tuesday night. I'd missed two nights in a row at my home group, which was unusual for me, and I hadn't gone to any daytime meetings to pick up the slack. More to the point, I had spent an uncharacteristic amount of time around alcohol in the past fifty-six hours. I was sleeping with a woman who drank the stuff, and I'd whiled away the afternoon in a saloon, and a pretty lowlife one at that. The thing to do was go to a meeting and talk about it.

I went to the meeting, getting there just in time to grab a cup of coffee and a seat before it got started. The speaker was sober less than six months, still what they call mocus — mixed up, confused, uncentered. It was hard to track his story, and my mind kept flitting around, wandering down avenues of its own.

Afterward I couldn't make myself raise my hand. I had visions of some soberer-than-thou asshole giving me a lot of advice I didn't want or need. I already knew what kind of advice I'd get from Jim Faber, say, or from Frank. *If you don't want to slip, stay out of slippery places. Don't go in bars without a reason. Bars are for drinking. You want to watch TV, you got a set in your room. You want to play darts, go buy a dart board.*

Jesus, I knew what anyone with a few years in the program would tell me. It was the same advice I'd give to anyone in my position. *Call your sponsor. Stay close to the program. Double up on your meetings. When you get up in the morning, ask God to help you stay sober. When you go to bed at night, thank Him. If you can't get to a meeting, read the Big Book, read the Twelve & Twelve, pick up the phone and call somebody. Don't isolate, because when you're by yourself you're in bad company. And let people know what's going on with you, because you're as sick as your secrets. And remember this: You're an alcoholic. You're not all better now. You'll never be cured. All you are, all you'll ever be, is one drink away from a drunk.*

I didn't want to hear that shit.

I left on the break. I don't usually do that, but it was late and I was tired. And I felt uncomfortable in that room, anyway. I'd liked the old midnight meeting better, even if I'd had to take a cab to get there.

Walking home, I thought about George Bohan, who'd wanted me to open a detective agency with him. I'd known him years back in Brooklyn, we'd been partnered for a while when I first got a detective's gold shield, and he'd retired and worked for one of the national agencies long enough to learn the business and get his PI license.

I hadn't answered when that particular opportunity had knocked. But maybe it was time to do that, or something like it. Maybe I had let myself get into a groove and wear it down into a rut. It was comfortable enough, but the months had a way of slipping by and before you knew it years had passed. Did I really want to be an old man living alone in a hotel, queueing up for food stamps, standing in line for a hot meal at the senior center?

Jesus, what a thought.

I walked north on Broadway, shaking off bums before they could launch their spiel. If I was part of a real detective agency, I thought, maybe I could give clients better value for their money, maybe I could operate effectively and efficiently instead

191

of fumbling around like some trench-coated refugee from a 1940's film. If it occurred to me, say, that Paula Hoeldtke might have left the country, I could interface with a Washington-based agency and find out if she'd applied for a passport. I could hire as many operatives as her father's budget could stand and check airline manifests for the couple of weeks around the date of her probable disappearance. I could —

Hell, there were lots of things I could do.

Maybe nothing would work. Maybe any further effort to track down Paula was just a waste of time and money. If so, I could drop the case and pick up something else.

The way things stood, I was holding on to the damn thing because I didn't have anything better to do. Durkin had said I was like a dog with a bone, and he was right, but there was more to it than that. I was a dog who didn't have but one bone, and when I put it down I had no choice but to pick it back up again.

Stupid way to go through life. Sifting through thin air, trying to find a girl who'd disappeared into it. Troubling the final sleep of a dead friend, trying to establish that he'd been in a sober state of grace when he died, probably because I hadn't been able to do anything for him while he was alive.

And, when I wasn't doing one of those two things, I could go hide out at a meeting.

The program, they told you, was supposed to be a bridge back to life. And maybe it was for

192

some people. For me it was turning out to be a tunnel, with another meeting at the end of it.

They said you couldn't go to too many meetings. They said the more meetings you went to, the faster and more comfortably you recovered.

But that was for newcomers. Most people reduced their attendance at meetings after a couple of years of sobriety. Some of us lived in meetings at the beginning, going to four or five a day, but nobody went on like that forever. People had lives to get on with, and they set about getting on with them.

For Christ's sake, what was I going to hear at a meeting that I hadn't already heard? I'd been coming for more than three years. I'd heard the same things over and over until the whole rap was coming out of my ears. If I had a life of my own, if I was ever going to have one, it was time to get on with it.

I could have said all of this to Jim, but it was too late to call him. Besides, all I'd get in response would be the party line. *Easy does it. Keep it simple. One day at a time. Let go and let God. Live and let live.*

The fucking wisdom of the ages.

I could have popped off at the meeting. That's what the meetings are there for. And I'm sure all those twenty-year-old junkies would have had lots of useful advice for me.

Jesus, I'd do as well talking to house plants.

Instead, I walked up Broadway and said it all to myself.

At Fiftieth Street, waiting for the light to change, it occurred to me that it might be interesting to see what Grogan's was like at night. It wasn't one yet. I could go over and have a Coke before they closed.

The hell, I was always a guy who felt at home in a saloon. I didn't have to drink to enjoy the atmosphere.

Why not?

11

"Zero blood alcohol," Bellamy said. "I didn't know anybody in this town ever had zero blood alcohol."

I could have introduced him to hundreds, starting with myself. Of course I might have had to start with someone else if I'd acted on impulse and gone to Grogan's. The inner voice urging me there had been perfectly reasonable and logical, and I hadn't tried to argue with it. I'd just kept walking north, keeping my options open, and I took a left at Fifty-seventh, and when I got to my hotel I went in and up to bed. I was brushing my teeth when he called in the morning to tell me about Eddie's blood alcohol, or lack thereof.

I asked what else was in the report, and one item caught my attention. I asked him to repeat it, and then I asked a couple of other questions, and an hour later I was sitting in a hospital cafeteria in the East Twenties, sipping a cup of coffee that was better than Willa's, but just barely.

Michael Sternlicht, the assistant medical examiner who had performed the autopsy, was about

Eddie's age. He had a round face, and the shape was echoed by the circular lenses of his heavy horn-rimmed glasses to give him a faintly owlish look. He was balding, and called attention to it by combing his remaining hair over the bald spot.

"He didn't have a lot of chloral in him," he told me. "I'd have to say it was insignificant."

"He was a sober alcoholic."

"Meaning he wouldn't take any mood-altering drugs? Not even a sleeping pill?" He sipped his coffee, made a face. "Maybe he wasn't that strict about it. I can assure you he couldn't have taken it to get high, not with the very low level in his bloodstream. Chloral hydrate doesn't much lend itself to abuse anyway, unlike the barbiturates and minor tranquilizers. There are people who take heavy doses of barbiturates and force themselves to stay awake, and the drug has a paradoxical effect of energizing and exhilarating them. If you take a lot of chloral, all that happens is you fall down and pass out."

"But he didn't take enough for that?"

"Nowhere near enough. His blood levels suggest he took in the neighborhood of a thousand milligrams, which is a normal dose to bring on sleep. It would make it a little easier for him to get drowsy and nod off, and it would aid him in sleeping through the night if he was prone to restlessness."

"Could it have been a factor in his death?"

"I don't see how. All my findings point to a classic textbook case of autoerotic asphyxiation. I'd guess he took his sleeping pill not too long before he died. Maybe he was planning to go right to sleep, then changed his mind and decided to squeeze in a hand of sexual solitaire. Or he might have been in the habit of taking a pill first, so that he could just slip right off to sleep as soon as he finished his fun and games. Either way, I don't think the chloral would have had any real effect. You know how it works?"

"More or less."

"They do it," he said, "and they get away with it. They have their heightened orgasm and they evidently enjoy it, so they make a regular practice of it. Even when they know about the dangers, their survival seems to prove to them that they know the right way to do it."

He took off his glasses, polished them with the tail of his lab coat. "The thing is," he said, "there *is* no right way to do it, and sooner or later your luck runs out. You see, a little pressure on the carotid" — he reached across to touch the side of my neck — "and it triggers a reflex that slows the heartbeat way down. That evidently has something to do with boosting the thrill of orgasm, but what it can also do is make you lose consciousness, and you have no control over that. When that happens, gravity tightens the noose, and you can't do anything about it because you're out of it, you don't know what's happening. Trying to be careful doing it is like exercising caution during Russian roulette. No matter how successful you've been in the past, you've got the same chance of blowing it the next time. The only careful way to do it is not to do it at all."

I had taken a cab downtown to see Sternlicht.
I took a couple of buses back, and got to Willa's
just as she was on her way out.

She was wearing a pair of jeans I hadn't seen
before, paint-smeared, ragged at the cuffs. Her
hair was pinned up and tucked out of sight behind
a beige scarf. She was wearing a man's white
button-down shirt with a frayed collar, and her
blue tennis shoes were paint-spattered to match
the jeans. She carried a gray metal toolbox, rusty
around the locks and hinges.

"I must have known you were coming," she
said. "That's why I dressed. I've got a plumbing
emergency across the street."

"Don't they have a super over there?"

"Sure, and I'm it. I've got three buildings to
take care of besides this one. That way I don't
just have a place to live, I also have something
to live on." She shifted the toolbox from one hand
to the other. "I can't stand and chat, they'll have
a full-scale flood over there. Do you want to come
watch or would you rather make yourself a cup
of coffee and wait for me?"

I told her I'd wait, and she walked inside with
me and let me into her apartment. I asked her
if I could have Eddie's key.

"You want to go up there? What for?"

"Just to look around."

She worked his key off her ring, then gave me
one for her apartment as well. "So you can get

back in," she said. "It's the top lock, it locks automatically when you pull the door shut. Don't forget to double-lock the door upstairs when you're through."

Eddie's windows had been wide open ever since Andreotti and I had opened them. The smell of death was still in the air, but it had grown faint, and wasn't really unpleasant unless you happened to recognize it for what it was.

It would be easy enough to get rid of the rest of the smell. Once the curtains and bedding were gone, once the furniture and clothing and personal effects were out on the street for the trash pickup, you probably wouldn't be able to smell a thing. Swab down the floors and spray a little Lysol around and the last traces would vanish. People die every day, and landlords clean up after them, and new tenants are in their place by the first of the month.

Life goes on.

I was looking for chloral hydrate, but I didn't know where he kept it. There was no medicine cabinet. The lavatory, in a tiny closet off the bedroom, held a commode and nothing else. His toothbrush hung in a holder above the kitchen sink, and there was half a tube of toothpaste, neatly rolled, on the window ledge nearby. In the cupboard nearest to the sink I found a couple of plastic razors, a can of shaving foam, a bottle of Rexall aspirin, and a pocket tin of Anacin. I opened the aspirin bottle and dumped its contents into my palm, and all I had was a handful of five-grain aspirin tablets. I put them back and tackled the Anacin tin, pressing the rear corners as indicated. Getting it open was enough to give you a headache, but all I found for my troubles were the white tablets the label had promised.

The upended orange crate beside his bed held a stack of AA literature — the Big Book, the Twelve & Twelve, some pamphlets, and a slender paperback called *Living Sober*. There was a Bible, the Douay Reims version, with a bookplate indicating it had been a first communion gift to Mary Scanlan. On another page, a family tree indicated that Mary Scanlan had been married to Peter John Dunphy, and that a son, Edward Thomas Dunphy, had been born a year and four months after the wedding date.

I flipped through the Bible and it opened to a chapter in Second Chronicles where Eddie had stashed a pair of twenty-dollar bills. I couldn't think what to do with them. I didn't want to take the money, but it felt odd to leave it. I gave the whole question a good forty dollars worth of thought, then returned the bills to the Bible and put the Bible back where I'd found it.

His dresser top held a small tin with a couple of spot Band-Aids left in it, a single shoelace, an empty cigarette pack, forty-three cents in change, and a pair of subway tokens. The dresser's top drawer contained mostly socks, but there was also a pair of gloves, wool with leather palms, a Colt .45 brass belt buckle, and a plush-lined box of the sort cuff-link sets come in. This one held a high school ring with a blue stone, a gold-plated tie bar, and a single cuff link with three small garnets on it. There had been a fourth garnet but it was gone.

The underwear drawer contained, along with shorts and T-shirts, a Gruen wristwatch with half its strap missing.

The erotic magazines were gone. I guessed they'd been bagged and tagged and taken along as evidence, and they'd probably spend eternity in a warehouse somewhere. I didn't come across any other erotica, or any sex aids, either.

I found his wallet in his trousers pocket. It held thirty-two dollars in cash, a foil-wrapped condom, and one of those all-purpose identification cards they sell in schlock shops around Times Square. They're usually bought by people who want fake ID, although they wouldn't fool anyone. Eddie had filled his out legitimately with his correct name and address and the same date of birth as the one in the family Bible, along with height and weight and hair and eye color. It seemed to be the only ID he had. No driver's license, and no Social Security card. If they gave him one at Green Haven, he hadn't troubled to hang on to it.

I went through the other drawers in the dresser, I checked the refrigerator. There was some milk that was starting to turn and I poured it out. I left a loaf of Roman Meal bread, jars of peanut butter and jelly. I stood on a chair and checked the closet shelf. I found old newspapers, a baseball glove that must have been his when he was a kid, and an unopened box of votive candles in small clear glass holders. I didn't find anything in the pockets of the clothes in the closet, or in the two pairs of shoes or the rubber overshoes on the closet floor.

After a while I took a plastic grocery bag and put in the Bible and the AA books and his wallet. I left everything else and let myself out of there.

I was locking the door when I heard a noise, someone behind me clearing her throat. I turned to see a woman standing at the head of the stairs. She was a tiny thing with wispy gray hair and eyes huge behind thick cataract lenses. She wanted to know who I was. I told her my name, and that I was a detective.

"For poor Dr. Dunphy," she said. "That I knew all his days, and his parents before him." She had groceries in a bag like the one I was carrying. She set her bag down, rummaged in her purse for her key. "They killed him," she said, dolefully.

"They?"

"Ach, they'll kill us all. Poor Mrs. Grod on the floor above, that they crept in off the fire escape and cut her ould throat."

"When did this happen?"

"And Mr. White," she said. "Dead of the cancer, and him so wasted and yellow at the end you'd take him for a Chinaman. We'll all be dead and gone soon enough," she said, wringing her hands with horror or with relish. "Every last one of us."

When Willa returned I was sitting at the kitchen table with a cup of coffee. She let herself in, put down her toolbox, and said, "Don't kiss me, I'm a mess. God, that's filthy work. I had to open up the bathroom ceiling, and all kinds of crap comes down on you when you do that."

"How did you learn plumbing?"

"I didn't, really. I'm good at fixing things and I picked up a lot of different skills over the years. I'm not a plumber, but I know how to shut a system down and find a leak, and I can patch it, and sometimes the patch holds. For a while, anyway." She opened the refrigerator and got herself a bottle of Beck's. "Thirsty work. That plaster dust gets in your throat. I'm sure it's carcinogenic."

"Almost everything is."

She uncapped the beer, took a long swallow straight from the bottle, then got a glass from the drainboard and filled it. She said, "I need a shower, but first I need to sit down for a minute. Were you waiting long?"

"Just a few minutes."

"You must have spent a long time upstairs."

"I guess I must have. And then I spent a minute or two in a strange conversation." I recounted my meeting with the little wispy-haired woman and she nodded in recognition.

"That's Mrs. Mangan," she said. " 'Shure, an' we'll all be molderin' in our graves, an' the wee banshees howlin' at our heels.' "

203

"You do a good Mrs. Mangan impression."

"It's a less useful talent than fixing leaky pipes. She's our resident crepe-hanger. She's been here forever, I think she may have been born in the building, and she has to be over eighty, wouldn't you say?"

"I'm not a good judge."

"Well, would you ask her for proof of age if she was trying to get the senior citizen rate at the movies? She knows everybody in the neighborhood, all the old people anyway, and that means she's always got a funeral to go to." She drained her glass, poured the rest of the bottle into it. "I'll tell you something," she said. "I don't want to live forever."

"Forever's a long way off."

"I mean it, Matt. There's such a thing as livming too long. It's tragic when somebody Eddie Dunphy's age dies. Or your Paula, with her whole life ahead of her. But when you get to be Mrs. Mangan's age, and living alone, with all her old friends gone — "

"How did Mrs. Grod die?"

"I'm trying to remember when that was. Over a year ago, I think, because it was in warm weather. A burglar killed her, he came in through the window. The apartments have window gates, but not all the tenants use them."

"There was a gate on Eddie's bedroom window, the one that opens into the fire escape. But it wasn't in use."

"People leave them open because it's harder to

open and close the windows otherwise. Evidently someone went over the roofs and down the fire escape and got into Mrs. Grod's apartment that way. She was in bed and must have awakened and surprised him. And he stabbed her." She sipped her beer. "Did you find what you were looking for? For that matter, what *were* you looking for?"

"Pills."

"Pills?"

"But I couldn't find anything stronger than aspirin." I explained what Sternlicht had found, and the implications of his findings. "I was taught how to search an apartment, and I learned to do it thoroughly. I didn't pry up floorboards or take the furniture apart, but I made a pretty systematic search of the premises. If there was chloral hydrate there, I would have found it."

"Maybe it was his last pill."

"Then there'd be an empty vial somewhere."

"He might have thrown it out."

"It wasn't in his wastebasket. It wasn't in the garbage under the kitchen sink. Where else would he have tossed it?"

"Maybe somebody gave him a single pill, or a couple of pills. 'You can't sleep? Here, take one of these, they work every time.' As far as that goes, you said he was streetwise, didn't you? Not every pill sold in this neighborhood gets dispensed by a pharmacist. You can buy everything else on the street. I wouldn't be surprised if you could buy coral hydrate."

"Chloral hydrate."

"Chloral hydrate, then. Sounds like something a welfare mother would name her kid. 'Chloral, now you leave off pickin' on yo' brother!' What's the matter?"

"Nothing."

"You seem moody, though."

"Do I? Maybe I caught it upstairs. And what you said about people living too long. I was thinking last night that I don't want to wind up an old man living alone in a hotel room. And here I am, well on the way."

"Some old man."

I sat there and nursed my mood while she took a shower. When she came out I said, "I must have been looking for more than pills, because what good would it have done me to find them?"

"I was wondering that myself."

"I just wish I knew what he wanted to tell me. He had something on his mind and he was just about ready to unload it, but I told him to take his time, to think it over. I should have sat down with him then and there."

"And then he'd still be alive?"

"No, but — "

"Matt, he didn't die because of what he said or didn't say. He died because he did something stupid and dangerous and his luck ran out."

"I know."

"There was nothing you could have done. And nothing you can do for him now."

"I know. He didn't — "

"Didn't what?"

"Say anything to you?"

"I hardly knew him, Matt. I can't remember the last time I talked to him. I don't know if I ever talked to him, beyond 'How's the weather?' and 'Here's the rent.' "

"He had something on his mind," I said. "I wish to hell I knew what it was."

12

I dropped into Grogan's in the middle of the afternoon. The dart board wasn't in use and I didn't see Andy Buckley anywhere, but otherwise the crowd was much the same. Tom was behind the stick, and he put a magazine down long enough to draw me a Coke. An old man with a cloth cap was talking about the Mets, lamenting a trade they'd made fifteen years earlier. "They got Jim Fregosi," he said scornfully, "and they gave up Nolan Ryan. Nolan Ryan!"

On the television screen, John Wayne was putting someone in his place. I tried to picture him pushing through the swinging doors of a saloon, bellying up to the bar, telling the barkeep to bring him a Coke and a chloral hydrate.

I nursed my Coke, bided my time. When my glass was almost empty I crooked a finger for Tom. He came over and reached for my glass but I covered it with my palm. He looked at me, expressionless as ever, and I asked if Mickey Ballou had been in.

"There's people in and out," he said. "I

208

wouldn't know their names."

There was a north-of-Ireland edge to his speech. I hadn't noticed it earlier. "You'd know him," I said. "He's the owner, isn't he?"

"It's called Grogan's. Wouldn't it be Grogan that owns it?"

"He's a big man," I said. "Sometimes he wears a butcher's apron."

"I'm off at six. Perhaps he comes here nights."

"Perhaps he does. I'd like to leave word for him."

"Oh?"

"I want to talk to him. Tell him, will you?"

"I don't know him. And I don't know yourself, so what would I tell him?"

"My name is Scudder, Matt Scudder. I want to talk to him about Eddie Dunphy."

"I may not remember," he said, his eyes flat, his voice toneless. "I'm not good with names."

I left, walked around, dropped in again around six-thirty. The crowd was larger, with half a dozen after-work drinkers ranged along the bar. Tom was gone, his place taken by a tall fellow with a lot of curly dark brown hair. He wore an open cowhide vest over a red-and-black flannel shirt.

I asked if Mickey Ballou had been in.

"I haven't seen him," he said. "I just got on myself. Who wants him?"

"Scudder," I said.

"I'll tell him."

I got out of there, had a sandwich by myself

at the Flame, and went over to St. Paul's. It was Friday night, which meant a step meeting, and this week we were on the sixth step, in the course of which one becomes ready on some inner level to have one's defects of character removed. As far as I can tell, there's nothing in particular that you do to bring this about. It's just supposed to happen to you. It hasn't happened to me.

I was impatient for the meeting to end but I made myself stay for the whole thing anyway. During the break I took Jim Faber aside and told him I wasn't sure whether or not Eddie had died sober, that the autopsy had found chloral hydrate in his bloodstream.

"The proverbial Mickey Finn," he said. "You don't hear about it much anymore, now that the drug industry has given us so many more advanced little blessings. I only once heard of an alcoholic who used to take chloral hydrate for recreational purposes. She went through a period of controlled solitary drinking; every night she took a dose of chloral, pills or drops, I don't remember, and drank two beers. Whereupon she passed out and slept for eight or ten hours."

"What happened to her?"

"Either she lost her taste for chloral hydrate or her source dried up, so she moved on to Jack Daniel's. When she got up to a quart and a half of it daily, something told her she might have a problem. I wouldn't make too much of the chloral hydrate Eddie took, Matt. It might not bode well for his long-term sobriety, but where he is now it's no longer an issue. What's done is done."

Afterward I passed up the Flame and went straight to Grogan's. I spotted Ballou the minute I cleared the threshold. He wasn't wearing his white apron, but I recognized him without it.

He'd have been hard to miss. He stood well over six feet and carried a lot of flesh on a large frame. His head was like a boulder, massive and monolithic, with planes to it like the stone heads at Easter Island.

He was standing at the bar, one foot on the brass rail, leaning in to talk to the bartender, the same fellow in the unbuttoned leather vest I'd seen a few hours ago. The crowd had thinned out since then. There were a couple of old men in a booth, a pair of solitary drinkers strung out at the far end of the bar. In the back, two men were playing darts. One was Andy Buckley.

I went over to the bar. Three stools separated me from Ballou. I was watching him in the mirrored back bar when he turned and looked directly at me. He studied me for a moment, then turned to say something to the bartender.

I walked toward him, and his head swung around at my approach. His face was pitted like weathered granite, and there were patches of broken blood vessels on his cheekbones, and across the bridge of his nose. His eyes were a surprising green, and there was a lot of scar tissue around them.

"You're Scudder," he said.

"Yes."

"I don't know you, but I've seen you. And you've seen me."

"Yes."

"You were asking for me. And now you're here." He had thin lips, and they curled in what might have been a smile. He said, "What will you drink, man?"

He had a bottle of Jameson on the bar in front of him, the twelve-year-old. In a glass beside it, two small ice cubes bobbed in an amber sea. I said I'd have coffee, if they happened to have any made. Ballou looked at the bartender, who shook his head.

"The draught Guinness is as good as you'll get this side of the ocean," Ballou said. "I wouldn't carry the bottled stuff, it's thick as syrup."

"I'll have a Coke."

"You don't drink," he said.

"Not today."

"You don't drink at all, or you don't drink with me?"

"I don't drink at all."

"And how is that?" he asked. "Not drinking at all."

"It's all right."

"Is it hard?"

"Sometimes. But sometimes drinking was hard."

"Ah," he said. "That's the fucking truth." He looked at the bartender, who responded by drawing a Coke for me. He put it in front of me and moved off out of hearing range.

Ballou picked up his glass and looked at me over

the top of it. He said, "Back when the Morrisseys had their place around the corner. Their after-hours. I used to see you there."

"I remember."

"You drank with both hands, those days."

"That was then."

"And this is now, eh?" He put his glass down, looked at his hand, wiped it across his shirtfront, and extended it toward me. There was something oddly solemn about our handshake. His hand was large, his grip firm but not aggressively so. We shook hands, and then he took up his whiskey and I reached for my Coke.

He said, "Is that what ties you to Eddie Dunphy?" He lifted his glass, looked into it. "Hell of a thing when the booze turns on you. Eddie, though, I'd say he never could handle it, the poor bastard. Did you know him when he drank?"

"No."

"He never had the head for it. Then I heard he stopped drinking. And now he's gone and hanged himself."

"A day or so before he did it," I said, "we had a talk."

"Did you now?"

"There was something eating him, something he wanted to get off his chest but was afraid to tell me."

"What was it?"

"I was hoping you might be able to answer that."

"I don't take your meaning."

"What did he know that was dangerous knowledge? What did he ever do that would weigh on his conscience?"

The big head swung from side to side. "He was a neighborhood boy. He was a thief, he had a mouth on him when he drank, he raised a little hell. That's all he ever did."

"He said he used to spend a lot of time here."

"Here? In Grogan's?" He shrugged. "It's a public house. All sorts of people come in, drink their beer or whiskey, pass the time, go on their way. Some have a glass of wine. Or a Coca-Cola, if it comes to that."

"Eddie said this was where he used to hang out. We were walking one night, and he crossed the street to avoid walking past this place."

The green eyes widened. "He did? Why?"

"Because it was so much a part of his drinking life. I guess he was afraid it would pull him in if he got too close."

"My God," he said. He uncapped the bottle, topped up his drink. The two ice cubes had melted but he didn't seem bothered by their absence. He picked up the glass. Staring into it he said, "Eddie was my brother's friend. Did you know my brother Dennis?"

"No."

"Very different from me, Dennis was. He had our mother's looks. She was Irish. The old man was French, he came from a fishing village half an hour from Marseilles. I went there once, a couple of years ago, just to see what it looked like.

214

I could see why he left. There was nothing there." He took a pack of cigarettes from his breast pocket, lit one, blew out smoke. "I look just like the old man," he said. "Except for the eyes. Dennis and I both got our mother's eyes."

"Eddie said Dennis was killed in Vietnam."

He turned the green eyes on me. "I don't know why the hell he went. It would have been nothing at all to get him out of it. I told him, I said, 'Dennis, for Christ's sake, all I have to do is pick up a phone.' He wouldn't have it." He took the cigarette and ground it out in an ashtray. "So he went over there," he said, "and they shot his ass off for him, the dumb bastard."

I didn't say anything, and we let the silence stretch. For a moment I had the thought that the room was filling up with dead people — Eddie, Dennis, Ballou's parents, and a few ghosts of my own, all the people who'd passed on but still lingered on the edge of consciousness. If I turned my head quickly, I thought, I might see my aunt Peg, or my own dead parents.

"Dennis was gentle," he said. "Maybe that was why he went, to prove a hardness he didn't have. He was Eddie's friend, and Eddie came to the service for him. After that he would come around sometimes. I never had much for him to do."

"He told me he watched you beat a man to death one night."

He looked at me. Surprise showed in his eyes. I didn't know if it was surprise that Eddie had told me this or that I was repeating it. He said,

"He told you that, did he?"

"In a basement somewhere around here, he said it was. He said you were in a furnace room and you had some guy tied to a post with a length of clothesline, and you beat him to death with a baseball bat."

"Who was it?"

"He didn't say."

"And when did it happen?"

"Some years ago. He didn't get any more specific than that."

"And was he there?"

"So he said."

"Or do you suppose he just put himself into the story?" He picked up his glass but didn't drink from it. "Though I don't think much of it as a story, do you? One man beats another with a ball bat. It's nasty, but it doesn't make much of a story. You couldn't dine out on a story like that."

"There was a better story going around a couple of years ago."

"Oh?"

"A fellow disappeared, a man named Farrelly."

"Paddy Farrelly," he said. "A difficult man."

"They said he gave you trouble, and then he disappeared."

"Is that what they said?"

"And they said you went into half the saloons on Ninth and Tenth Avenues carrying a bowling bag, and you would open the bag and show everybody Farrelly's head."

He drank some whiskey. "The stories they tell," he said.

"Was Eddie around when that happened?"

He looked at me. There was no one anywhere near us now. The bartender was all the way down at the end of the bar, and the men who'd been closest had left. "It's godawful warm in here," he said. "What do you need that suit jacket for?"

He was wearing a jacket himself, tweed, heavier than mine. "I'm comfortable," I said.

"Take it off."

I looked at him, took off the jacket. I hung it over the back of the stool next to me.

"The shirt, too," he said.

I took it off, and the T-shirt after it. "Good man," he said. "God's sake, put your clothes back on before you catch cold. You got to be careful, a bastard'll come in and start talking about old times, and the next thing you know it's all recorded, he's wearing a fucking wire. Paddy Farrelly's head? My mother's father was from Sligo, he used to say it was the hardest thing in the world to find a man alive in Dublin that wasn't in the GPO during the Easter Rising. Twenty brave men marched into that post office, he said, and thirty thousand marched out. Well, it's that hard to find a son of a bitch on Tenth Avenue who didn't see me showing round the bloody head of poor Farrelly."

"Are you saying it didn't happen?"

"Oh, Jesus," he said. "What happened and what didn't? Maybe I never opened the fucking bowling

217

bag. Maybe a fucking bowling ball was all it ever contained. They all love a story, you know. They love to hear it, they love to tell it, they love the little shiver it puts between their shoulder blades. The Irish are the worst that way. Especially in this fucking neighborhood." He drank, set the glass down. "It's rich soil around here, you know. Plant a seed and a story grows like weeds."

"What happened to Farrelly?"

"Why should I know? Maybe he's in Tahiti, drinking the milk of coconuts and fucking little brown-skinned girls. Did anyone ever find his body? Or the legendary fucking head?"

"What did Eddie know that made him dangerous?"

"Nothing. He didn't know a damn thing. He was no danger to me."

"Who could he have been a danger to?"

"Nobody I can think of. What did he ever do? He did some thieving. He went along with some boys who took a load of furs out of a loft on Twenty-seventh Street. That's the biggest thing I can think of that he was a part of, and there'd be no stink coming off that one. It was all arranged, the owner let them have the key. He wanted the insurance. And it was years ago, years ago. Who was he a danger to? Jesus, didn't he hang himself? Wasn't it himself he was a danger to?"

Something happened between us, something that I find hard to explain, or even to understand. We were silent for a few minutes, having run out of things to say about Eddie Dunphy. Then he told a story about his brother Dennis, how he'd taken the blame for something Dennis had done when they were children. Then I told a couple of cop stories from when I was attached to the Sixth Precinct in the Village.

Somehow or other something bonded us. At one point he walked all the way to the back end of the bar and came around behind it. He filled two glasses with ice cubes, then ran them both full of Coca-Cola and passed them over the bar to me. He took a fresh fifth of the twelve-year-old Jameson from the back bar, put a couple of ice cubes in a clean glass, and came around the bar again, leading me to a booth in the corner. I put my two Cokes on the table in front of me, and he cracked the seal on the whiskey bottle and filled his glass, and we sat there for the next hour or so, telling stories, sharing silences.

It didn't happen all that often in the drinking days and it hasn't happened often since. I don't think you could say that we became friends. Friendship is something different. It was as if some inner barrier that each of us ordinarily maintained was, for the moment, dissolved. Some internal truce had been declared, with hostilities suspended for the holidays. For an hour we were easier with each other than old friends, than brothers. It was not the sort of thing that could last much longer than an hour, but that made it no less real.

At length he said, "By God, I wish you drank."

"Sometimes I wish it myself. But most of the

time I'm glad I don't."

"You must miss it."

"Now and then."

"I'd miss it like fury. I don't know if I could live without it."

"I had more trouble living with it," I said. "The last time I drank I wound up with a grand mal seizure. I fell down in the street and woke up in the hospital with no idea of where I was or how I got there."

"Christ," he said, and shook his head. "But until then," he said, "you had a good long run at it."

"That I did."

"Then you can't complain," he said. "We can't any of us complain, can we?"

Around midnight it began to wear thin. I was starting to have the feeling that I'd stayed too long at the dance. I stood up and told Ballou I had to get on home.

"Are you all right to walk? Do you want me to call a car for you?" He caught himself and laughed. He said, "Jesus, all you've been drinking is Coca-Cola. Why shouldn't you be all right to get home under your own power?"

"I'm fine."

He hauled himself to his feet. "Now that you know where we are," he said, "come back and see us again."

"I'll do that."

"I enjoyed this, Scudder." He laid a hand on my shoulder. "You're all right."

"You're all right yourself."

"It's a damn shame about Eddie. Did he have any family at all? Will there be a wake for him, do you know?"

"I don't know. The city's holding the body for the time being."

"Hell of a way to end up." He sighed, then straightened up. "We'll talk again, you and I."

"I'd like that."

"I'm here most nights, off and on. Or they know how to reach me."

"Your early-shift bartender wouldn't even admit he knew who you were."

He laughed. "That's Tom. He's a close one, isn't he? But he gave me your message, and so did Neil. Whoever's behind the bar here can get word to me."

I reached into my pocket, got out a card. "I'm at the Northwestern Hotel," I said. "Here's the number. I'm not there much, but they'll take messages."

"What's this?"

"My number."

"This," he said. I looked, and he had the card turned and was looking at the picture of Paula Hoeldtke. "The girl," he said. "Who is she?"

"Her name's Paula Hoeldtke. She's from Indiana, and she disappeared over the summer. She lived in the neighborhood, she worked at a few restaurants nearby. Her father hired me to find her."

"Why give me her picture?"

"It's the only thing I've got with my name and number on it. Why? Do you know her?"

He studied her picture, then raised his green eyes to meet mine. "No," he said. "I never saw her."

13

The phone woke me, wrenching me out of a dream. I sat up in bed, grabbed for the phone, got it to my ear. A voice, half in a whisper, said, "Scudder?"

"Who is this?"

"Forget about the girl."

There'd been a girl in the dream but the dream was melting off like snow in the sun. I couldn't bring her image into focus. I didn't know where the dream ended and the phone call began. I said, "What girl? I don't know what you're talking about."

"Forget about Paula. You'll never find her, you can't bring her back."

"From where? What happened to her?"

"Quit looking for her, quit showing her picture around. Drop the whole thing."

"Who is this?"

The phone clicked in my ear. I said hello a couple of times, but it was useless. He was gone.

I switched on the bedside lamp, found my watch. It was a quarter to five. It had been past two by

223

the time I turned the light out, so I'd had less than three hours. I sat on the edge of the bed and went over the conversation in my mind, trying to find a deeper message behind the words, trying to place the voice. I had the feeling I'd heard it before but couldn't draw a bead on it.

I went into the bathroom and caught sight of my reflection in the mirror over the sink. All my years looked back at me, and I could feel their weight, pressing down on my shoulders. I ran the shower hot and stood under it for a long time, got out, toweled dry, got back into bed.

"You'll never find her, you can't bring her back."

It was too late or too early, there was no one I could call. The only person I knew who might be awake was Mickey Ballou, and he'd be too drunk by now, and I didn't have a number for him. And what would I say to him anyway?

"Forget about the girl."

Was it Paula I'd been dreaming about? I closed my eyes and tried to picture her.

When I awoke a second time it was ten o'clock and the sun was shining. I was up and half-dressed before I remembered the phone call, and at first I wasn't entirely certain if it had actually happened. My towel, tossed over a chair and still damp from my shower, provided physical evidence. I hadn't dreamed it. Someone had called me, urging me off a case I had already pretty much dropped.

The phone rang again as I was tying a shoe-

224

lace. I answered it and said a guarded "Hello," and Willa said, "Matt?"

"Oh, hi," I said.

"Did I wake you? You didn't sound like yourself."

"I was being cagey."

"I beg your pardon?"

"I woke up to an anonymous call in the middle of the night, telling me to stop looking for Paula Hoeldtke. When it rang just now I thought I might be in for more of the same."

"It wasn't me before."

"I know that. It was a man."

"Although I'll admit I was thinking of you. I sort of thought I might see you last night."

"I was tied up until late. I spent half the night at an AA meeting and the rest in a ginmill."

"That's a nice balanced existence."

"Isn't it? By the time I was done, it was too late to call."

"Did you find out anything about what was bothering Eddie?"

"No. But all of a sudden the other case is alive again."

"The other case? You mean Paula?"

"That's right."

"Just because someone told you to drop it? That's given you a reason to pick it up again?"

"That's just part of it."

Durkin said, "Christ, Mickey Ballou. The Butcher Boy. How does he fit into it?"

225

"I don't know. I spent a couple of hours with him last night."

"Oh yeah? You're really moving up in class these days, aren't you? Wha'd you do, take him out to dinner, watch him eat with his hands?"

"We were at a place called Grogan's."

"A few blocks from here, right? I know the joint. It's a dive. They say he owns it."

"So I understand."

"Except of course he can't, since the SLA doesn't like to let convicted felons put their names on liquor licenses, so somebody must be fronting it for him. What were the two of you doing, playing canasta?"

"Drinking and telling lies. He was drinking Irish whiskey."

"You were drinking coffee."

"Coke. They didn't have coffee."

"You're lucky they had Coke, a pigpen like that. What the hell has he got to do with Pauline? Not Pauline, Paula. What's he got to do with her?"

"I'm not sure," I said, "but the machine went *tilt* when he saw her picture, and a couple of hours later somebody woke me up to tell me to drop the case."

"Ballou?"

"No, it wasn't his voice. I don't know who it was. I have some ideas, but nothing solid. Tell me about Ballou, Joe."

"Tell you what?"

"What do you know about him?"

226

"I know he's an animal. I know he belongs in a fucking cage."

"Then why isn't he in one?"

"The worst ones never are. Nothing sticks to them. You can't ever find a witness, or you find one and he gets amnesia. Or he disappears. It's funny the way they disappear. You ever hear the story, Ballou's running all over town showing people a guy's head?"

"I know the story."

"The head never turned up. Or the body. Gone, no forwarding. *Finito*."

"How does he make his money?"

"Not running a ginmill. He started out doing some enforcing for some of the Italians. He's as big as a house and he was always a tough bastard and he liked the work. All those Westies, tough Irish mugs from the Kitchen, they've been hiring out as muscle for generations. I suspect he was good at it, Ballou. Say you borrowed money from a shy and you're a few weeks behind with the vig, and this hulk walks in on you wearing a bloody apron and swinging a cleaver in his hand. What are you going to do? You want to tell him see me next week or are you gonna come up with the cash?"

"You said he was a convicted felon. What did he go away for?"

"Assault. That was early, I don't think he was out of his teens. I'm pretty sure he only went away the once. I could look it up."

"It's not important. Is that what he's done ever

since? Strongarm work?"

He leaned back. "I don't think he hires out any-more," he said. "You call him, tell him So-and-so needs his legs broken, I don't think Ballou grabs a hunk of pipe and goes out and does the job him-self. But he might send somebody. What else does he do? I think he's got a few dollars on the street, earning that six-for-five. There's joints he's sup-posed to have a piece of, but you hear all sorts of shit along those lines, you never know what to believe. His name comes up in connection with a lot of things. Trucks getting hijacked, a couple of heavy heists. You remember a couple of years ago, five guys with masks and guns took off Wells Fargo for three mil?"

"They had somebody on the inside, didn't they?"

"Yeah, but he happened to die before anybody had a chance to ask him the right questions. And his wife died, and he had a girlfriend on the side, and you'll never guess what happened to her."

"She died?"

"She disappeared. A few other people disap-peared, too, and a couple more turned up in car trunks out at JFK. We'd hear that this guy or that guy was one of the guns and masks on the Wells Fargo thing, and before we could go out looking for him we'd get a call that he was in the trunk of his Chevy Monte Carlo out at Kennedy."

"And Ballou — "

"Was supposed to be the man at the top. That was the word, but nobody said it too loud because it was a dangerous thing to do, you could wind up in Long Term Parking along with all your friends and relations. But that was the word, Ballou set it up and ran it, and he may have come out with the whole three mil because there wasn't anybody around to share it with."

"He have anything to do with drugs?"

"Not that I ever heard of."

"Prostitution? White slaving?"

"Not his style." He yawned, ran a hand through his hair. "There was another one they called Butcher. A mob guy, out in Brooklyn if I remember it right."

"Dom the Butcher."

"That's the one."

"Bensonhurst."

"Yeah, right. Under Carlo G., if I remember it right. And they called him the Butcher because he had some kind of no-show job in the meat-cutter's union, that's what he paid his taxes on. Dominic something or other, I forget his last name. Something Italian."

"No kidding."

"Somebody shot him a couple of years ago. His line of work, you call that dying of natural causes. The thing is, they called him the Butcher because of his cover job, but all the same he was a brutal bastard. There was a story, some kids robbed a church and he had 'em skinned alive."

"To teach respect for the cloth."

"Yeah, well, he must have been a deeply spiritual guy. All I'm getting at, Matt, is when you got a guy they call the Butcher, or the Butcher Boy, or whatever the fuck they call him, you're talking about an animal oughta be in a cage, you're talking about the kind of guy eats raw meat for breakfast."

"I know."

"What I'd do in your position," he said, "is I'd take the biggest gun I could find, and right away I'd shoot him in the back of the neck. Either that or I'd stay the fuck away from him."

The Mets were back home for a weekend series with the Pirates. They'd won last night and it didn't look as though anyone was going to catch them. I called Willa but she had chores to do and wasn't enough of a fan to shirk them. Jim Faber was at his shop, with a job he'd promised a client by six. I flipped through my book and called a couple of other fellows I knew from St. Paul's, but either they weren't home or they didn't feel like shlepping out to Shea.

I could just stay home. The game would be televised, NBC was carrying it as the game of the week. But I didn't want to sit around all day. I had things to do and I couldn't do them. Some of them had to wait until dark, and some until after the weekend, and I wanted to get up and go somewhere in the meantime, not sit around looking at my watch. I tried to think who to go to the game with, and I could only come up with two people.

First was Ballou, and I had to laugh at myself

for thinking of him. I didn't have a number for him, and wouldn't have called it if I had. He probably didn't like baseball. Even if he did, I somehow couldn't see the two of us palling around, eating hot dogs and booing a bad call at first base. It just showed how strong if illusory the bond between us had been the previous evening for me to have thought of him at all.

The other person was Jan Keane. I didn't have to look up her number, and I dialed it and let it ring twice, then rang off before either she or her machine could answer.

I rode the subway down to Times Square, switched to the Flushing line and rode all the way out to Shea. The cashiers were sold out, but there were plenty of kids out front with tickets to sell, and I got a decent seat, up high behind third base. Ojeda pitched a three-hit shutout and for a change the team got him some runs, and the weather was just the way it ought to be. The new kid, Jefferies, went four-for-five with a double and a home run, and he went to his left for a low liner off Van Slyke's bat and saved Ojeda's shutout for him.

The fellow on my right said he'd seen Willie Mays in his rookie season at the Polo Grounds, and he'd been exciting in the same way. He'd come by himself, too, and he had a lot to say over nine innings, but it was better than sitting home and listening to Scully and Garagiola and Bud Light commercials. The fellow on my left had a beer each inning until they stopped selling it in the seventh. He had an extra in the fourth, too, to make up for the half of one that he spilled on his shoes and mine. I was annoyed at having to sit there and smell it, and then I reminded myself that I had a lady friend who generally smelled of beer when she didn't smell of scotch, and that I'd spent the previous night voluntarily breathing stale beer fumes in a lowlife saloon and had a grand time of it. So I had no real reason to sulk if my neighbor wanted to sink a few while he watched the home team win one.

I had a couple of hot dogs myself, and drank a root beer, and stood up for the national anthem and the seventh-inning stretch, and to give Ojeda a hand when he got the last Pirate to swing at a curveball low and away. "They'll roll right over the Dodgers in the playoffs," my new friend assured me. "But I don't know about Oakland."

I'd made a dinner date with Willa earlier. I stopped at my hotel to shave and put on a suit, then went over to her place. She had her hair braided again, and the braid coiled across her forehead like a tiara. I told her how nice it looked.

She still had the flowers on the kitchen table. They were past their prime, and some were losing their petals. I mentioned this, and she said she wanted to keep them another day. "It seems cruel to throw them out," she said.

She tasted of booze when I kissed her, and she had a small scotch while we decided where to go. We both wanted meat, so I suggested the Slate, a steak house on Tenth Avenue that always drew a lot of cops from Midtown North and John Jay College.

We walked over there and got a table in front near the bar. I didn't see anyone I recognized, but several faces were vaguely familiar and almost every man in the room looked to be on the job. If anyone had been fool enough to hold the place up, he'd have been surrounded by men with drawn revolvers, a fair percentage of them half in the bag.

I mentioned this to Willa, and she tried to calculate our chances of being gunned down in a crossfire. "A few years ago," she said, "I wouldn't have been able to sit still in a place like this."

"For fear of being caught in a crossfire?"

"For fear they'd be shooting at me on purpose. It's still hard for me to believe I'm dating a guy who used to be a cop."

"Did you have a lot of trouble with cops?"

"Well, I lost two teeth," she said, and fingered the two upper incisors that replaced the ones knocked out in Chicago. "And we were always getting hassled. We were presumably undercover, but we always figured the FBI had somebody in the organization reporting to them, and I can't tell you the number of times the Feebies showed up to question me. Or to have long sessions with the neighbors."

"That must have been a hell of a way to live."

"It was crazy. But it almost killed me to leave."

"They wouldn't let you go?"

"No, it wasn't like that. But the PCP gave my

life all the meaning it had for a whole lot of years, and when I left it was like admitting all those years were a waste. And on top of that I would find myself doubting my actions. I would think that the PCP was right, and that I was just copping out, and missing my chance to make a difference in the world. That was what kept you sucked in, you know. The chance it gave you to see yourself as being one of the ones who mattered, out there on the cutting edge of history."

We took our time over dinner. She had a sirloin and a baked potato. I ordered the mixed grill, and we split a Caesar salad. She started off with a scotch, then drank red wine with her dinner. I got a cup of coffee right away and let them keep filling it up for me. She wanted a pony of Armagnac with her coffee. The waitress came back and said the bartender didn't have any, so she settled for a cognac. It couldn't have been too bad, because she drank it and ordered a second one.

The check came to a fairly impressive sum. She wanted to split it and I didn't work too hard trying to talk her out of it. "Actually," she said, checking the waitress's arithmetic, "I should be paying about two-thirds of this. More than that. I had a million drinks and you had a cup of coffee."

"Cut it out."

"And my entrée was more than yours."

I told her to stop it, and we halved the check and the tip. Outside, she wanted to walk a little to clear her head. It was a little late for panhandlers, but some of them were still hard at it. I passed out a few dollars. The wild-eyed woman in the shawl got one of them. She had her baby in her arms, but I didn't see her other child, and I tried not to wonder where it had gone to.

We walked downtown a few blocks and I asked Willa if she'd mind stopping at Paris Green. She looked at me, amused. "For a guy who doesn't drink," she said, "you sure do a lot of barhopping."

"Somebody I want to talk to."

We cut across to Ninth, walked down to Paris Green and took seats at the bar. My friend with the bird's-nest beard wasn't working, and the fellow on duty was no one I'd seen before. He was very young, with a lot of curly hair and a sort of vague and unfocused look about him. He didn't know how I could get hold of the other bartender. I went over and talked to the manager, describing the bartender I was looking for.

"That's Gary," he said. "He's not working tonight. Come around tomorrow, I think he's working tomorrow."

I asked if he had a number for him. He said he couldn't give that out. I asked if he'd call Gary for me and see if he'd be willing to take the call.

"I really don't have time for that," he said. "I'm trying to run a restaurant here."

If I still carried a badge he'd have given me the number with no argument. If I'd been Mickey Ballou I'd have come back with a couple of friends and let him watch while we threw all his chairs and tables out into the street. There was another way, I could give him five or ten dollars for his time, but somehow that went against the grain.

I said, "Make the phone call."

"I just told you — "

"I know what you told me. Either make the phone call for me or give me the fucking number."

I don't know what the hell I could have done if he'd refused, but something in my voice or face must have gotten through to him. He said, "Just a moment," and disappeared into the back. I went and stood next to Willa, who was working on a brandy. She wanted to know if everything was all right. I told her everything was fine.

When the manager reappeared I walked over to meet him. "There's no answer," he said. "Here's the number, if you don't believe me you can try it yourself."

I took the slip of paper he handed me. I said, "Why shouldn't I believe you? Of course I believe you."

He looked at me, his eyes wary.

"I'm sorry," I said. "I was out of line there, and I apologize. It's been a rough couple of days."

He wavered, then went with the flow. "Hey, that's cool," he said. "Don't worry about it."

"This city," I said, as if that explained everything, and he nodded, as if indeed it did.

He wound up buying us a drink. We had survived a tense moment together, and that seemed to carry more weight than the fact that we had created the tension ourselves. I didn't really want another Perrier, but Willa managed to find room for another brandy.

When we stepped outside, the fresh air sucker-punched her and almost knocked her down. She grabbed my arm, caught her balance. "I can feel that last brandy," she announced.

"No kidding."

"What's that supposed to mean?"

"Nothing."

She drew away from me, her nostrils flaring, her face dark. "I'm quite all right," she said. "I can get home under my own power."

"Take it easy, Willa."

"Don't tell me to take it easy. Mr. Holier-than-thou. Mr. Soberer-than-thou."

She stalked off down the street. I walked alongside her and didn't say anything.

"I'm sorry," she said.

"Forget it."

"You're not mad?"

"No, of course not."

She didn't say much the rest of the way home. When we got into her apartment she swept up the faded flowers from the kitchen table and started dancing around the floor with them. She was humming something but I couldn't recognize the tune. After a few turns she stopped and began to cry. I took the flowers from her and put them on the table. I held her and she sobbed. When the tears stopped I let go of her and she stepped back. She began undressing, dropping her clothes on the floor as she removed them. She took off everything and walked straight back to the bedroom and got into the bed.

"I'm sorry," she said. "I'm sorry, I'm sorry, I'm sorry."

"It's all right."

"Stay with me."

I stayed until I was sure she was sleeping soundly. Then I let myself out and went home.

14

I tried Gary's number in the morning. I let it ring and no one answered, neither man nor machine. I tried him again after breakfast with the same result. I took a long walk and tried the number a third time when I got back to the hotel. I put the television on, but all I could find were economists talking about the deficit and evangelists talking about the Day of Judgment. I turned them all off and the phone rang.

It was Willa. "I would have called you a little earlier," she said, "but I wanted to make sure I was going to live."

"Rough morning?"

"God. Was I impossible last night?"

"You weren't so bad."

"You could say anything and I couldn't prove you wrong. I don't remember the end of the evening."

"Well, you were a little fuzzy there toward the end."

"I remember having a second brandy at Paris Green. I remember telling myself that I didn't have to drink it just because it was free. He bought us a round, didn't he?"

"He did indeed."

"Maybe he put arsenic in it. I almost wish he had. I don't remember anything after that. How did I get home?"

"We walked."

"Did I turn nasty?"

"Don't worry about it," I said. "You were drunk and you were in a blackout. You didn't throw up, turn violent, or say anything indiscreet."

"You're sure of that?"

"Positive."

"I hate not remembering. I hate losing control."

"I know."

There's a Sunday afternoon meeting in SoHo that I've always liked. I hadn't been there in months. I usually would spend Saturdays with Jan. We'd make the rounds of the galleries and go out for dinner, and I'd stay over, and in the morning she'd fix a big brunch. We'd walk around and look in shops and, when the time came, go to the meeting.

When we stopped seeing each other, I stopped going.

I took a subway downtown and walked in and out of a lot of shops on Spring Street and West Broadway. Most of the SoHo art galleries close on Sunday, but a few stay open, and there was one show I liked, realistic landscapes, all of them of Central Park. Most of them showed only grass and trees and benches, with no buildings looming in the background, but it was nonetheless clear that you were looking at a distinctly urban environment no matter how peaceful and green it appeared. Somehow the artist had managed to instill the city's hard-edged energy in the canvases, and I couldn't figure out how he'd done it.

I went to the meeting, and Jan was there. I managed to focus on the qualification, and then during the break I went over and sat next to her.

"It's funny," she said. "I was thinking of you just this morning."

"I almost called you yesterday."

"Oh?"

"To see if you wanted to go out to Shea."

"That's really funny. I watched that game."

"You were out there?"

"On television. You really almost called?"

"I did call."

"When? I was home all day."

"I let it ring twice and hung up."

"I remember the call. I wondered who that was. As a matter of fact — "

"You wondered if it was me?"

"Uh-huh. The thought crossed my mind." She had her hands in her lap and she was looking at them. "I don't think I'd have gone."

"To the game?"

She nodded. "But it's hard to say, isn't it? How I might have reacted. What you'd have said, what I'd have said."

241

"Do you want to have coffee after the meeting?"

She looked at me, then looked away. "Oh, I don't know, Matthew," she said. "I don't know."

I started to say something, but the chairperson was rapping on the table with a glass ashtray to indicate that it was time to resume the meeting. I went back to where I'd been sitting. Toward the end I started raising my hand, and when I got called on I said, "My name is Matt and I'm an alcoholic. Over the past couple of weeks I've been spending a lot of time around people who are drinking. Some of it's professional and some is social, and it's not always easy to tell which is which. I spent an hour or two in a ginmill the other night having one of those rambling conversations, and it was just like old times except I was drinking Coke."

I went on for another minute or two, saying what came to mind. Then someone else got called on and talked about how her building was going co-op and she didn't see how she could afford to buy her apartment.

After the prayer, after the chairs were folded and stacked, I asked Jan if she felt like coffee. "Some of us go to the place around the corner," she said. "Do you want to come along?"

"I thought just the two of us."

"I don't know if that's a good idea."

I told her I'd walk her to where she was going and we could talk on the way. Once we were outside and had fallen into step together, I couldn't

242

think what it was I had wanted to say, and so we walked a little ways in silence.

I've missed you, I said a couple of times in my mind. Finally I said it aloud.

"Have you? Sometimes I miss you. Sometimes I think of the two of us and I feel sad."

"Yes."

"Have you been getting out?"

"I couldn't get interested. Until the past week or so."

"And?"

"I fell into something. Without looking for it, which I guess is the way it happens."

"She's not in the program."

"Not hardly."

"Does that mean she ought to be?"

"I don't know who ought to be anymore. It doesn't matter, the whole thing's not going anywhere."

After a moment she said, "I think I'd be afraid to spend a lot of time with someone who was drinking."

"That's probably a healthy fear."

"Do you know about Tom?" We went back and forth for a moment, with her trying to describe a long-term member of downtown AA and me unable to place him. "Anyway," she said, "he was sober for twenty-two years, kept up on his meetings, sponsored a lot of people, everything. And he was in Paris for three weeks over the summer, and he was walking down the street, and he fell into a conversation with this pretty French girl, and she said, 'Would you like to have a glass of wine?' "

"And he said?"

"And he said, 'Why not?' "

"Just like that."

"Just like that, after twenty-two years and God knows how many thousands of meetings. 'Why not?' "

"Did he make it back?"

"He can't seem to. He's sober for two days, three days, and then he goes out and drinks. He looks terrible. His drunks don't last long because he can't stay out, he winds up in a hospital after a couple of days. But he can't stay sober, and when he shows up at a meeting I can't bear to look at him. I think he's probably going to die."

"The cutting edge," I said.

"How's that?"

"Just something somebody said."

We turned the corner, reached the coffee shop where she was to meet her friends. She said, "Don't you want to join us for a cup of coffee?" I said I didn't think so, and she didn't try to talk me into it.

I said, "I wish — "

"I know," she said. She reached out a hand and held mine for a moment. "Eventually," she said, "I think we'll probably be able to feel easier with each other. Now's too soon."

"Evidently."

"It's too *sad*," she said. "It hurts too much."

She turned from me, headed for the coffee shop.

I stood there until she was through the door. Then I started walking, not paying much attention to where I was going. Not much caring.

Once I'd walked out from under my mood I found a pay phone and tried Gary's number. No one answered. I caught a subway uptown and walked over to Paris Green and found him behind the bar. The bar was empty but there were several tables of people who'd come for a late brunch. I watched as he made up a tray of Bloody Marys, then filled a pair of tulip-shaped glasses half with orange juice and half with champagne.

"The mimosa," he said to me. "Reverse synergy, the whole less than the sum of its parts. Drink orange juice or drink champagne, I say, but not the two at once out of the same glass." He proffered a rag and made a show of wiping the bar in front of me. "And what may I get you?"

"Is there coffee?"

He called to a waiter, ordered a cup of coffee for the bar. Leaning toward me, he said, "Bryce said you were looking for me."

"Last night. And I called you at home a couple of times since then."

"Ah," he said. "Never made it home last night, I'm afraid. Thank God there are still ladies left in the world who find a poor barkeep a creature of romance and intrigue." He grinned richly behind his beard. "If you'd reached me, what would you have said?"

I told him what I had in mind. He listened, nodded. "Sure," he said. "I could do that. Thing is, I'm on until eight tonight. It's slow enough right now but there's nobody around who could cover for me. Unless — "

"Unless what?"

"How accomplished a bartender are you?"

"No," I said. "I'll come by for you around eight."

I went back to my hotel and tried to watch the end of a football game but I couldn't sit still. I got out of there and walked around. At some point I realized I hadn't eaten since breakfast, and I made myself stop for a slice of pizza. I put a lot of the crushed red pepper on it, hoping it would stir me up a little.

A few minutes before eight I went back to Paris Green and drank a Coke while Gary evened out his cash and checks and turned it all over to his relief. We walked out together and he asked me the name of the place again. I told him, and he said he'd never noticed it. "But I'm not on Tenth Avenue much," he said. "Grogan's Open House? It sounds like your basic Irish saloon."

"It pretty much is."

We went over what I wanted him to do, and then I waited across the street while he ambled over to Grogan's front entrance and walked in. I stood in a doorway and waited. The minutes crawled, and I was starting to worry that something had unaccountably gone wrong, that I'd pushed him into a dangerous situation. I was trying to decide whether I'd make things worse by going in myself. I was still mulling it over when the door swung open and he emerged. He had his hands in his pockets and he sauntered along, looking almost too carefree to be true.

I matched his pace for half a block, then crossed over to his side of the street. He said, "Do I know you? What's the password?"

"Recognize anybody?"

"Oh, no question," he said. "I wasn't that certain I'd know him again, but I took one look and knew him right off. And he knew me."

"What did he say?"

"Didn't say much of anything, just stood in front of me waiting for me to order. I didn't let on that I knew him."

"Good."

"But, see, he didn't let on that he knew me, either, but I could see he did. The way he sent little glances my way. Ha! Guilty knowledge, isn't that what they call it?"

"That's what they call it."

"It's not a bad little store. I like the tile floor and all the dark wood. I had a bottle of Harp, and then I took a second bottle and watched two fellows shooting darts. One of them, I'm sure he must have spent a past life as the Leaning Tower of Pisa. I kept thinking he was going to fall on the floor, but he never did."

"I know who you mean."

"He was drinking Guinness. That's a shade too primal a flavor for my tastebuds to come to terms with. I suppose you could mix it with orange juice." He shuddered. "I wonder what it's like to work in a place like that, where the closest you get to a mixed drink is scotch and water or the odd vodka tonic. You could live your whole life and never hear anyone order a mimosa. Or a Harvey Wallbanger. Or a hickory dickory daiquiri."

"What the hell is that?"

"You don't want to know." He shuddered again. I asked him if he'd recognized anyone else in the room. "No," he said. "Only the bartender."

"And he was the one you saw with Paula."

"The very lad himself, as the boyos in Grogan's might put it." He mused again on the delights of working in a simple, honest bar, unadorned with potted ferns or earnest yuppies. "Of course," he reminded himself, "the tips are pretty awful."

And that reminded me. I'd set aside a bill earlier, and now I dug it out and slipped it to him.

I couldn't get him to take it. "You brought a little excitement into my life," he said. "What did it cost me, ten minutes and the price of two beers? Someday we'll sit down and you can tell me how the whole thing turns out, and I'll even let you buy the beers that night. Fair enough?"

"Fair enough. But they don't always turn out. Sometimes they just trail off."

"I'll take my chances," he said.

I killed fifteen minutes, then went back to Grogan's myself. I didn't see Mickey Ballou in the room. Andy Buckley was in the back at the dart board, and Neil was behind the bar. He was dressed as he'd been Friday night, with the leather vest over the red buffalo-plaid shirt.

I stood at the bar and ordered a glass of plain soda water. When he brought it I asked if Ballou had been around. "He looked in earlier," he said. "He might be back later on. You want me to tell him you were looking for him?"

I said it wasn't important.

He moved off to the far end of the bar. I took a sip or two of my soda water and glanced his way from time to time. Guilty knowledge, Gary had called it, and that was what it felt like. It was hard to be sure of his voice, my caller the other morning had spoken in a hoarse half-whisper, but I had to figure it was him.

I didn't know how much more I could find out. Or what I could possibly do with whatever I learned.

I must have stood there for half an hour, and he spent all that time down at the other end of the bar. When I left, my glass of soda wasn't down more than half an inch from the top. He'd forgotten to charge me for it, and I didn't bother to leave him a tip.

The manager at the Druid's Castle said, "Oh, sure, Neil. Neil Tillman, sure. What about him?"

"He used to work here?"

"For around six months, something like that. He left sometime in the spring."

"So he would have been here the same time Paula was here."

"I think so, but I couldn't say for certain without looking it up. And the book's in the owner's office, and that's locked up right now."

"Why did he leave?"

His hesitation was brief. "People come and go," he said. "Our turnover rate would amaze you."

"Why did you let him go?"

"I didn't say we did."

"But you did, didn't you?"

He shifted uncomfortably. "I'd rather not say."

"What was his problem? Was he dealing out of the restaurant? Stealing too much of what came in over the bar?"

"I really don't feel right talking about it. If you come back tomorrow during the day, you can probably learn what you want to know from the owner. But — "

"He's a possible suspect," I said, "in a possible homicide."

"She's dead?"

"It's beginning to look that way."

He frowned. "I really shouldn't say anything."

"You're not talking for the record. It'll just be for my own information."

"Credit cards," he said. "There was no hard evidence, that's why I didn't want to say anything. But it looked as though he was running duplicate slips with customers' cards. I don't know just what he was doing or how he was doing it, but there was something shady going on."

"What did you say when you fired him?"

"I didn't do it, the owner did. He just told Neil it wasn't working out, and Neil didn't push it. That looked pretty much like an admission of guilt, don't you think? He'd worked here long enough so that you wouldn't fire him without telling him the reason, but he didn't want to know."

"How did Paula fit in?"

"Did she? It never occurred to me that she did. She left on her own, she wasn't fired, and I'm pretty sure she was still here after we let him go. If she was working with him — well, she could have been, but they never seemed close, you didn't see them whispering in corners. I never thought of the two of them as involved in any way. There was no gossip, and I certainly didn't pick up on anything."

Around midnight I picked up a couple containers of coffee and planted myself diagonally across the street from Grogan's. I found a doorway and sat there, drinking coffee and keeping an eye on the place. I figured I was reasonably inconspicuous there. There were a lot of guys in doorways, some of them sitting up, some lying down. I was better dressed than most of them, but not by all that much.

Time passed a little faster than when I'd stood around waiting for Gary. My mind would drift, working on a thread of the yarnball it had to grapple with, and ten or fifteen minutes would slip by before I knew it. Throughout it all I kept my eyes pointed at the entrance to Grogan's. You have to let your mind wander on a stakeout, otherwise you drive yourself crazy with boredom, but you learn to program yourself so that your eyes will bring you back to basics if they register anything you ought to be paying attention to. Now and then someone would walk in or out of Grogan's, and that would bring me back from my reverie and I would take note of who it was.

A few minutes after one several people left at once, and moments after that the door opened to release four or five more. The only one I recognized in either batch was Andy Buckley. The door closed after the second group, and a few seconds later the overhead lights went out, leaving the place very dimly lit.

I crossed the street so that I was standing opposite the place. I could see better now, although the doorway I had to lurk in was shallower and not as comfortable. Neil looked to be moving around inside, doing whatever he did to shut the place down for the night. I drew back a little when the door opened and he dragged a Hefty bag out to the street and swung it up into a green dumpster. Then he went back inside, and I heard the snick of the lock. It was faint, but you could hear it across the street if you were listening for it.

More time passed at a crawl. Then the door opened again and he came out. He drew the steel gates across and locked them. The saloon was still dimly illuminated inside. Evidently those lights stayed on all night for security.

When he had all the padlocks fastened I got to my feet, ready to move off after him. If he took a cab I could forget it, and if he wound up going down into the subway I would probably let him go, but I figured he was odds-on to live somewhere in the neighborhood, and if he walked home it wouldn't be terribly difficult to tag him. I hadn't been able to find him listed in the Manhattan phone book, so the easiest way to locate his residence was to let him lead me to it.

I wasn't sure how I'd play it after that. By ear, probably. Maybe I'd catch up with him on his doorstep and see if he was rattled enough to spill anything. Maybe I'd wait and try to get into his apartment when he was out of it. First, though, I'd follow him and see where he went.

Except he didn't go anywhere. He just stood there, lurking in his doorway even as I lurked in mine, drawing in his shoulders against the cold, bringing his hands to his mouth and blowing on them. It wasn't all that cold, but then he didn't have anything on over the shirt and the vest.

He lit a cigarette, smoked half of it, threw it away. It landed at the curb and sent up a little shower of sparks. As they were dying out, a car heading uptown on Tenth made a right and pulled up in front of Grogan's, blocking my view of Neil. It was a Cadillac, a long one, silver. The glass was tinted all around and I couldn't see who was driving, or how many people it held.

For a minute I expected gunshots. I thought I'd hear them, and then the car would pull away fast, and I'd see Neil clutching his middle and sinking to the pavement. But nothing like that happened. He trotted over to the car. The passenger door opened. He got in, closed the door.

The Cadillac pulled away, leaving me there.

15

I thought I heard the phone while I was in the shower. It was ringing again when I got out. I wrapped a towel around my middle and went to answer it.

"Scudder? Mick Ballou. Did I wake you, man?"

"I was already up."

"Good man. It's early, but I have to see you. Say ten minutes? In front of your hotel?"

"Better make it twenty."

"Sooner if you can," he said. "We don't want to be late."

Late for what? I shaved quickly, put on a suit. I'd spent a restless night, dream-ridden, my dreams full of doorway stakeouts and drive-by shootings. Now it was seven-thirty in the morning and I had a date with the Butcher. Why? For what?

I tied my tie, grabbed up my keys and wallet. There was nobody waiting for me in the lobby. I went outside and saw the car at the curb, parked next to a hydrant directly in front of the hotel. The big silver Cadillac. Tinted glass all around, but I could see him behind the wheel now because he had lowered the window on the passenger side and was leaning halfway across the front seat, motioning me over.

I crossed the pavement, opened the door. He was wearing a white butcher's apron that covered him from the neck down. There were rust-colored stains on the white cotton, some of them vivid, some of them bleached and faded. I found myself wondering at the wisdom of getting into a car with a man so dressed, but there was nothing in his manner to lead me to fear that I was going to be taken for that sort of ride. His hand was out and I shook it, then got in and drew the door shut.

He pulled away from the curb, drove to the corner of Ninth and waited for the light. He asked again if he'd awakened me and I said he hadn't. "Your man at the desk said you weren't answering," he said, "but I made him ring again."

"I was in the shower."

"But you had a night's sleep?"

"A few hours."

"I never got to bed," he said. The light turned and he made a fast left in front of oncoming traffic, then had to stop for the light at Fifty-sixth. He had touched a button to raise my windshield, and I looked through tinted glass at the morning. It was an overcast day, with the threat of rain in the air, and through the dark window the sky looked ominous.

I asked where we were going.

"The butchers' mass," he said.

I thought of some weird heretical rite, men in bloody aprons brandishing cleavers; a lamb sacrificed.

"At St. Bernard's. You know it?"

"Fourteenth Street?"

He nodded. "They have daily mass at seven in the main sanctuary. And then there's another mass at eight in a small room off to the left, and there's only a handful ever come to it. My father went every morning before work. Sometimes he'd take me with him. He was a butcher, he worked in the markets down there. This was his apron."

The light turned and we cruised down the avenue. The lights were timed, and when one was out of sync he slowed, looked left and right, and sailed on through it. We caught a light we couldn't run at one of the approaches to the Lincoln Tunnel, then made them all clear to Fourteenth Street, where he hung a left turn. St. Bernard's was a third of the way down the block on the downtown side of the street. He pulled up just short of it and parked in front of a storefront funeral parlor. Signs at the curb prohibited parking during business hours.

We got out of the car and Ballou waved at someone inside the funeral parlor. Twomey & Sons, the sign said, and I suppose it was Twomey or one of his sons who waved back. I kept pace with Ballou, up the steps and through the main doors of the church.

He led me down a side aisle and into a small

room on the left, where perhaps a dozen worshipers occupied three rows of folding chairs. He took a seat in the last row and motioned for me to sit next to him.

Another half-dozen people found their way into the room during the next few minutes. There were several elderly nuns in the group, a couple of older women, two men in business suits and one in olive work clothes, and four men beside Ballou in butchers' aprons.

At eight the priest entered. He looked Filipino, and his English was lightly accented. Ballou opened a book for me and showed me how to follow the service. I stood when the others stood, sat when they sat, knelt when they knelt. There was a reading from Isaiah, another from Luke.

When they gave out communion, I stayed where I was. So did Ballou. Everyone else took the wafer, except for a nun and one of the butchers.

The whole thing didn't take all that long. When it was over Ballou strode from the room and on out of the church, and I tagged along in his wake.

On the street he lit a cigarette and said, "My father went every morning before work."

"So you said."

"It was in Latin then. They took the mystery out when they put it in English. He went every morning. I wonder what he got out of it."

"What do you get out of it?"

"I don't know. I don't go that often. Maybe ten or twenty times in a year. I'll go three days in a row and then I'll stay away for a month or two." He took another drag on his cigarette and threw the butt into the street. "I don't go to confession, I don't take communion, I don't pray. Do you believe in God?"

"Sometimes."

"Sometimes. Good enough." He took my arm. "Come on," he said. "The car's all right where it is. Twomey won't let them tow it or ticket it. He knows me, and he knows the car."

"I know it, too."

"How's that?"

"I saw it last night. I copied the plate number, I was going to run it through Motor Vehicles today. Now I won't have to."

"You wouldn't have learned much," he said. "I'm not the owner. There's another name on the registration."

"There's another name on the license at Grogan's."

"There is. Where did you see the car?"

"On Fiftieth Street a little after one. Neil Tillman got into it and you drove away."

"Where were you?"

"Across the street."

"Keeping an eye out?"

"That's right."

We were walking west on Fourteenth. We crossed Hudson and Greenwich and I asked where we were going. "I was up all night," he said. "I need a drink. After a butchers' mass where would you go but a butchers' bar?" He looked over at me, and something glinted in his green eyes. "You'll likely be the only man there in a suit. Salesmen come in there, but not this early. But you'll be all right. Meatcutters are a broadminded lot. Nobody'll hold it against you."

"I'm glad to hear that."

We were in the meat district now. Markets and packing houses lined both sides of the street and men in aprons like Ballou's unloaded carcasses from big trucks and hooked them up onto the overhead racks. The raw stink of the dead meat hung in the air like smoke, overriding the burnt reek of the trucks' exhaust. Beyond, at the end of the street, you could see dark clouds lowering over the Hudson, and high-rise apartments on the Jersey side. But for these last, the whole scene looked as though it had sprung from an earlier time. The trucks should have been horse-drawn; then you'd have sworn you were in the nineteenth century.

The bar he took me to was on Washington Street at the corner of Thirteenth. The sign said BAR, and if it had more of a name than that they were keeping it a secret. It was a small room, its board floor liberally strewn with sawdust. There was a sandwich menu posted, and a pot of coffee made. I was glad to see that. It was a little early in the day for Coca-Cola.

The bartender was a beefy fellow with a flattop haircut and a brushy moustache. There were three men standing at the bar, two of them in butcher's aprons, both of the aprons richly bloodstained. There were half a dozen square tables of dark wood, all of them empty. Ballou got a glass of whiskey and a cup of black coffee from the bar and led me to the table that was farthest from the door. I sat down. He started to sit, then looked at his glass and saw that it didn't hold enough. He went back to the bar and returned with the bottle. It was Jameson, but not the premium stuff he drank at his own place.

He wrapped his big hand around his glass and raised it a few inches from the tabletop in a wordless toast. I raised my coffee mug in acknowledgment. He drank half the whiskey. It might have been water for all the effect it had on him.

He said, "We have to talk."

"All right."

"You knew the minute I looked at the girl's picture. Didn't you?"

"I knew something."

"Took me on the blind side, it did. You came in talking about poor Eddie Dunphy. And then we talked about every damned thing, didn't we?"

"Just about."

"I thought what a devious bastard you were, leading me round the barn and then dropping her picture on the table. But that wasn't it at all, was it?"

"No. I didn't have anything to connect her to you or to Neil. I was just trying to find out what was on Eddie's mind."

"And I had no reason to have my guard up. I didn't know a fucking thing about Eddie or his mind or what he might have had on it." He drank the rest of the whiskey and put the glass on the table. "Matt, I have to do this. Come into the men's room so I can be certain you're not wearing a wire."

"Jesus," I said.

"I don't want to talk around the point. I want to say whatever comes to mind and I can't do that unless I know you're clean."

The lavatory was small and dank and foul. It wouldn't hold us both comfortably, so he stood outside and held the door open. I took off my jacket and shirt and tie and lowered my trousers while he apologized for the indignity of it all. Then he held my jacket while I got dressed. I took my time getting my tie knotted right, then took my jacket from him and put it on. We went back to the table and sat down, and he poured more whiskey into his glass.

"The girl's dead," he said.

Something settled lower within me. I had known she was dead, had sensed it and reasoned it both, but evidently there had been a part of me that had gone on hoping.

I said, "When?"

"Sometime in July. I don't know the date." He gripped his glass but didn't lift it. "Before Neil came to work for me he was behind the bar at a tourist place."

"The Druid's Castle."

"You'd know that, of course. He had a racket there."

"Credit cards."

He nodded. "He came to me with it, I put him in touch with someone. There's a lot of money in it, those little plastic cards, though it's not the kind of business I care for, not for myself. You can't get your hands into it, it's moving numbers around. But it was a good thing for all concerned, and then they caught on at the restaurant and they let him go."

"That's where he met Paula."

He nodded. "She was in it with him. She would run an impression of the cards on her own machine before she took the cards to the cashier. Or they'd give her their carbons to tear up, only she wouldn't do it, she'd pass them on to Neil. After he left she stayed on there, and he had her bringing slips and carbons to him, he had girls at a couple of places doing that. But then she quit, she didn't care to wait on tables anymore."

He picked up the glass and took a drink. "She moved in with him. She kept her room so that her parents wouldn't know what she was doing. Sometimes she came to the bar when he was working, but more often she'd wait and come by for him when his shift was over. He didn't just tend bar."

"He still had his credit card scam?"

"That didn't last. But hanging around, you know, he found things to do. You could tell him the make and model and he'd steal you a car. He went along a couple of times when some boys took off a truck. There's good money in that."

"I'm sure there is."

263

"The details don't matter. He was all right, you know, for what he was. But it bothered me, having her around."

"Why?"

"Because she didn't fit. She was along for the ride but she didn't belong. What does her father do?"

"He sells Japanese cars."

"And not stolen ones, either."

"I wouldn't think so, no."

He uncapped the bottle, raised it. He asked me if I wanted more coffee.

"I'm fine," I said.

"I should be drinking coffee myself. When I'm up this long, though, the whiskey is like coffee to me, it fuels it and keeps it all rolling." He filled his glass. "She was a nice Protestant girl from Indiana," he said. "She'd steal, but she stole for the thrill of it. You can't trust that, it's almost as bad as a man who kills for the thrill of it. A good thief doesn't steal for the thrill. He steals for the money. And the best thief of all steals because he's a thief."

"What happened to Paula?"

"She heard something she shouldn't have heard."

"What?"

"You don't have to know. Ah, what's the difference? There were these dago bastards brought in a load of heroin and sold it, and someone shot the whole fucking lot of them and took their money. There was something in the papers. They

264

got it all wrong, but maybe you remember it."

"I remember it."

"He had her out at the farm. There's a farm up in Ulster County, it has another man's name on the deed, but it's mine the way the car and Grogan's are mine." He took a drink. He said, "I don't own a fucking thing, can you believe that? One fellow lets me drive his car, another lets me live in an apartment even if his name's on the lease. And there's this couple, his people are from County Westmeath, he's always liked the country. He and his wife live there and the deed says they own it, and he milks the cows and slops the hogs and she feeds the chickens and collects the eggs, and I can go and stay up there anytime I want. And if some bastard from Internal Revenue ever wants to know where my money came from, why, what money? What do I own I ever had to buy?"

"Neil had Paula at the farm," I prompted.

"And everyone was relaxed, and talking freely, and she heard too damn much. And she wouldn't stand up, you know. If anyone was to ask her a question, she'd be the white-bread Protestant girl from Indiana, you know, and she'd tell them everything. So I told Neil he had to get rid of her."

"You ordered him to kill her?"

"The hell I did!" He slammed the glass on the table, and at first I thought his anger was for me, that the question itself enraged him. "I never told him to kill her," he said. "I said he should send her to hell and gone out of New York. She'd be no danger if she wasn't around. She wouldn't have

265

anybody asking her questions back in Indiana, not the cops nor the fucking guineas either. But if she was around, you know, there was always the chance she could turn out to be a problem."

"But he mistook your orders?"

"He did not. Because he came back and told me it was all taken care of. She'd got on a plane to Indianapolis and we'd never be seeing her again. She was all checked out of her room, all on her way back home, and she was no loose end for anybody to be nervous about." He picked up his glass again, put it down, pushed it a few inches away from him. "The other night," he said, "when I turned over the card you gave me and saw her picture staring back at me, it gave me a turn. Because why would anyone come around looking for a girl who was back home with her mother and father?"

"What happened?"

"That's what I asked him. 'What happened, Neil? If you've sent the girl home, why have her parents hired a man to search for her?' She went home to Indiana, he said, but she didn't stay. She got right on a plane to Los Angeles to make her fortune in Hollywood. And never so much as called her parents? Well, he said, perhaps something happened to her out there. Perhaps she took to drugs, or fell in with a bad lot. After all, she'd got into the fast life here, so she might have gone looking for it out there. I knew he was lying."

"Yes."

"But I let it go for then."

266

"He called me," I said. "It must have been Saturday morning, early. Probably just a few hours after he closed up at Grogan's."

"I talked with him that night. We locked the door and turned down the lights and drank whiskey and he told me how she'd gone to Hollywood to be a movie star. And then he called you? What did he say?"

"That I should stop looking for her. That I was wasting my time."

"Stupid lad. Stupid call to make. Just let you know you were getting on to something, wouldn't it?"

"I already knew."

He nodded. "Gave it all away myself, didn't I? But I never knew I had anything to give away. Thought for all the world she was home in Indiana. What's the name of the town?"

"Muncie."

"Muncie, that's it." He looked at his whiskey, then drank some of it. I never drank Irish much but I got a sudden sense-memory of it now, not as smoky as scotch or as oily as bourbon. I drank the rest of my coffee, gulping it as if it were an antidote.

He said, "I knew he was lying. I gave him a little time to let his nerves get the better of him, and then last night I took him for a long ride upstate and got it all out of him. We went up to Ellenville. That's where the farm is. That's where he took her."

"When?"

"Whenever it was. July. He took her there for a last weekend, he said, a treat before she went back home where she came from. And he gave her a little cocaine, he said, and her heart failed. She didn't take that much, he said, but you can't predict with cocaine, it will get the better of you now and then."

"And that's how she died?"

"No. Because the bastard was lying. I got the story out of him. He took her up to the farm and told her how she had to go home. And she refused, and she got drunk and angry and started threatening to go to the police. And she was making a lot of noise, and he was afraid she'd rouse the couple who take care of the place. And, trying to quiet her, he hit her too hard and she died."

"But that wasn't it either," I said. "Was it?"

"No. Because why would he drive her a hundred miles to tell her she had to get on an airplane? Christ, what a liar he was!" He flashed a shark's grin. "But, you know, I didn't have to read him his rights. He didn't have the right to remain silent. He didn't have the right to an attorney." Unconsciously his hand moved to touch one of the darker stains on the front of his apron. "He talked."

"And?"

"He took her up there to kill her, of course. He claimed she never would have agreed to go home, that he'd sounded her out on it, that all she did was swear she could be counted on to keep her mouth shut. He took her up to the farm and gave her a lot to drink and then took her outside and made love to her in the grass. Had all her clothes off, laid with her in the moonlight. And then while she was lying there afterward he took out a knife and let her see it. 'What's that?' she said. 'What are you going to do?' And he stabbed her."

My coffee cup was empty. I left Ballou at the table and took my cup to the bar and let the barman fill it up again. Crossing the floor, I fancied the sawdust underfoot was blood-soaked. I thought I could see it and smell it. But it was just spilled beer that I was seeing, and the smell was the meat smell from the street outside.

When I got back Ballou was looking at the picture I'd given him. "She was a pretty girl," he said evenly. "Prettier than you'd know from her picture. Lively, she was."

"Until he killed her."

"Until then."

"He left her there? I'll want to get the body, arrange to ship it back to them."

"You can't."

"There'd be a way to do it without opening an investigation. I think her parents would cooperate if I explained it to them. Especially if I could tell them that justice had been done." The phrase sounded stilted, but it said what I wanted to say. I glanced at him. "It has been done, hasn't it?"

He said, "Justice? Is justice ever done?" He frowned, following the thought through the fumes of his whiskey. "The answer to your ques-

269

tion," he said, "is yes."

"I thought so. But the body — "

"You can't take it, man."

"Why not? Wouldn't he say where he buried it?"

"He never buried her." His hand, resting on the table between us, tightened into a fist. His fingers went white at the knuckles.

I waited.

He said, "I told you about the farm. All it's supposed to be is a place in the country, but the two of them, O'Mara's their name, they like to farm it. She has a garden, and all summer long they're giving me corn and tomatoes. And zucchini, they're always after me to take zucchini." He opened his fist, spread his hand palm-down on the tabletop. "He has a dairy herd, two dozen head. Holsteins, they are. He sells the milk and keeps what it brings him. They try to give me milk, but what do I want with it? The eggs, though, are the best you'll ever have. They're free range chickens. Do you know what that means? It means they have to scratch for a living. Christ, I'd say it does them good. The yolks are deep yellow, close to orange. Someday I'll bring you some of those eggs."

I didn't say anything.

"He keeps hogs there, too."

I took a sip of my coffee. For a moment I tasted bourbon in it, and I thought he might have added it to my cup while I was away from the table. But of course that was nonsense, I'd had the cup with me, and the bottle on the table held Irish whiskey, not bourbon. But I used to take my coffee that way, and my memory was pitching me curves and sliders, showing me blood on the sawdust underfoot, putting a bourbon taste in my coffee.

He said, "Every year there are farmers who pass out drunk in the hog pen, or fall and knock themselves out, and do you know what happens to them?"

"Tell me."

"The hogs eat them. Hogs will do that. There's men in the country who advertise that they'll pick up dead cows and horses, dispose of them for you. A hog needs a certain amount of animal matter in his diet, you see. He craves it, thrives better if he has it."

"And Paula — "

"Ah, Jesus," he said.

I wanted a drink. There are a hundred reasons why a man will want a drink, but I wanted one now for the most elementary reason of all. I didn't want to feel what I was feeling, and a voice within was telling me that I needed the drink, that I couldn't bear it without it.

But that voice is a liar. You can always bear the pain. It'll hurt, it'll burn like acid in an open wound, but you can stand it. And, as long as you can make yourself go on choosing the pain over the relief, you can keep going.

"I believe he wanted to do it," Mickey Ballou said. "To kill her with his knife and hoist her into the pen, to stand with his arms against the rail fence and watch the swine go at her. He had no call to do it. She would have gone home where she belonged and nobody would ever have heard of her again. He might have thrown a scare into her if he had to, but he never had any call to kill her. So I have to think he did it to take delight in it."

"He's not the first."

"No," he said fervently, "and sometimes there's joy to be found in it. Have you known that joy?"

"No."

"I have," he said. He turned the bottle so that he could read the label. Without looking up he said, "But you don't kill for no good reason. You don't make up reasons to give yourself an excuse to shed blood. And you don't fucking lie about it to them you shouldn't lie to. He killed her on my fucking farm and fed her to my fucking hogs, and then he let me go on thinking she was baking cookies in her mother's kitchen in fucking Muncie, Indiana."

"You picked him up at the bar last night."

"I did."

"And drove up to Ulster County, I think you said. To the farm."

"Yes."

"And you were up all night."

"I was. It's a long drive there and a long drive back, and I wanted to get to mass this morning."

"The butchers' mass."

"The butchers' mass," he agreed.

"It must have been tiring," I said. "Driving all

the way there and back, and I suppose you'd been drinking."

"I had for a fact, and it's true it was a tiring drive. But, you know, there's no traffic at that hour."

"That's true."

"And on the way up," he said, "I had him along for company."

"And on the way back?"

"I played the radio."

"I suppose that helped."

"It did," he said. "It's a wonderful radio they put in a Cadillac. Speakers front and back, the sound as clear as good whiskey. You know, hers wasn't the first body ever went in that hog pen."

"Nor the last?"

He nodded, lips set, eyes like green flint. "Nor the last," he said.

16

We left the meat market bar and walked over Thirteenth to Greenwich Street, then up to Fourteenth and east to where he'd left the car. He wanted to give me a ride uptown but I wasn't going that way, and I told him it was easier for me to take the subway than for him to fight the traffic in lower Manhattan. We stood there for a moment. Then he clapped me on the shoulder and walked around his car to the driver's side, and I headed off toward Eighth Avenue and the subway.

I rode downtown, and after I got off the first thing I did was look for a telephone. I didn't want to call from a booth on the street. I found one in the lobby of an office building. It even had a door you could draw shut, unlike the open-air booths they have outside.

I called Willa first. We went through the hellos and the how are yous, and I cut into the middle of a sentence of hers and said, "Paula Hoeldtke's dead."

"Oh. You suspected that."

"And now I've confirmed it."

"Do you know how it happened?"

"I know more than I want to know. I don't want to go into it over the phone. Anyway, I have to call her father."

"I don't envy you that."

"No," I said. "And I have other things to do, but I'd like to see you later. I don't know how long I'll be. Suppose I come by around five or six?"

"I'll be here."

I hung up and sat in the booth for a few minutes. The air got close and I cracked the door. Then after a while I closed it again and the little light came on overhead and I lifted the receiver and dialed 0 and 317 and the rest of his number, and when the operator came on I gave her his name and my name and told her I wanted to make a collect call.

When I had him on the line I said, "It's Scudder. I spent a long time getting nowhere and then things loosened up all of a sudden. I don't have everything yet, but I thought I'd better call you. It doesn't look good."

"I see."

"In fact it looks pretty bad, Mr. Hoeldtke."

"Well, I was afraid of that," he said. "My wife and I, that's what we were afraid of."

"I should know more later today, or possibly tomorrow. I'll call you then. But I know you and Mrs. Hoeldtke have been sitting around hoping for good news, and I wanted to tell you, well, that there isn't going to be any."

"I appreciate that," he said. "I'll be here until six, and then I'll be home all evening."

"You'll hear from me."

I spent the next several hours going in and out of a bunch of offices. The information I wanted was mostly available, but I had to shell out a few dollars here and there in order to get my hands on it. New York is like that, and a sizable percentage of the people who work for the local government regard their salaries as a sort of base they get in return for reporting to work every morning. If they actually do anything, they expect to be paid extra for it. Elevator inspectors expect a bribe to certify that an elevator is safe. Other functionaries expect payment before they'll issue a building permit, or overlook a real or imagined restaurant violation, or otherwise do the job they've been hired to do. It must baffle people from out of town, although those who've lived in Arab countries probably find it familiar and comprehensible.

The favors I wanted were routine, and the baksheesh required was nominal. I paid out around fifty dollars, maybe a few dollars more than that. And, gradually, I began to learn what I needed to know.

Just before noon I called the AA Intergroup number and told the volunteer who answered that I didn't have my meeting book with me and needed a lunchtime meeting near City Hall. He gave me an address on Chambers Street and I got there while they were reading the preamble. I sat there for the rest of the hour. I don't know if I heard a word anybody said, and I didn't contribute anything myself beyond the physical fact of my presence and the dollar I put in the basket, but I left the room glad I'd come to it.

I had a hamburger and a glass of milk after the meeting and went to some more offices and bribed some more municipal employees. It was raining when I left the last office and walked to the subway, and it was clear when I got out at Fiftieth Street and walked up to Midtown North.

I got there around three-thirty. Joe Durkin was out. I said I'd wait for him, and I said that if he called in they should tell him I was waiting, and that it was important. Evidently he did, and got the message, because when he breezed in forty-five minutes later the first thing he did was ask what was so important.

"Everything's important," I said. "You know what my time is worth."

"About a buck an hour, isn't it?"

"Sometimes even more."

"I can't wait until I got my twenty years in," he said. "Then I can move into the private sector and start knocking down those big bucks."

We went upstairs and sat at his desk. I took out a slip of paper with a name and address and set it down in front of him. He looked at it, then at me, and said, "So?"

"Victim of a burglary and homicide."

"I know," he said. "I remember the case. We closed it."

"You got the guy?"

"No, but we know who did it. Twitchy little junkie, pulled a lot of jobs the same way, over the rooftops and down the fire escapes. We couldn't make a case against him for this one, but we hung a batch of other ones on him where we had good hard evidence. His Legal Aid lawyer plea-bargained him, but he still went away for — I don't know, a few years. I could look it up."

"But you didn't have any hard evidence against him for this one?"

"No, but it fit close enough for us to close the file. We weren't doing a whole lot with it anyway. No witnesses, no physical evidence. Why?"

"I'd like to see the autopsy report."

"Why?"

"I'll tell you later."

"She was stabbed and she died of it. What else do you want to know?"

"I'll tell you later. And while you're at it — "

"What?"

I took out another slip of paper and laid it on his desk. "Some more autopsy reports," I said.

He stared at me. "What the hell are you onto?"

"Oh, you know. Just working away like a dog at a bone. If I had more things to occupy me I wouldn't hang on like this, but you know what they say about idle hands doing the devil's work."

"Don't fuck around, Matt. Have you really

got something here?"

"See if you can pull the autopsy reports," I said. "And we'll see what I've got."

17

When I got to Willa's she was wearing the white Levi's with another silk blouse, this one lime green. Her hair was down, flowing over her shoulders. She'd buzzed me in and she met me at the door of her apartment, giving me a quick kiss, then drawing back, concern showing on her face. "You look drained," she said. "Exhausted."

"I didn't get a lot of sleep last night. And I've been going all day after an early start."

She drew me inside, closed the door. "Why don't you take a nap right away," she urged. "Do you think you could do that?"

"I'm wound too tight. And I've still got things I have to do."

"Well, at least I can give you a decent cup of coffee. I went out today to one of those yuppie havens where they sell fifty different blends, one more expensive than the next. I think they price it by the bean, and they can tell you where it came from and what kind of animal crap they spread on the fields. I bought a pound each of three different coffees and this electric drip machine that does everything but drink it for you."

"Sounds great."

"I'll pour you a cup. I had them grind it for me. They wanted to sell me a grinder so that every cup I brewed would be at the peak of freshness, but I figured you have to draw the line somewhere."

"I'm sure you're right."

"Taste it, see what you think."

I took a sip, set the cup down on the table. "It's good," I said.

"Just good? Oh, God, I'm sorry, Matt. You had a long day and it was a hard one, too, wasn't it? And I'm running off at the mouth. Why don't you sit down? I'll try to shut up."

"It's all right," I said. "But I'd like to make a phone call first, if you don't mind. I want to call Warren Hoeldtke."

"Paula's father?"

"He should be home now."

"Would you like me to go out while you make the call?"

"No," I said. "Stick around. In fact, you can listen while I talk to him. It'll save saying the same thing twice."

"If you're sure."

I nodded, and she sat down while I picked up the phone and dialed his home number, not bothering to make it collect this time. Mrs. Hoeldtke answered, and when I asked for him she said, "Mr. Scudder? He's expecting your call. Just a moment, I'll get him."

When Hoeldtke came on the line he said hello as if bracing himself. "I'm afraid the news is bad," I said.

"Tell me."

"Paula is dead," I said. "She died the second weekend in July. I can't be sure of the precise date."

"How did it happen?"

"She spent the weekend on a boat, she and a gentleman friend and another couple. The other man had a speedboat, some sort of cabin cruiser that he kept at a marine on City Island. The four of them went out on open water."

"And there was an accident?"

"Not exactly," I said. I reached for my cup and had some of my coffee. It was very good coffee. "Boats, fast ones, are in demand these days. I'm sure I don't have to tell you that drug smuggling is a big business."

"Were these other people drug smugglers?"

"No. Paula's companion was a securities analyst. The other man was also on Wall Street, and the other woman ran a crafts gallery on Amsterdam Avenue. They were respectable people. There's no evidence that they even used drugs, let alone dealt in them."

"I see."

"Their boat, however, was one that would lend itself to smuggling. That made it an attractive target for pirates. This sort of piracy has become very common in the Caribbean. Boat owners down there have learned to carry firearms on board and fire at any other vessel that comes too close. Piracy is less common in northern waters, but it's getting to be a problem. A gang of pirates approached the boat Paula was on, pretending to be a ship in distress. They managed to get on board, and then they did what pirates have always done. They killed everyone and made off with the ship."

"My God," he said.

"I'm sorry," I said. "There's no gentle way to say it. From what I've been able to determine, it was over very quickly. They came onto the ship with their guns drawn and they didn't waste any time before firing them. She wouldn't have suffered long. None of them would have."

"Dear God. How can things like this happen in this day and age? Piracy, you think of men with gold earrings and peg legs and, and, parrots. Errol Flynn in the movies. It seems like something out of another time."

"I know."

"Was there anything in the newspapers about this? I don't recall seeing anything."

"No," I said. "There's no official record of the incident."

"Who was the man? And the other couple?"

"I promised someone I'd keep their names out of it. I'll violate that promise if you insist, but I'd rather not."

"Why? Oh, I can probably guess."

"The man was married."

"That was my guess."

"And the other couple was married as well, but

not to each other. So there doesn't seem to be any purpose served by revealing their names, and their surviving families would prefer being spared the embarrassment."

"I can appreciate that," he said.

"I wouldn't keep it under wraps if there were an investigation to pursue, something for the police or the Coast Guard to go after. But the case is closed before it could ever be opened."

"How do you mean? Because Paula and the others are dead?"

"No. Because the pirates themselves are dead. They were all shot down in a dope deal that went sour. It happened a couple of weeks after the piracy, and otherwise I very likely would never have found out anything substantial. But someone I met who knew people on the other end of that dope deal felt free to talk about what he knew, and I got as much of the story as I did."

He had a few more questions and I answered them. I'd had all day to get my story right, so I was prepared for the questions he raised. The last question took a long time coming; I'd expected it early on, but I guess he was reluctant to ask it.

"And the bodies?"

"Overboard."

"Burial at sea," he said. He was silent for a moment, and then he said, "She always loved the water. When she — " and his voice broke. "When she was a little girl," he said, back in control again, "we spent our summers at the lake, and you couldn't get her out of the water. I called her a water rat, she would swim all day if we let her. She loved it."

He asked if I would hold on while he passed on what I'd reported to his wife. He must have covered the mouthpiece with his hand because I didn't hear anything at all for several minutes. Then she came on and said, "Mr. Scudder? I want to thank you for all you've done."

"I'm sorry to bring you this kind of news, Mrs. Hoeldtke."

"I must have known," she said. "I must have known ever since it happened. Don't you think so? On some level, I think I must have known all along."

"Perhaps."

"At least I don't have to worry anymore," she said. "At least now I know where she is."

Hoeldtke came on again to thank me, and to ask if he owed me money. I told him he didn't. He asked if I was sure of that and I said I was.

I hung up, and Willa said, "That was quite a story. You found out all that today?"

"Last night and this morning. I called him this morning to let him know it looked bad. I wanted to let him prepare himself and his wife before I gave him the details."

" 'Your mother is on the roof.' "

I looked at her.

"You don't know that story? A man's on a business trip and his wife calls him and tells him the cat is dead. And he has a fit. 'How can you say something flat out like that, you could give a person a heart attack. What you have to do is break it to a person gently. You don't call up and say in one breath that the cat climbed up on the roof and fell off and died. First you call up and tell me the cat is on the roof. Then you call a second time and say people are trying to get the cat down, the Fire Department and all, but it doesn't look good. Then, by the time you call me a third time, I've prepared myself. Then you can tell me the cat is dead.' "

"I think I can see where this is going."

"Of course, because I led off with the punch line. He goes on a business trip and he gets another phone call from his wife, and he says hello, how are you, what's new, and she says, 'Your mother is on the roof.' "

"I guess that's what I was doing. Telling him his daughter was on the roof. Were you able to follow the whole thing by hearing one side of the conversation?"

"I think so. How did you find all this out? I thought you went looking for a crook who used to know Eddie."

"I did."

"How did that lead to Paula?"

"Luck. He didn't know anything about Eddie, but he knew people who took off the pirates in a dope deal. He put me on to somebody, and I asked the right questions, and I learned what I had to learn."

"Pirates on the open sea," she said. "It sounds like something out of an old movie."

"That's what Hoeldtke said."

"Serendipity."

"How's that?"

"Serendipity. Isn't that what you call it when you look for one thing and find something else?"

"It happens all the time in the kind of work I do. But I didn't know there was a word for it."

"Well, there is. What about all that business with her phone and answering machine? And all her clothes and things moved out, but the bed linens left."

"None of it amounted to anything. My guess is she took a lot of her clothes along on the weekend, and probably had other things stowed at an apartment her boyfriend was maintaining. When Flo Edderling went into her room, it looked empty to her, with nothing much visible except for the bedclothing. Then, while the room was open, one of the other tenants probably appropriated whatever was left, thinking that Paula had left it behind on purpose. The answering machine was left on because she thought she was coming back. None of it turned out to be a clue to anything, but it kept me playing with the case, and then I lucked out and found the solution almost by accident. Or whatever you called it."

"Serendipity. Don't you like the coffee? Is it too strong?"

"There is no such thing. And it's fine."

"You're not drinking it."

"I'm sipping it. I've had gallons of coffee already today, it's been that kind of a day. But I'm enjoying it."

"I guess I don't have too much confidence in it," she said. "After all those months of instant decaf."

"Well, this is a big improvement."

"I'm glad. So you didn't learn anything more about Eddie? And what was on his mind?"

"No," I said. "But then I didn't really expect to."

"Oh."

"Because I already knew."

"I don't follow you."

"Don't you?" I got to my feet. "I already knew what was on Eddie's mind, and what happened to him. Mrs. Hoeldtke just now told me that she knew all along that her daughter was dead, that the knowledge had to have existed on some level. I knew about Eddie on a more conscious level than the one she was talking about, but I didn't want to know about it. I tried to shut out the knowledge, and I went out there hoping I'd learn something that would prove me wrong."

"Wrong about what?"

"Wrong about what was eating at him. Wrong about how he got killed."

"I thought it was autoerotic asphyxiation." She frowned. "Or are you saying that it was actually suicide? That he really had the intention of killing himself?"

" 'Your mother is on the roof.' " She looked at me. "I can't break it gently, Willa. I know what happened and I know why. You killed him."

18

"It was the chloral hydrate," I said. "And the funny thing is it wouldn't have flagged anybody's attention but mine. He only had a very small dose of chloral in him, not enough to have any pronounced effect on him. Certainly not enough to kill him.

"But he was a sober alcoholic, and that meant he shouldn't have *any* chloral hydrate in him. As far as Eddie was concerned, sobriety was unequivocal. It meant no alcohol and no mood-changing or sedative drugs. He'd tried dicking around with marijuana shortly after he came into the program and he knew that didn't work. He wouldn't take something to help him sleep, not even one of those over-the-counter preparations, let alone a real drug like chloral hydrate. If he couldn't sleep he'd have stayed awake. Nobody ever died from lack of sleep. That's what they tell you when you first get sober, and God knows I heard it enough myself. 'Nobody ever died from lack of sleep.' Sometimes I wanted to throw a chair at the person who said it, but it turned out they were right."

She was standing with her back to the refrigerator, one hand pressed palm-first against the white surface.

"I'd wanted to find out if he died sober," I went on. "It seemed important to me, maybe because it would have been his one victory in a life that had been nothing but a chain of small defeats. And when I learned about the chloral I couldn't let go of it. I went up to his apartment and I gave it a pretty decent search. If he'd had any pills there, I think I would have found them. Then I came downstairs and found a bottle of chloral hydrate in your medicine cabinet."

"He said he couldn't sleep, that he was going nuts. He wouldn't take a drink or a bottle of beer so I gave him a couple of drops in a cup of coffee."

"That's no good, Willa. I gave you a chance to tell me that after I searched his place."

"Well, you made such a big deal out of it. You made it sound as though giving a sedative to an alcoholic was like giving apples with razor blades in them to Halloween trick-or-treaters. I sort of hinted at it. I said he might have bought a pill on the street, or somebody might have given him one."

"Coral hydrate."

She looked at me.

"That's what you called it. We had a conversation about it, and you were very good about getting the name of the drug wrong, as though this were the first time you were hearing about it. That was a nice touch, casual as could be, but the timing

291

wasn't so good. Because I was hearing it all just a few minutes after seeing a bottle of liquid chloral in your medicine chest."

"I just knew it was something to take to go to sleep. I didn't know the name of it."

"It was typed right on the label."

"Maybe I never read it properly in the first place. Maybe it never registered, maybe I haven't got a mind for that kind of detail."

"You? The woman who knew what Paris green was? The woman who would know how to poison a municipal water system if the word came down from the party leadership?"

"Then maybe it was just a slip of the tongue."

"Just a slip of the tongue. And then, the next time I looked, the bottle was gone from the medicine cabinet."

She sighed. "I can explain. It's going to make me sound stupid, but I can explain."

"Let's hear it."

"I gave him the chloral hydrate. I didn't know any reason not to, for God's sake. He came in to talk and he wasn't going to have any coffee because he told me he was having a terrible time sleeping. I guess there was something on his mind, the same thing he was going to tell you about, but he didn't give any indication what it was."

"And?"

"I told him decaf wouldn't keep him awake, and that this particular brand seemed to help people to sleep, at least it had that effect on me. And then I put a couple of drops of the chloral hydrate in his cup but didn't let him know what I was doing. And he drank it right down and went up to bed, and the next time I saw him was when I walked in there with you and he was dead."

"And the reason you didn't say anything — "

"Was because I thought I'd killed him! I thought the dose I gave him made him drowsy, and then as a result he lost consciousness while he was half strangling himself, and that was why he died. And by this time you and I were sleeping together, and I was terrified you'd hold it against me, I knew what a fanatic you are about sobriety, and I couldn't see what purpose it would serve to admit that I'd done something that might have contributed to his death." She held her hands at her sides. "That may make me guilty of something, Matt. But it doesn't mean I killed him."

"Jesus," I said.

"Do you see, darling? Do you see what — "

"What I'm beginning to see is how good you are at improvisation. I suppose you had good training, living under false colors for all those years, putting up one front after another for your neighbors and co-workers. It must have been a great education."

"You're talking about the lies I told earlier. I'm not proud of that but I guess it's true, I guess I've learned to lie as a reflex. And now I have to learn a new way of behavior, now that I'm involved with someone who's really important to me. It's a different ball game now, isn't it, and I — "

"Cut the shit, Willa."

She recoiled as if from a blow. "It won't work," I told her. "You didn't just slip him a Mickey. You knotted the clothesline around the neck and hanged him from the pipe. It wouldn't have been hard for you to do. You're a big strong woman and he was a little guy, and he wouldn't have put up a fight once you'd knocked him out with the chloral. You set the stage nicely, you stripped him, you put a couple of bondage magazines where they'd tell a good story. Where did you buy the magazines? Times Square?"

"I didn't buy the magazines. I didn't do any of the things you just said."

"One of the clerks down there might remember you. You're a striking woman, and they don't get that many female customers in the first place. I don't suppose it would take a whole lot of legwork to turn up a clerk who remembers you."

"Matt, if you could hear yourself. The awful things you're accusing me of. I know you're tired, I know the kind of day you've had, but — "

"I told you to cut the crap. I know you killed him, Willa. You closed the windows to hold the smell in a little longer, to make the medical evidence a little less precise. Then you waited for someone to notice the stench and report it, to you or to the cops. You were in no hurry. You didn't really care how long it took before the body was discovered. What mattered was that he was dead. That way his secret could die with him."

"What secret?"

"The one he had trouble living with. The one you didn't dare let him tell me. About all the other people you killed."

I said, "Poor Mrs. Mangan. All her old friends are dying while she sits around waiting for her own death. And the ones who don't die are moving away. There was a landlord around the corner who moved junkies into the building so that they would terrorize his rent-controlled tenants. He got fined for it. He should have gone to jail, the son of a bitch."

She looked right at me. It was hard to read her face, hard to guess what was going on behind it.

"But a lot of people have been moving out of the neighborhood willingly," I went on. "Their landlords buy them out, offer them five or ten or twenty thousand dollars to give up their apartments. It must confuse the hell out of them, to get offered more to vacate an apartment than they've paid all their lives to live in it. Of course, once they take the money, they can't find a place they can afford to live in."

"That's the system."

"It's a funny system. You pay steady rent on a couple of rooms for twenty or thirty years and the guy who owns the building pays a small fortune to get rid of you. You'd think he'd want to hang on to a good steady tenant, but then the same kind of thing happens in business. Companies pay their best employees big bonuses to take early retirement and get the hell out. That way they can replace them with young kids who'll work for lower salaries. You wouldn't think it would work that way, but it does."

"I don't know what you're getting at."

"Don't you? I managed to get hold of the autopsy report on Gertrude Grod. She had the apartment directly above Eddie's, and she died right around the time he was starting to get sober. She had just about as much chloral hydrate in her as Eddie did. And her physician never prescribed the drug for her, and neither did anyone on staff at Roosevelt or St. Clare's. I figure you knocked on her door and got her to invite you in for a cup of tea, and when she was looking the other way you dosed her cup. On your way out you could have made sure the window gates were unlocked, so that Eddie could slip in a few hours later with a knife."

"Why would he do this for me?"

"My guess is you had a sexual hold on him, but it could have been anything. He was just starting to get sober and he wasn't a model of mental health at the time. And you're pretty good at getting people to do what you want them to do. You probably convinced Eddie he'd be doing the old lady a favor. I've heard you rap on the subject, how nobody should have to grow old that way. And she'd never know what happened to her, the drug would keep her from waking up, and so she'd never feel a thing. All he had to do was go out his window, climb up a flight, and stick a knife into a sleeping woman."

"Why wouldn't I just knife her myself? If I was already in her apartment and I got her to drink a dose of chloral."

"You wanted it to go in the books as a burglary. Eddie could make it a lot more convincing. He could lock her door from the inside and put the chain latch on before he went back out the window. I saw the police report. They had to break the door down. That was a nice touch, made it look a lot less like a possible inside job."

"Why would I want her dead?"

"That's easy. You wanted her apartment."

"Look around you," she said. "I've already got an apartment. Ground floor, no stairs to climb. What did I need with hers?"

"I spent a lot of time downtown today. Most of the morning and a good part of the afternoon. It's hard to chase things through the municipal record system, but if you know how to do it and what you're looking for, there's a lot you can find out. I found out who owns this building. An outfit called Daskap Realty Corp."

"I could have told you that."

"I also found out who owns Daskap. A woman named Wilma Rosser. I don't suppose it would be terribly hard to prove that Wilma Rosser and Willa Rossiter are the same person. You bought the building and moved in, but you told everybody that you were just the super, that you got the apartment in return for your services."

"You have to do that," she said. "No landlord can live on the premises unless you hide the fact

297

from your tenants. Otherwise they're after you all the time for one thing or another. I had to be able to shrug and say the landlord says no or I can't reach the landlord or whatever I had to say."

"It must have been tough," I said. "Trying to generate a positive cash flow here, with all of the tenants paying rent way below market."

"It *is* tough," she admitted. "The woman you mentioned, Gertrude Grod. She was rent-controlled, of course. Her annual rent came to less than what it cost to heat her place during the winter. But you can't believe I'd kill her because of that."

"Her among others. You don't own just this building. You're the principal in two other corporations besides Daskap. One of them, also owned ultimately by Wilma Rosser, owns the building next door. Another, owned by W. P. Taggart, owns two buildings across the street, the ones where you're the superintendent. Wilma P. Rosser was divorced from Elroy Hugh Taggart three years ago in New Mexico."

"I got in the habit of using different names. My political background and all."

"The buildings across the street have been a very unsafe place to live since you bought them. Five people have died over there in the past year and a half. One was a suicide. They found her with her head in the oven. The rest all died of natural causes. Heart attacks, respiratory failure. When frail old people die alone, no one looks too hard to see what did it. You can smother an old man in his sleep, you can haul an old lady across the floor and leave her with her head in the gas oven. That's a little dangerous because there's always the possibility of an explosion, and you wouldn't want to blow up the building just to kill a tenant. That's probably why you only used that method once."

"There's no evidence of any of this," she said. "Old people die all the time. It's not my fault if the actuarial tables caught up with some of my tenants."

"They were all full of chloral hydrate, Willa."

She started to say something. Her mouth opened, but something stopped the words. She breathed heavily, in and out, and then her hand moved to her mouth and her index finger rubbed at the gum above the two false teeth, replacements for the ones she'd lost in Chicago. She sighed again, heavily, and something went out of her face and the set of her shoulders.

She picked up her coffee cup, took it over to the sink and emptied it. She got the bottle of Teacher's from the cabinet and filled the cup. She drank deeply and shuddered. "God," she said, "you must miss this stuff."

"Sometimes."

"I'd miss it. Matt, they were just waiting to die, just hanging on and hanging on."

"And you were doing them a favor."

"I was doing everybody a favor, myself included. There are twenty-four apartments in this building, all with pretty much the same layout. Renovated and sold as co-ops, every apartment in the building would bring a minimum of a hundred and twenty-five thousand dollars. You could probably get a little more for the front ones. They're a little nicer, they're airier, the light's better. Maybe you could up the numbers a little if you did a really nice renovation. Do you know what that comes to?"

"Two million dollars?"

"Closer to three. That's for each building. Buying them cost me every cent I inherited from my parents, and they're mortgaged to the hilt. The rent roll barely covers payments and taxes and maintenance. I have a few tenants in each building who are paying close to market, and otherwise I couldn't keep the buildings. Matt, do you think it's fair that a landlord has to subsidize tenants by letting them hang on to an apartment for a tenth of what it's worth?"

"Of course not. The fair thing is for them to die and for you to make twelve million dollars."

"I wouldn't be making that much. Once I've got a large percentage of vacant apartments I can sell the buildings to somebody who specializes in co-op conversions. If everything comes together the way it should, my profit will be about a million dollars a building."

"So you'll make four million."

"I might hang on to one of the buildings. I'm not sure, I haven't decided. But either way I'll make a lot of money."

"It sounds like a lot to me."

"It's actually less than it sounds like. A millionaire used to be a really rich person. Now when the top prize in a lottery is a million dollars it's considered small-time. But I could live nicely on a couple of million dollars."

"It's a shame you won't be able to."

"Why won't I?" She reached out and took my hand, and I felt her energy. "Matt, there won't be any more killings. That ended a long time ago."

"A tenant in this building died not two months ago."

"In this building? Matt, that was Carl White, he died of cancer, for God's sake!"

"He was full of chloral, Willa."

Her shoulders sagged. "He was dying of cancer," she said. "He would have died of his own accord in another month or two. He was in pain all the time." She raised her eyes to mine. "You can believe what you want about me, Matt. You can think I'm the reincarnation of Lucrezia Borgia, but you really can't turn Carl White's death into a murder for gain. All I did was lose whatever rent he would have paid in however many months of life he'd have had left to him."

"Then why did you kill him?"

"You'll try to find a way to twist this, but it was an act of mercy."

"What about Eddie Dunphy? Was that an act of mercy?"

"Oh, God," she said. "That was the only one

I regret. The others were people who would have killed themselves if they'd had the wit to think of it. No, Eddie wasn't an act of mercy. Killing him was an act of self-preservation."

"You were afraid he would talk."

"I knew he would talk. He actually waltzed in here and *told* me he would talk. He was in AA, the poor damned fool, and he was babbling like some kind of religious convert who had Jesus Christ appear to him on the side of his toaster oven. He said he had to sit down with someone and tell him everything, but that I didn't have anything to worry about because he would keep my name out of it. 'I killed somebody in my building so the landlady could get her apartment, but I won't tell you who put me up to it.' He said the person he was going to tell wouldn't tell anyone."

"He was right. I wouldn't have."

"You'd have overlooked multiple homicide?"

I nodded. "I'd have been breaking the law, but it wouldn't be the first law I ever broke or the first homicide I overlooked. God never appointed me to go around the world righting wrongs. I'm not a priest, but anything he said to me would have been under the seal of the confessional as far as I was concerned. I told him I'd keep his confidence and I would have."

"Will you keep mine?" She moved closer to me, and her hands fastened first on my wrists, then moved to my forearms. "Matt," she said, "I invited you in here the first day to find out how much you knew. But I didn't have to take you to bed to manage that. I went to bed with you because I wanted to."

I didn't say anything.

"I didn't count on falling in love with you," she said, "but it happened. I feel foolish saying it now because you'll twist it, but it happens to be the truth. I don't know if you're in love with me. I think you were starting to be, and I think that's why you're angry with me now. But there's been something real and strong between us from the beginning, and I feel it now, and I know you do, too. Don't you?"

"I don't know what I feel."

"I think you do. And you're a good influence on me, you've already got me making real coffee. Matt, why don't you give us a chance?"

"How can I do that?"

"It's the easiest thing in the world. All you have to do is forget everything we said tonight. Matt, you just told me you weren't put on the planet to right all wrongs. You'd have let it go if Eddie had told you about it. Why can't you do as much for me?"

"I don't know."

"Why not?" She leaned a little closer, and I could smell the scotch on her breath, and remember how her mouth tasted. She said, "Matt, I'm not going to kill anybody else. That's over forever, I swear it is. And there's no real proof I ever killed anyone, is there? A couple of people had a non-lethal dose of a common drug in their systems. Nobody can prove I gave it to them. Nobody can even prove I had it in my possession."

"I copied the label the other day. I've got the number of the prescription, the issuing pharmacy, the date of issue, the physician's name — "

"The doctor will tell you I have trouble getting to sleep. I bought the chloral for my own consumption. Matt, there's no real physical evidence. And I'm a respectable citizen, I'm a property owner, I can afford good lawyers. How good a case could they make against me when all they have is circumstantial evidence?"

"That's a good question."

"And why should we go through all of that?" She laid a hand on my cheek, stroked along the grain of my beard. "Matt, darling, we're both tense, it's all crazy, it's a crazy day. Why don't we go to bed? Right now, the two of us, why don't we take off our clothes and go to bed and see how we feel afterward. How does that sound to you?"

"Tell me how you killed him, Willa."

"I swear he never felt a thing, he never knew what was happening. I went up to his room to talk with him. He let me in. I gave him a cup of tea and put the drops in it. Then I came back downstairs, and when I went up again later he was sleeping like a lamb."

"And what did you do?"

"What you said. It was clever of you to figure it out. You're a good detective."

"How'd you manage it?"

"He was already stripped. All he was wearing was the T-shirt. I got the clothesline hooked up, and then I sat him up and fixed the noose around his neck. He never woke up. I just pulled up on the clothesline and let his own body weight shut off his oxygen. That's all."

"And Mrs. Grod?"

"It was the way you figured it. I got her to take the chloral and I unlocked her window gates. I didn't kill her. Eddie did that. He made it look like a struggle, too, and he locked the doors from inside and went back downstairs on the fire escape. Matt, they were all tired of life, the ones I killed. I just gave them a hand in the direction they were already heading."

"The merciful angel of death."

"Matt?"

I took her hands from my shoulders, stepped back. Her eyes widened, and I could see her trying to gauge which way I was leaning. I took a full breath and let it out and took off my suit jacket and hung it over the back of the chair.

"Ah, my darling," she said.

I took off my tie and strung it over the jacket. I unbuttoned my shirt, tugged it out of the waistband of my slacks. She smiled and moved to embrace me. I lifted a hand to hold her off.

"Matt — "

I drew my undershirt up over my head and off. She couldn't miss the wire. She saw it right away, wrapped around my middle, taped to my skin, but it took a minute or two for the implications to sink in.

Then she got it, and her shoulders sagged with the knowledge and her face collapsed. One hand reached out, gripping the table to keep her from falling.

While she was pouring herself more scotch, I got back into my clothes.

19

I brought her in. It was a nice collar for Joe Durkin, with an assist for Bellamy and Andreotti. Willa didn't stay inside long. The equity in her buildings allowed her to make bond, and she's out on bail now pending disposition of her case.

I don't think it'll come to trial. The newspaper coverage was heavy, and neither her good looks nor her radical past got in the way of the story. The recording I made of our conversation should prove to be admissible evidence, although her lawyer will do what he can to hold it back, but aside from that there's not a wealth of physical evidence, so the betting right now is that her lawyer will want to plea-bargain the case and the Manhattan DA's office will be agreeable. She'll probably have to go away for a year or two. Most people would very likely say she'll be getting off too easy, but then most people haven't spent very much time in prison.

I had taken a few things from Eddie's apartment — books, mostly, and his wallet. I brought all his AA literature along to St. Paul's one night, and added the pamphlets to the stack on the free table. I gave his copies of the Big Book and the Twelve & Twelve to a newcomer named Ray, whom I haven't laid eyes on since. I don't know if he's going to other meetings, or if he's staying sober, but I don't suppose the books drove him to drink.

I kept his mother's Bible. I have one of my own, the King James version, and I figured it wouldn't hurt to have a Catholic Bible to keep it company. I still like the King James better, but I don't open either of them all that often.

I spent more than seventy-two dollars' worth of mental energy trying to decide what to do with the forty bucks in the Bible and the thirty-two dollars in his wallet. Ultimately I appointed myself his executor and hired myself retroactively to solve his murder, and paid myself seventy-two dollars for my services on his behalf. I dropped the empty wallet in a trash basket, where it no doubt proved a major disappointment for some sharp-eyed scavenger.

Eddie was buried out of Twomey & Sons funeral parlor, on Fourteenth Street next to St. Bernard's. Mickey Ballou arranged for the service and footed the bill for it. "At least he'll have a priest reading over him and a decent burial in a proper cemetery," he said, "though you and I'll probably be the only ones there for him." But I mentioned the event at a meeting, and as it turned out there were about two dozen of us who came to see him off.

Ballou was astonished, and drew me aside. "I

thought it'd just be you and me," he said. "If I'd known there'd be all this turnout I'd have laid on something after, a couple of bottles and some food. Do you suppose we could ask them all to come back to Grogan's for a few jars?"

"These people won't want to do that," I said.

"Ah," he said, and looked thoughtfully around the room. "They don't drink."

"Not today."

"And that's where they knew him from. And they're here for him now." He considered this for a moment, then nodded shortly. "I guess he came out of it all right," he said.

"I guess he did."

Not long after Eddie's funeral I got a call from Warren Hoeldtke. They'd just had a small service for Paula, and I guess his call to me was a part of the mourning process.

"We announced that she'd died in a boating accident," he said. "We talked it over, and that seemed like the best way to handle it. And I suppose it's the truth, if not the whole truth."

He said he and his wife had agreed that I hadn't been paid enough for my services. "I've put a check in the mail to you," he said. I didn't argue with him. I'd been a New York cop long enough not to argue with people who wanted to give me money.

"And if you ever want a car," he said, "you're more than welcome to anything on the lot at actual cost. It would be a genuine pleasure for me."

"I wouldn't know where to park it."

"I know," he said. "Personally I wouldn't own a car in New York if someone gave it to me. But then I wouldn't care to live there either, with or without a car. Well. You should have that check in a few days."

It took three days, and it was for $1,500. I tried to decide if it bothered me to take it, and I concluded that it didn't. I had earned it, had put in sufficient effort to justify it and had produced sufficient results. I had pushed against the wall, and the wall had moved a little, so I had done real work and deserved real pay for it.

I put the check in the bank and drew some cash and paid some bills. And I took a tenth of the sum in singles and made sure I always had a supply in my pocket, and I went on giving them out haphazardly to some of the people who stood on the street and asked for them.

The same day the check came, I had dinner with Jim Faber and told him the whole story. I needed an ear to pour it all into, and he was decent enough to listen to it. "I figured out how the payment breaks down," I told him. "A thousand dollars for finding out how Paula died and fifteen hundred for lying about it."

"You couldn't tell him the truth."

"I don't see how I could have, no. I told him *a* truth. I told him that she died because she was in the wrong place at the wrong time, and I told him that the person who killed her was dead. Burial

310

at sea sounds a lot more wholesome than getting dumped in a pigpen, but what's the real difference? Either way you're dead, and either way something eats you."

"I suppose."

"Fish or hogs," I said. "What's the difference, when you come right down to it?"

He nodded. "Why did you want Willa to listen in on your conversation with the Hoeldtkes?"

"I wanted to start with the focus on Paula instead of on Eddie, so I could come up on her blind side. And I wanted her to have the same version they were getting, so she couldn't blurt anything out after she was in police custody." I thought about it. "Maybe I just wanted to lie to her," I said.

"Why?"

"Because I'd already shared a lot of myself with her, before I got Eddie's autopsy results and found the chloral hydrate in her medicine chest. From that point I started drawing away. I never slept with her after that. The one time we went out, I think I encouraged her to drink. I wanted her to pass out, I wanted us to keep our clothes on. I wasn't sure she'd done it, I didn't know everything at that point, but I was afraid of it and I didn't want the intimacy, or the illusion of intimacy."

"You cared about her."

"I was starting to."

"How do you feel now?"

"Not great."

He nodded and poured himself another cup of tea. We were in a Chinese place, and they'd refilled the teapot twice already. "Oh, before I forget," he said, and reached into a pocket of his army jacket and came out with a small cardboard box. "This may not cheer you up," he said, "but it's something. It's a present. Go on, open it."

The box contained business cards, nice ones, with raised lettering. They had my name, Matthew Scudder, and my telephone number. Nothing else.

"Thank you," I said. "These are nice."

"I thought to myself that you ought to have cards, for God's sake. You've got a buddy with a printshop, you really ought to have cards."

I thanked him again, then started to laugh. He asked what was so funny.

"If I'd had them earlier," I said, "I never would have found out who killed Paula."

And that was that. The Mets went ahead and clinched their division, and they'll start the play-offs next week against the Dodgers. The Yankees still have a mathematical chance, but it looks as though it'll be the Red Sox and Oakland in the American League.

The night the Mets clinched, I had a call from Mickey Ballou. "I was thinking about you," he said. "You ought to come round to Grogan's one of these nights. We could sit up all night telling lies and sad stories."

"That sounds good."

"And in the morning we'll catch the butchers' mass."

"One of these days," I said.

"I was thinking," he went on, "about all those people who came to say goodbye to Eddie. You go to those meetings yourself, don't you?"

"Yes, I do."

After a moment he said, "One of these days I might ask you to take me along with you. Just for curiosity, don't you know. Just to see what it's like."

"Anytime at all, Mick."

"Ah, there's no hurry," he said. "It's nothing you'd want to rush into, is it? But one of these days."

"Just let me know when."

"Ah," he said. "We'll see."

I'll probably get out to Shea for a game or two during the playoffs. They shouldn't have trouble with the Dodgers. They beat them eleven games out of twelve during the regular season, so they ought to breeze right past them.

Still, you can never tell. Anything can happen in a short series.

The employees of G.K. HALL hope you have enjoyed this Large Print book. All our Large Print titles are designed for easy reading, and all our books are made to last. Other G.K. Hall Large Print books are available at your library, through selected bookstores, or directly from us. For more information about current and up-coming titles, please call or mail your name and address to:

G.K. HALL
PO Box 159
Thorndike, Maine 04986
800/223-6121
207/948-2962